Praise for EXODUS

'A miracle of a novel . . . a book
you will remember for the rest of your life'
Guardian

'Like all the best fantasies, this one
confronts some very real issues, and it's the
most exciting book I've read all year'
Mail on Sunday

'Intellectually rigorous and bursting with humanity,
this is a book to read again and again'
Sunday Herald

'An ambitious, futuristic, environmental wake-up call'
Scotsman

'Haunted by the past, this is a novel that reminds
us what matters: the power of storytelling
and that age-old spirit of survival'
Irish Times

Also by Julie Bertagna

EXODUS

THE OPPOSITE OF CHOCOLATE

SOUNDTRACK

THE SPARK GAP

For younger readers

THE ICE-CREAM MACHINE

THE ICE-CREAM MACHINE:
TOTALLY FIZZBOMBED

Zenith

Julie Bertagna

YOUNG PICADOR

First published 2007 by Young Picador
an imprint of Pan Macmillan Limited
20 New Wharf Road, London N1 9RR
Basingstoke and Oxford
www.panmacmillan.com

Associated companies throughout the world

ISBN: 978-0-230-01534-0

3 5 7 9 8 6 4 2

A CIP catalogue record for this book is available from
the British Library.

Typeset by Intype Libra Ltd
Printed and bound in Great Britain by Mackays of Chatham plc, Kent

In memory of two inspirational women:
Miriam Hodgson and Jan Mark.

And for Natalie, my inspiration
for the future.

AVANNA

TARTOQ

IMAQA

What lasts, what changes, what survives?

The Play of Gilgamesh by Edwin Morgan,
adapted from the world's oldest surviving poem

Hurt not the earth, nor the sea, nor the trees

Revelation 7:3

AVANNA north

The sea is as near as we come to another world.

'North Sea Off Carnoustie' by Anne Stevenson

LODESTAR

Out on the world's ocean, night is a black war-horse. The white ship bucks upon it like a ghost rider with no reins.

A lone figure at the bow keeps watch, her eyes as dark as the night. She has lost the star. All through the night she tracked it, even when it vanished behind cloud.

The North Star is an old friend. A steering star for the island fishermen, it was their lodestar to guide them home. For Mara, it was a stray jewel dropped from Queen Cassiopeia's crown, falling towards the Long-Handled Ladle that scoops up the soup of the stars. On clear, calm nights Granny Mary would take her out on to the island hills of Wing and show her the stories of the stars. With a finger, Mara would pretend to join the dots of the Long-Handled Ladle, the studs on the belt of Orion the Hunter and the zigzag of Queen Cass's crown.

If you stood at the North Pole, at the very top of the world, said Granny, the Star of the North would be right overhead. It never moves. All the other stars wheel around that anchor in the sky. You can't stand at the North Pole any more though, Granny would sigh, now the ice has melted into the sea.

Back then, when she was little, Mara couldn't fathom the crack of sadness in the old woman's voice.

Now the North Star is her only anchor. A flickering point of hope in a drowned world. The ice cap has melted, but if she can track the North Star it just might lead her shipful of refugees, a floating village of desperate people, to land at the top of the world.

The world's wind rises, boiling up a black brew of sea and sky. The refugees huddle closer as the wind wraps the ship in warrior arms and rides it across galloping waves. Mara clings to the ship's rail as her lodestar vanishes in the wild ocean night.

TUCK

The ocean has eaten the stars.

All that's left are their crumbs. They litter a sea as dark as squid ink or the depths of a whale's eye.

Tuck thanks his lucky stars for the dark and prays for the curfew bell. Meantime, he's running so fast the tail of his faded blue windwrap streams out behind him like a tiny gas flare from the oil rig that anchors the gypsea city of Pomperoy.

The oil lanterns on the boat masts above him glow like a host of shivering souls. If he keeps running till curfew he'll be safe. As soon as the bell clangs the rig flame and the boat lanterns snuff out and there won't be a wink of light left in the ocean night. The gang of Salters on his heels will need cat's eyes to catch him then.

There's a shout close behind. Tuck rakes air into his lungs and makes a leap on to the nearest bridge. The bridge wire twangs and sways. His long, gangly legs are shaking so hard they almost topple him into the water. He steadies his nerve, and his legs, runs along the bridge on to one of the ferries and – aah! – he's knee-deep in squelchy sea tangle outside the reeking, rickety Weeder shacks that cram the broad deck. Tuck turns around and – *whack!* – gets a face full of stringy ocean wrack that's drying on a line of rope. He fights his way out of the thick, knotty strands only to skid on a litter of sea cabbage – and ends up on his knees.

A Salter's skittering on the cabbage too, right behind, close enough to grab a fistful of Tuck's windwrap, when a great *clang* sends a shudder through Tuck's bones. He shakes off the Salter as the curfew bell tolls across Pomperoy. Now the rig's great oil flare dwindles and snuffs out, along with every last lamp and lantern in the boats and masts.

A whole floating city vanishes into the night.

All that's left is a vast percussion beat. The *clink-chank* and *knockety-knock* of chained boats, cradling a huge human cargo, rocking them to sleep on the world's sea.

Tuck makes it through the ferries and heads into the heart of a noisy throng spilling out of the casino ship, hoping to lose the Salters in the crowd. From here, he's into the maze of boats and bridgeways of Doycha. He keeps running and leaping till he reaches the slum barges then clambers on to the flat roof of one of the boat shacks that crowd the deck of the nearest barge.

He lies on his stomach and covers himself with his windwrap. The sack of stolen salt cakes are digging him in the ribs but he dare not move. A *clatter-clang* of feet are chasing along the bridgeways. Soon, the shouts of the Salter gang are hot in his ears and the barge is swarming with men. Tuck crosses all his fingers and begs The Man in the Middle to send him a wink of looter's luck.

And Great Skua, he gets it. The clang of feet on the bridge to the next-door barge tells him the Salters are moving on.

8

The stolen salt cakes are making a hard pain in his side. Tuck shifts on his stomach and swallows a groan as the cakes begin to crumble under his weight. He feels the sack burst and deflate. Salt pours out over the shack roof.

Still he dare not move. A stray Salter might have lagged behind. Tuck listens so hard his ears tingle and once he's as sure as he can be that the gang are all gone, he sits up.

What a waste of a night. Chased all across Pomperoy by a gang of Salters and all for a burst sack of salt. Tuck scoops up as much of the spill as he can stuff into the pockets of his windwrap.

'Gotcha, scummy barge rat!'

There's a hard scrape of a laugh and a burning grip on his foot. A Salter's got him by the ankle and he's not letting go.

The worst crime in a city whose roots are pirate is not killing (there's often a reason for that). It's looting. Tuck has seen people rope-lashed and hung from the Middle Bridges, all for a loot gone wrong. Ransack and plunder were once the lifeblood of Pomperoy, but there was a time when boats of prey grew scarce and the city's taste for piracy turned in on itself. Pomperoy almost ate itself up.

So every night that Tuck goes out on the loot, he's risking *his* blood, if he's caught.

Tuck kicks hard against the Salter's grip. He doesn't want to be rope-lashed or hung. It doesn't matter that he's only taken a single sack tonight – looted night after night and resold on the barges, Tuck's stolen sackfuls have been undercutting the Salters' market price for weeks now.

They've been keeping Tuck and his Ma in style, those little salt cakes. Great Skua, so what? Tuck kicks harder. After Da died the Salters took their boat and he and Ma ended up in a barge shack so he's only taking back a

9

snitch of what's his. He and Ma have gorged on every delicacy he could spy on the market gondolas: sugar-kelp snaps, tangles of ocean noodles, rainbow baskets of briny cucumbers, the finest seaweed bread, crisp-baked anemones. For the first time in a while, Tuck's started to see some flesh on his skinny bones.

The Salter yanks on Tuck's ankle so hard he's brought crashing on to the deck. Tuck chokes as his neck is locked by an iron grip. Blood rushes to his head. The sting of a knife grazes the skin of his throat.

Tuck feels his looter's luck running out, faster than a trickle of salt.

MARA

Dawn reveals a brutal ocean, a roaring grey desert of sea.

'Mara.'

The ocean is so loud it almost drowns out Rowan's voice.

Mara turns from the ship's bow where she has been all night, though there's been nothing to see but the dark. And now, as day breaks, there is nothing but grey. She tries to smile at Rowan, but the blasting wind has made her face feel as rigid as stone.

Rowan throws a dirty blanket around her shoulders and hands her a plastic packet full of powdery yellow stuff.

NOOSOUP, she reads on the garish label.

'Gulp it down fast with some water.' Rowan makes a face and hands her a water bottle. 'Horrible. But it's food. There's crates full of it below in the hold.'

Mara wipes her wind-streamed eyes with the blanket, smearing her cheeks with its dirt. She scrapes a dark tangle of hair from her face and grimaces as she puts the packet to her lips, recoiling from the synthetic smell. But she's weak with hunger so she forces it down.

'Now,' says Rowan, as she wipes her mouth, 'tell me what happened. You vanished from the boat camp. I thought you must be dead. But here you are with a fleet of ships in a mass break-out from the city.' His haggard face breaks into a grin. 'I'm impressed.'

Mara returns a wry smile, but it disappears as she begins her extraordinary tale.

After the loss of her family on the journey to the New World, then more deaths in the boat camp around the city walls, Mara wished she were dead too. She was the one who convinced her people to flee their sinking island and make an exodus to the sky-scraping city of New Mungo. But inside the city wall she found a drowned netherworld at the foot of New Mungo's great towers. There Gorbals, Broomielaw, Candleriggs, Molendinar and the others survived as Treenesters in the ruins of a lost city. Mara saw the rooftops glimmering with ghostly phosphorescence under the sea. When Gorbals and the urchins were snatched by the sea police, Mara stole into the sky city to find them. And there she met Fox, the grandson of Caledon, the architect of the New World.

'Fox didn't know about the boat camp,' Mara insists. 'He knew nothing about the outside world. The City Fathers make sure of that. Up in New Mungo,' she remembers, 'it's like living on an island in the sky. You forget about the outside world, just like we did on Wing.'

'If refugees arrived on Wing, we wouldn't have built a great big wall to keep them out,' Rowan retorts.

'What if thousands landed on our shores? What would we have done?'

After a long moment, filled by the roar of the sea, Rowan returns to the here and now.

'How on Earth did you steal a fleet of ships?'

'Fox wiped out the city's communications. It was a big risk but he – he—'

Mara bites her lip, hoping the noise of the wind and the ocean drowned out the tremor in her voice.

'The grandson of the man who created the New World helped you break out of the city?' Rowan looks puzzled.

'Fox wants to change his world. That's why he had to stay.' She feels Rowan's eyes studying her face, trying to read the meaning behind the catch in her voice. Mara rushes on; there's plenty more to tell. Rowan looks increasingly bewildered as Mara tells him about the statue in the netherworld that is her image and the story the Treenesters say is carved into the drowned city's stone. It's a promise left by their ancestors, they believe, that one day they would be rescued from the deathly netherworld. When Mara arrived and they saw her face, the face in the stone, they were convinced that she must be the one to do that.

And strangely enough, she has. Though whether they will all find a home in the world, luck and fate will decide.

Mara has still to tell the tragic story of Candleriggs, the ancient Treenester, but Rowan looks exhausted and so is she. It's far too much to tell all at once.

And there are some things too painful to tell.

'It's crazy,' says Rowan. 'Our life on Wing was so hard and there were people dying in the boat camp and living in trees. Yet all the while the people of the New World were . . . are . . .' He breaks off, swallows hard, beyond words.

'Living in castles in the sky,' Mara finishes. 'In luxury you wouldn't believe, built by slaves the people know nothing about.'

'So who do they think built their walls and towers?

13

Who builds bridges all across the sea?' Rowan demands. There's a spark of anger in his weary eyes.

'They never think about that.' Mara grabs his arm. 'If you'd ever been inside a sky city you'd see why. Rowan, it's *amazing* . . .'

In her mind's eye she sees the vast cybercathedral which seemed to be created out of light and air, the silver sky tunnels sparking with speed-skaters, the wild and savage beauty of the Noos.

Rowan is frowning into the wind. 'This Fox . . .'

Mara's heart skips a beat, but she is rescued from questions she is not ready to answer by a sudden cry. She turns to see her friend, Broomielaw, struggling across the heaving deck with her baby in his papoose on her back.

'What if the world is all ocean?' says Broomielaw, crashing into Mara. They grip on to each other as the ship rolls up over a wave. The other girl's large eyes are shadowed and scared. 'What if there's no land? What if this is all there is? Ocean and ocean and ocean. I don't like it, Mara. I hate this wild world. I wish we were all back inside the wall on the Hill of Doves, safe and sound in our trees.'

Mara keeps a steadying arm across the sleep-slumped baby on Broomielaw's back.

'You *weren't* safe,' she reminds her friend. 'The sea was rising. Sooner or later, it'll swallow up the Hill of Doves just like it swallowed my island, and then what would you have done? There's land, Broomielaw, I'm sure there is, at the top of the world. It's in my book.'

'What if it's a drowned land too?'

It chills Mara's heart, that thought.

'And it's only the word of an old b—' Broomielaw grimaces as if she's swallowed an insect and spits out the

14

word '–book. What's that worth? You shouldn't trust those *things*.'

'You lot trusted your whole future to a story set in stone,' Mara retorts. 'It's your stone-telling legend as much as anything that's brought us here. You'll believe in an old stone statue but not a book.'

'You can trust stone.'

There's an edge of granite in Broomielaw's soft face.

'A vast land of mountains locked in ice.' Mara murmurs the words. She knows them off by heart; she's been chanting them like a mantra, over and over, to make herself believe they're true. 'If the Arctic ice is melted, the land must be free.'

But those mountains worry her. After all, the reason Mara's people abandoned their island, Wing, was because the rising sea had forced them further and further upland towards barren mountain rock. And they couldn't survive on that.

Broomielaw squeezes her hand. 'Sorry, Mara. I'm just so tired and the sea is making me sick. Baby Clayslaps couldn't settle all night.' She gives Mara a look. 'Like you.'

'Oh, me.' Mara pulls away.

Broomielaw grabs her arm. 'Tell me about the sky city. What happened to you up there? Something bad, I can tell.'

Mara shakes her head. How could she describe the wonders and horrors of a New World city to a girl who has lived her whole life in the ruins of the drowned world? Yet Broomielaw knows all about the cruelty of New Mungo towards those beyond its sky-scraping towers.

She also knows the pain of a broken heart.

'Tell me,' Broomielaw urges.

Mara hesitates. Rowan has gone into the control cabin and is deep in conversation with some of the boat-camp refugees.

'I – I had to leave someone behind.'

And she killed someone, but she can't tell anyone that. There wasn't time to dwell on that in the panic to escape New Mungo but there was time enough on the ship in the depths of the night.

She is rescued from Broomielaw's probing by the ship lurching over a wave almost as sheer as a cliff. They hang on to the rail and hope for their lives. Clayslaps howls, hurled out of his sleep.

'Take the baby below deck!' The wind whips away Mara's words.

'Come with me,' Broomielaw yells back, fighting the wind to make for the stairs.

'I'll be down soon,' Mara promises.

She turns back to the ocean. The exhilaration of escaping the city is gone. All last night, blanketed in darkness, she still felt close to Fox, felt the ghost of him beside her, his kiss, the heat of his fingerprints on her skin. Now, in daylight, she is confronted with the ocean that lies between them. The adrenalin is gone and the only thing left is rock-hard grief that feels as if it is crushing her from the inside out.

The wind calms a little. And so does Mara. Head thumping, she scrubs her eyes, turns around and rubs them again.

A long line of jagged grey teeth bite the horizon. The southern horizon. Not North, where the ship heads.

Mara races to the stairwell.

'Land!' she shouts.

A mass of sleepers rouses in an instant. When they

16

surge on deck Mara curses at the stampede she has caused. There's a dangerous rush to the ship's starboard.

Mara searches the mob and grabs Rowan. 'It's behind us. We need to turn back.'

But Rowan is shaking his head. 'No, no, that land's no good for us.'

'We've sailed too far!' The shouts go up all over the ship. 'Back, turn back!'

'It's no good.' Rowan tries to make himself heard above the din. 'It's all New World land.'

His voice is as frail as his body. No one hears – except Mara, who climbs on to the ship's rail to look over the heads of the other refugees.

'You sure, Rowan? How do you know?'

But Rowan is pushing through the crowd, still trying to be heard. Yes, it's high land, he's shouting, but it all belongs to the New World. Look! The sky above those mountains is swarming with air ships. They take off and land all day and night. There's no chance of refuge there, he insists, not unless you want to be a New World slave.

Word spreads across the ship and people slump on deck or troop dejectedly back below stairs to the hold. Mara jumps down from her unsteady perch on the rail.

'I thought I'd got it all wrong again,' she confesses, 'but why didn't we see it on the journey *into* New Mungo?'

She doesn't want to think about that journey, when the sea claimed almost everything and everyone she loved.

But she has Rowan. He is the last link with her island people and the life she lost. She has the Treenesters too and the urchins. She must keep reminding herself of what she still has in the world because what is lost is more than she can bear.

'We missed it in the dark,' said Rowan. 'We reached

New Mungo at sunrise, remember? It was only when I was working on the sea bridge that I saw there were high lands and found out it was a New World colony.'

That spell of slave labour has wrecked him. Mara wishes she could magic back the old Rowan: quick-witted, never-say-die Rowan, who explored worlds through his hoard of books. Not this broken boy who, like her, has lost *his* world.

He's watching her as she looks at the endless sea, trying to catch the tails of her thoughts. He always could, just as she could always sense the weather of his moods. Now, Rowan's misery engulfs her like an icy wind.

'We'd never find it, Mara.'

He means Wing, their island, where Tain and the other old ones were abandoned to the rising sea.

'We could try.' Her voice cracks. It's an empty hope.

A wave thunders on to the deck, crashing over Rowan's head and knocking Mara off her feet. Another sends her shooting across the deck until she smashes into the wall of the control cabin. Weak as he is, Rowan scutters across the slippery deck and grabs her. Together, they scramble into the shelter of the cabin.

Mara rubs a bashed shoulder, shakes soaking hair out of her eyes.

'You want to play hide and seek with an island and a great big ship?' Rowan wipes his streaming face on his arm. 'In a sea like this?'

They are sailing across the very ocean their island lies in yet it's impossible to find it and rescue anyone who might have survived. Like so much of the Earth's land, Wing might already have slipped into oblivion under the waves.

Mara looks at the switches and buttons of the control

deck, at the flashing numbers and symbols on the radar screen. Fox programmed the navigation disk to take them due North; beyond that, they are on their own.

The reek of the ocean fills the cabin. Rowan thumps a fist on the control deck. Seawater splashes from his hair into bitter blue eyes and drips on to the radar screen like tears.

THE MOST
IMPORTANT THING

'The sea is killing me.'

Gorbals the Treenester hangs over the side of the ship, making a noise like a clogged drain. His face is as grey as the day. A spell of slave labour in New Mungo has left him a shaven-headed ragbag of bones, just like Rowan. But Rowan is a sea-hardy boy, used to the ocean. Gorbals has only ever known the dank waters of the netherworld within New Mungo's walls.

Mara rubs his shoulder. 'You're alive. Remember how much you wanted to be free in the world.'

Gorbals groans and grips the ship's rail as they ride an ocean surge. 'I never thought the free world would feel so bad.'

A band of urchins barges past, almost toppling him over the rail.

'Time we boiled them up and had them for supper.' Gorbals eyes the urchins grimly. 'Though the little rats would be tough even if you boiled them till sundown.'

'They're just kids gone wild,' says Mara, though she is as exasperated as everyone else. Abandoned by the world, the urchins survived like human water rats under the bridges and in the drowned ruins around New Mungo. They seem almost as much animal as human with their thick, feral skin and wordless grunts. Yet they touch Mara's heart. Despite their wild nature the little ones, especially Wing, remind her of Corey, the young brother she lost.

Ibrox, the Treenester's firekeeper, taps Mara on the shoulder. 'They've got your bag.'

Mara glances down at her feet. Her backpack is gone. 'Oh, the little . . . hey! Come back here.'

But the urchins have vanished, along with her bag.

'My backpack – it's got everything . . .'

Her cyberwizz, the precious books, all her treasured things.

'Pollock and Possil,' says Ibrox. 'They're your men. They could hunt out a black beetle in the dead of night.'

Pollock and Possil are found down in the hold, fighting through scuffling refugees to grab a share of food for the Treenesters from the ship's cargo of crates. Crammed with packs of dried foodstuffs, tins and water, the crates are being emptied as fast as they are broken open. Glad to escape the mayhem, they set on the trail of Mara's bag.

Just as Mara is growing frantic, Possil brings it back to her. Pollock has the squirming culprit by the scruff of the neck.

'Want me to wring his skinny neck?' he asks, looking hopeful.

'Let him go,' says Mara, though right now she wouldn't mind doing it herself. 'They don't know right from wrong. They've had no one to look after them.'

Pollock narrows his eyes. '*I'll* look after them – I'll

truss them up like a puck of rabbits and teach them what's what.'

The urchin growls like a wild dog.

'*You'll* look after them?' Gorbals gives a hard laugh that ends in a sickly gurgle as the ship heaves over a wave. 'You don't even look after your own child.'

Pollock releases the urchin and strides over to Broomielaw and Clayslaps. He pulls a packet from a pocket of his tattered clothes, rips it open and gives a bar of food to his baby son. Clayslaps grabs the sticky bar and puts it to his mouth with a delighted squawk.

'Just as well Clayslaps doesn't have *you* for a father.' Pollock throws a sneer at Gorbals, who gives another nauseous groan over the side of the ship. 'What use would you be, you wet rag?'

'Will you two never stop?' mutters Broomielaw.

Mara exchanges a glance with Molendinar.

'Once we're settled, that lot will have to sort themselves out.' Mol shakes her head. 'Clay can't grow up with Pollock and Gorbals squabbling over his mother all the time.'

Despair crumples Broomielaw's soft face yet Mara feels a pang of envy. Broomielaw has a chance to heal the rift between her and Gorbals. Unlike herself and Fox, they have a whole future to sort themselves out.

But those kinds of thoughts engulf Mara in a misery she cannot bear. She must focus on here and now.

'Stroma?' She frowns down at the mucky urchin that Pollock set free. The child's face is layered in so much grime it's hard to tell who it is. Back in the netherworld, Mara named each urchin after the islands now lost to the sea. Isn't this Stroma? Or is it Hoy?

'Oy!' shouts the urchin.

22

'Hoy.' Mara smiles at the bedraggled child, then remembers he's the pest who took her bag.

She rummages in the backpack, checking her precious possessions, one by one. The book on Greenland is safe and so is Charles Dickens's *A Tale of Two Cities*; she found both in the wrecked book rooms of the old university tower in the netherworld sea. The tiny black meteorite from the ruined museum, older than Earth itself, is safe too. And here are the gifts old Candleriggs gave her when she fled the drowned city – a bottle of fizzy amber drink and a pair of red shoes. There are only crumbly fragments left of the sprig of herbs she took from the kitchen at home on Wing, but the bag is filled with the green, head-clearing scent of rosemary, her mother's namesake, and every time she opens it the ghost of her mother seems to waft through her.

Two things are missing: Gorbals's book of charcoal-scribbled poems; she left them with Fox. And the bone dagger – Mara doesn't want to remember what she did with that.

But the most important thing of all is safe.

Mara takes out an apple-sized globe from her bag and cradles it in her palm. The cyberwizz is a relic of the old technology. When the oceans rose and devastated the Earth, the vast datascape of the lost world was left in cyberspace. The Weave still hangs there like a cobweb in an abandoned house, a ghostly electronic network suspended between old satellites around the Earth. Once upon a time, cyberwizzing through the sparking boulevards of the Weave was a game for Mara. Now, it's her only connection with Fox.

The globe tingles to life at her touch. Colours drift across its surface like hazy clouds and the solar rods glow at its core. Mara clicks opens the globe and checks the small screen, keypad and wand inside. She digs into her bag and finds the halo, a sleek crescent that is her visor.

All fine.

She lets out a long breath. Tonight, the cyberwizz will be her escape. It will zip her out of the nightmare of real-world, deep into the Weave, where Fox will be waiting for her on the bridge.

That's her hope. Her dread is that he never got out of New Mungo or made it down to the netherworld, safe and sound.

Tonight, she'll find out.

A TRUE DUBYA

It's the looted salt that saves Tuck at the very last second from the lethal little knife at his throat.

He grabs a handful from the pocket of his windwrap and flings a crackle of salt. There's a roar as it hits the man in the eyes. The salt-knife slips from Tuck's throat. The instant the arm-lock loosens from his neck, Tuck breaks free.

His long, lean legs outrun the Salter's short, sturdy ones easy enough, but Tuck's a stride too far from the short suspension bridge that links to the next barge. Panic is a bad judge. He gambles on a leap. Against the odds he makes it but crash-lands on the bridge and hears his ankle crack. Now he has to hobble through a red blaze of pain. He struggles across the rusted wire bridge that links to his own barge. At last he's home on *The Grimby Gray*.

He'd be safer still if he was where he should be once the curfew bell has rung – inside his ramshackle barge shack, tucked up in his bunk. But Tuck's never one for doing what he should. So he hauls himself up on to the shack roof, his bad ankle jangling with pain, and scans the dark decks of the barges, just in case the Salter is lurking somewhere. But the decks are quiet and still.

He'll stay up here until his heart and his breathing calm. Ma doesn't want to hear him huffing and puffing. She knows fine well what he does. How else does he get his hands on all those extra rations of lamp oil, the baskets of smoked oysters and crabs, the best catch of the sea every day, not to mention those gluggets of seagrape beer Ma likes so much? Patching bridges and roof shacks? He'd earn grit for that. Great at fooling herself, is Ma. Her mind shuts snap-hard as an oyster shell if there's something she doesn't want to know. It's not the deaths that made her like that; it's just the way she is. But she never used to guzzle a glugget of seagrape bitterbeer every night.

She's had a good glug tonight, he can tell; she's snoring like one of the old dogs that snooze around the lagoon. The noise rattles the shack roof. Tuck knots his windwrap tight around him and lies on his back with only the blanket of the night sky above.

Better off up here.

He's still there when a slice of sunrise, thin as a wire, prises open his sleep-locked eyes. Tuck thinks he's in his bunk, turns away from the light, rolls off the roof and lands with a crash among the two buckets of looted eels he's forgotten he left outside the shack the other night.

'Urth!' he curses.

Landed right on his bad ankle too.

'Tuck?'

Ah, now Ma's up. And the buckets are spilt, the eels splattering on to the deck.

'Sodden *Urth.*'

'Tuck!'

26

There's a weary creak of wood as Ma struggles out of her bunk. She fiddles with the broken window latch, the one she's been asking him to fix for many a moon, and pushes the shutters open.

'Whassall the racket?' she croaks, rubbing bleary eyes. She spies Tuck among the spilt eels. 'In the name of The Man! You'd better catch those eels, Tuck, before I grab you by the neck and . . .'

Tuck doesn't wait to hear what she'll do. He runs a string of curses through his teeth as he limps along the deck of the barge, crashing into neighbouring shacks, tripping over fishing gear, seaweed stacks, pot plants and all kinds of junk, trying to catch the tail end of an eel.

He's just about to close his fingers on one when next-door's cat darts between his feet and trips him up. Now he's flat on his face, his bad ankle on fire, and it's too late.

The eels slick down a drain. Tuck hears the slither and *plop* as they escape back into the sea.

No eels, a few crumbs of salt in his pocket, a druxy ankle and there's no one to blame but himself.

The cat knows she's in for it and tries to slink into the eel bucket. Tuck kicks the bucket and grabs the cat's tail, yanks it hard in revenge. The cat gives an outraged yowl.

'*Tuck.*'

'Oy, cut the racket out there!' yells Arthus, the old grump from the next shack. A window shutter rattles open and Arthus's walrussy head looms out. 'What a dubya. That's what you are, boy, a true dubya.' Arthus surveys the mess Tuck has made and pulls the shutter closed again with a whack.

Tuck gets to his feet. From his own shack there's an outburst of wheezy coughs. No wonder he goes out looting. It's better than staying in this dump, getting yelled at and listening to Ma's snores and wheezes, night after night.

Tuck limps back to his own shack. The dawn light glints in his Ma's eye. With her beaky nose, pale face and nest of greying hair, she has the look of an orange-eyed gull. A gull with its nest on its head.

'Sorry, Ma.'

'A sorry excuse for a son, thass what you are, Tuck Culpy. *Phut – wheez.* All that creaking on the roof – you been up there all night again?'

Tuck shrugs.

Ma gives him a glinty glare. 'You can just set off early and find yourself some work 'cause there's no dinner now, is there? You just kicked it back in the sea. I never know how we'll live from one day till the – *phut wheez* – next.'

A fit of cough-wheezies halts her.

'Rubbish, Ma,' says Tuck. 'We're doing all right. Had a good glug of seagrape last night, didn't you, eh? And a nice basket of smoked oysters? Keeping you in luxury, I am.'

But she's decided, as the neighbours are no doubt listening in now he's woken them up, to pretend to be a proper Ma.

'D'you think I sailed across the ocean in a bottle? Think I – *phut-phut-wheez* – fell out of the sky? I know what you get up to. You wuzzn't on that roof all night, Tuck Culpy . . . *wheeez* . . . hanging out with a no-good lot of curfew breakers, thass where you were. Be a good lad now and knuckle down to some steady work, eh?'

Ah, he's sick of her. Sick of looking after her and getting no thanks. Sick of her gorging on whatever he brings home then moaning about how he got it. And most of all

28

he's sick of the strange guilt she somehow drums up in him, just because he's alive and the others died.

Last year's summer fever wiped out boatfuls of gypseas all over Pomperoy. It killed his little sister Beth and Grumpa, Ma's old Da. They'd hardly recovered from Tuck's own Da's death the year before, from a bone-rotting sickness he caught while raiding one of the toxic ships that ghost the oceans, ships full of scrap metal, oil and chemicals left over from the old world. Da was on a scavenge scoop for bridge metal and wire, but he ended up scavenging his own death.

He'd known the risk. That's why he wouldn't take Tuck.

Now Da and the others are gone, there's only Tuck left to look after Ma. Though they both survived the fever, Ma is a wretched shadow of her old self. Tuck knows he'll never be able to mend the great big rip in her life where little Beth and Da and Grumpa once were. All he can do is bring her home the fruits of his ill-gotten loot.

Ma's still grumbling. 'If there's one thing I want before I – *phut-phut PHUT* – lie down here on my bunk and die, it's my son anchored and settled in a rock-solid trade.'

Tuck almost laughs at the show Ma's putting on for the neighbours. Urth's sake, how can he settle when the world's all hurling and wheeling, when the windsnap in the rigging is loud as thunderclaps day and night, when the boats are in a tug of war with the chains that bind the city together against an ocean that's set on tearing it apart?

'In the name of The Man, Ma, gimme *peace*.'

Wheeez.

'Go back to sleep,' he mutters. 'I'll go find some work.'

Tuck clambers back on to the shack roof. His ankle's

still sore, but he tries a leap and lands, light as a cat, on one foot, on the roof next door.

But Ma's still going. He's a disgrace, she's yelling, always away out leaving his poor mother to fend for herself. One day he'll come back and she'll have died, she will, in a corner, all alone.

But the wind's against her. Soon she'll be right out of his ears.

THE MAN IN THE MIDDLE

Without a dodgy ankle, it's easy to leap and scuddy across the boat shacks. They're crammed close with rubbery roofs, good for foot-grip, made from tarred strips of sea-scavenged tyres. Today, Tuck tries to leap and land on his good foot. Eyes of The Man, who cares about a foot? He's alive! He might've been gutted like a fish by a Salter and ditched in the sea last night.

Pomperoy is the shape of a flat fish. *The Grimby Gray* is one of the wrecked, rusty barges crammed with shacks at the city's tail end. The lagoon around the oil rig in the middle, where Tuck is headed, is its pumping heart.

At the edge of *The Grimby Gray*, Tuck hops across the wire suspension bridge (built by his own Da and branded with the Culpy crescent) that connects to the neighbouring barge. He clears that, and the next. Now he's in the huge region of Doycha, a motley maze of small boats. It's said that Doycha has a thousand bridgeways, but Tuck knows there are exactly eight hundred and forty-one.

He leaps from boat to boat, laughing whenever he earns a yell. Every so often his ankle throbs too hard and he sits down on a roof or hobbles on to a swaying bridge for a rest, but cuts back to scuddying across the boats as soon as he can. They give him a straighter route than the bridgeways that link the boats. Though he could map a track across the bridgeways blind.

Beyond Doycha, he zigzags a route along the bridges that run between the rusted hulks of the ferries and take him into the higgledy squalor of Yewki. At last, he reaches the wooden walkways that surround the central lagoon. In the middle of the lagoon is the huge oil rig, the city's anchor and fuel source, linked by the five suspension bridges that radiate from it like the spokes of a great wheel.

All around the lagoon the market gondolas are being loaded up. By the time the sky has lightened the lagoon will be thronged with gondolas, each one piled with a harvest from the ocean or the sky: seafood and scrap metal, plastic and driftwood, birds and eggs. Tuck is overtired and achy. The buzz of the market workers irritates like a swarm of flies round his head. Creeping round the empty city after curfew is what he loves. Especially the lagoon.

Sometimes, deep in the night, strange winds whirl around the boat masts and upset the lagoon with scents of somewhere else. They fill Tuck with curiosity and send prickles down his spine. The restless ruffles inside him only calm when the wind flies off across the ocean and the lagoon smoothes to black glass.

Tuck knows about glass. He even owns a bit. It belonged to Grumpa. The fragment of glass is the shape of a raggedy, three-cornered boat sail and just fits into the creases of his closed hand. Once sharp enough to cut him, Tuck has rubbed the jagged edges smooth by scraping the Culpy crescent, his Da's trademark, into the wooden walkways around the lagoon. The power of the glass is that it can show you your very own self. And, better still, if you catch the sun's rays inside it, you can train it to make fire.

It's a mirror, Grumpa told him. *My old mum called it a looking-glass. Everyone used to have them, some big as your face, even as big as your whole self. First thing you'd do in the morning was take a look in your mirror, brush your hair and your teeth, have a shave.*

Grumpa would look wistful. The idea makes Tuck laugh. He can't imagine waking up and staring at your own face instead of rushing out to fish or load up a gondola or seal a leak in a rusted boat. Not that Tuck does any of that, himself.

He likes to look in the mirror, though it only shows his face in bits. Long, sun-bleached hair that blows across his face. Gypsea eyes, a deeper blue than his faded windwrap, narrowed by sharp winds and blades of sun. Weather-tanned cheeks, scoured by salty air. His Ma's mouth. His Da's strong nose.

Grumpa told strange stories of how people once lived fixed to the Earth. He'd always use the old word, no matter what Ma said.

Earth, he'd insist, rounding out the word. *Not Urth. Earth! A good old word. It's you youngsters who've made it a curse.*

It's you oldsters who cursed it, Da would mutter, just too low for Grumpa's crusty old ears. Tuck could hear, but Da would never explain what he meant.

Tuck never could get his head around the idea of Earth. A world steady underfoot? That didn't shift to the dance of the ocean? Even the word *Earth* is odd. It always made him snigger when Grumpa said it, all proud and defiant, because Tuck couldn't think of it as anything other than a curse.

There were cities, Grumpa would tell him, and he'd rub his watery blue eyes. Great cities with homes and shops and tall buildings fixed to the Land. The cities would stretch on and on, but the Land stretched further, as far as you could see. You'd have to walk for days until you reached the sea. Before the fuel ran out, he added, you'd just jump in a car or a plane and go anywhere you wanted, anywhere in the world, in no time at all.

Cars and planes? What are they? Tuck wanted to know.

A plane, Grumpa explained, was a boat with wings that flew across the skies like a giant bird. A car was a boat that travelled across Land. People lived in houses fixed to the Earth. Tuck has taken the biggest rock he ever dredged up with a catch of fish, held it in his hand and tried to imagine Land as a rock bigger than the whole of Pomperoy. He has even tried to imagine it stretching as far as the sea. But he can't.

Sometimes he wonders if Grumpa dreamed it all up.

Yet some people say there is still Land. Once, during a bad outbreak of sickness, one of the boats unchained from the rest and set out to sea. It was so long gone that everyone thought the family was lost. Many moons later the boat returned. Only some had survived and they were wounded and stunned with fear. They told a tale of a fiery island where a ferocious people live. A place where water thunders from the sky and boils up from the earth, they said. The ground runs with molten rivers and people bake to stone under a summer sun that burns day and night.

Since then the Pomperoy gypseas have stayed anchored to the rig, safe from the terrors of Land. This patch of ocean is home. An unbroken horizon means security and

34

peace. Tuck's gypsea heart beats to the rhythm of the waves. The spirit of the ocean dances in his soul.

Now, he strolls the walkways around the lagoon that is the bustling heart of Pomperoy. A richly patterned wind-wrap catches his eye.

That windwrap is a beauty. It belongs to his friend, Pendicle, and was sewn by his clan of industrious aunts. Tuck would do anything to have a windwrap like that. Instead of the Prender family emblem he'd have the Culpy crescent, a sharp silver moon, emblazoned on its back.

Pendicle is with his father, doing the early-morning stocktake of the Prenders' gondola fleet. Each boat is stocked with a jumble of old world goods, dredged up from the ocean. With a bit of ingenuity, any piece of junk can be crafted into something new. Tuck waves at Pendicle, but the look on his friend's face warns him not to get any closer, at least not until Pendicle's father has gone. Tuck is no longer welcome anywhere near Prender property, not since they discovered he'd been looting their stock.

Pendicle has been keeping a cool distance for a while now. Tuck knows he pushed his luck too far when he tried to loot Pendicle's mother's plush sealskin boots. He'd been eyeing them up for a while, maybe for his own Ma or maybe he'd trade them for gluggets of seagrape beer. He'd have shared the beer with Pendicle, of course. Tuck might be sly as a rat but he's not mean. What he hadn't planned on was Pendicle's Ma sneezing in her sleep so hard she woke herself up, just as Tuck was grabbing the sealskin boots from under her bed.

He feels bad about that. Just a bit, though. It's not as if Pendicle and his family are hard up, like Tuck. Yet he, Tuck reminds himself, wasn't always hard up. When Da was alive the Culpys had a plush enough home-boat of their own. Da's burial boat had hardly burned itself out on the ocean when a gang of Salters put a knife to Ma's throat and stole their boat. If it happened now, Tuck knows what he'd have done to those druxy Salters. But back then he was still a scared boy, so they ended up in a slum shack on a barge.

A shot of envy hits Tuck as he watches Pendicle with his father, one of the city's most powerful men. He is a striking man, with a strong brown face and his dark head covered in elegant furrows of plaits. His windwrap, like Pendicle's, is emblazoned with the Prender family emblem; an old world sign for power, Pendicle claims, though to Tuck it looks like an oily eel wrapped around a fishing rod.

But *his* Da, Tuck reminds himself, was once just as important. He was one of the best bridge-builders in Pomperoy. With hair as bright as winter sunshine and his windwrap with the Culpy crescent on its back, Jack Culpy was a striking man too. Da used to take Tuck along when he met the Prender brothers at the Oyster Bar; Tuck and Pendicle would play among the gondolas of sea junk while the men argued about bridges and oil.

Way back when Pomperoy was still at war with itself, the Prenders grabbed a share of the rig's oil. By the time the other gypseas had burned themselves out with pirating and wanted to be safe and settled instead, the Prenders had set themselves up as one of the city's oil families. Now they're one of the richest clans in Pomperoy. What does a bit of looting matter to them?

Tuck walks up on to a swaying arm of the Middle Bridges. He'd better steer clear of the Saltmarket at the head of the lagoon. The bridges are the highest point in Pomperoy, apart from the rig. Tuck looks across the city

36

to the ocean beyond. When he's overtired, like he is now, he sometimes gets spooked by a thought. What if a great storm uprooted the rig and unanchored the whole of Pomperoy? What if the boats were then tossed across the ocean until they slipped over the edge of the world?

The old people say the world is round. Even if the city's anchors failed, the boats would just keep floating round and round. You couldn't fall over the edge because there isn't an edge. If that's true, thinks Tuck, why don't things fall off? What keeps the sea on the underside stuck to the Earth?

Tuck yawns and shivers inside his windwrap as he looks at the line of the ocean where it meets the sky. It looks like an edge to him.

Once, people thought they knew the world. Not any more.

No one even knows if there are other gypsea cities, like Pomperoy. The only signs of life upon the ocean, though there's plenty underneath, are lone refugee boats, lost and adrift, ripe for raiding. But even they're more dead than alive, full of bones or rotting corpses.

Wind scuffs the lagoon and a popple sea threatens, but soon the water is as sleek as a seal again. Way up on the oil rig's chimney stack, The Man in the Middle beams down on Pomperoy, his face aglow in the rising sun.

Years ago, The Man surfaced in the lagoon. A couple of kids spotted the large plastic board with its smiling face. They fished it out of the water and ran home with it to their boat. The very next day the sickness that had struck the city left the family's boat. The Man was taken to a neighbouring boat where a mother and her baby were sick almost to death. Once again he seemed to chase the illness away. So they carried The Man across one of the arms of the Middle Bridges to the oil rig in the heart of the lagoon. They hung the face of The Man high on the chimney stack of the rig so that he could watch over the whole of Pomperoy and keep it safe.

None of the old people believe in The Man. Bit of plastic junk, they say, and ramble about a chicken called Kentucky that people used to eat, before the world was sea. But the old people tell so many tall tales about the past, no one knows what's true and what's not. Anyhow, the Kentucky name stuck to The Man and The Man stayed on the rig as the luck-keeper of Pomperoy.

When Ma named baby Tuck after The Man people said it was barefaced cheek. Ma, being Ma, didn't care. *But look*, they say, *what happened to the Culpy family when they took The Man's name. Jack Culpy died a horrible death, followed by his father and the little girl. Then Tuck and his Ma end up in a slum shack.*

Tuck's name has ruined his family. That's what everyone thinks. Tuck hears the whispers and they make him want to run. So he does, every night. Runs from the blame and the guilt, runs from his own lousy, wrecked life. Runs and leaps the whole of Pomperoy, looting as he goes, and only calls it a night when the flocks of Great Skua fill the dawn skies over the city, and call him home by name, *tuk-tuk, tuk-tuk*.

The Great Skua's cry makes him itch for their wings. He'd like to fly free of Pomperoy, soar all across the oceans and see what the world is. Tuck would rather risk a salt-knife at his throat than settle for a life of patching boats or mending bridges. It was bridging that killed Da in the end. If Tuck's going to gamble his life, it'll be for something more than a coil of bridgewire.

Or a pocketful of salt, come to that . . .

When the idea hits, Tuck stops breathing. It's either the best loot he's ever thought of, or the worst.

A fearful excitement zips through him, right down to his fingers and toes. Does he dare?

Great Skua, he dares!

Tuck's doubts about The Man's power have been growing for many a moon. For eleven moons, to be exact. Ever since Tuck stood on this same bridge and promised The Man he'd change his name, never glug another beer ever again, he'd do anything, anything at all, whatever The Man wanted, if only he'd save little Beth and Grumpa from the deadly fever that was burning them up. But The Man did nothing at all.

In nightmares, Tuck still sees their burial boat, blazing on the black sea like a dying sun. The sound of Ma screaming is seared into a corner of his mind.

And secretly, in the depths of his heart, Tuck hates The Man.

Last night, in his panic, he broke his own sullen promise never to ask The Man for another thing as long as he lived. He begged to be saved from the Salters. And he was. Did The Man do that? Or was it just a scrape of ordinary luck? Well, the idea that's ripped through him might reveal once and for all whether The Man is just a bit of old junk like Grumpa said – or not.

Tuck avoids looking at the inscrutable, beaming face as he unfolds the astounding idea in his head.

He'll steal The Man. In the dead of night when Pomperoy is sound asleep.

He'll hide The Man's face in his secret loot store, a murky cabin below deck in *The Grimby Gray*.

Pomperoy will wake up to find The Man gone. The city will grow frantic with fear. At last, The Man will reappear in the sea. Who will find him? Tuck, of course! He'll be an instant hero and *The Grimby Gray* will be known as the lucky place where The Man in the Middle rose once again – right outside Tuck Culpy's barge.

No more will folk mutter my name like a curse, Tuck vows. *I'll rescue the Culpy name. I'll make Ma happy again and do Da proud.*

Dawn bleeds across the sky and into the lagoon. The wind throws a punch at the market gondolas and they *knock-knock* against each other like a boxful of bones.

Tuck counts the knocks to keep himself calm. He knows he is gambling with his life because if he's caught . . . Tuck has seen people hang right here on this bridge, for less.

It's a gamble. But if he wins, it'll be the loot of his life.

Tuck lets out a long breath, counts twenty racing heartbeats.

He'll do it.

He will.

MISSING MIDNIGHT

At sundown the wind turns evil. The refugees hide below deck as the wind tries to hurl the ship against the sky.

Crushed between her friends, Mara snatches shreds of sleep but the striplights below deck keep flickering. Every time her eyes drop with exhaustion, the lights beat against her eyelids. Time and time again, she jolts awake and stares at the cavernous interior of the ship, wondering where on Earth she is. Each time it takes her long, giddy moments to remember, and immediately she wishes she could forget.

All around, refugees cry and bicker and curse at having landed up in such a foul place as this.

What have I done? Mara wonders. *What if we don't find land?*

The ship's hold is like a warehouse, piled with crates of food supplies meant for the New World. At least they managed to steal a stocked cargo ship, thinks Mara. They might have been unlucky and taken one that had already unloaded its supplies in the city's dock tower.

What about the other ships that escaped the city? Mara

has searched the ocean through all the hours of daylight but there has been no sign of them.

Mara looks at all the refugees crammed in between the crates in the hold. The urchins have made one corner their own and have filled it with the hoard of objects they stole from the museum in the netherworld. Scarwell is snuggled up asleep with her prize loot, the life-size model of an ape-man.

A small girl sits alone, hugging her knees. Every so often her face twitches. Mara goes over and tries to talk to the child but there's no response. The girl stares at the floor, lost in her own world. Better there than in this nightmare, thinks Mara.

She buries her face in her arms and tries to find her own escape. Sleep comes at last, ragged with dreams of her family and her old island home. Dad, clattering milk buckets in the barn. Her little brother Corey, chasing the chickens and running through billows of bed sheets that Mum is hanging out to dry. Rowan is a lone, distant figure among the crazy whirl of the field of windmills. And there's Tain, bolting the storm shutters of his stone cottage against a rising storm. His white hair is wild in the wind; he's bellowing about the rising sea but the weather drowns his words.

And she dreams of Fox, just for an instant. Fox, alone in the drowned ruins below the towers of New Mungo. Fox, with nightmares in his beautiful eyes.

When a surge of the ship slams her head against a crate, Mara tries to hold on to him but he crashes out of her dream. She's awake and he's gone, just as he crashed out of her life.

Mara sits up with a jolt. What time is it? She rushes up on deck into darkness, blasted by wind. There's no moon, not one lone star to help track the passage of the night. Has she missed midnight, when she promised to meet Fox in the Weave?

Mara slips into the control cabin to escape the wind. She unzips her backpack, opens the waterproof seal within and takes out the cyberwizz globe, feels the electric tingle as she nestles it in her hands and it powers up. She shoves the halo over her eyes and clicks open the globe. With the tiny wand, she scribbles a series of symbols on the small screenpad.

And in the flash of a thought, she's there . . .

. . . *magicked out of realworld and dropped into the vast, glittering cyberscape of the Weave.*

Mara zooms along the familiar wrecked boulevards lined with buzzing, sparking towerstacks that store the lost data of the old, drowned world. The boulevards end in a crumble of tumbledown stacks, rotting mountains of cyberjunk. There's a strange, flickering beauty, danger too sometimes, in these heaps of decay.

Deep in the the ruins looms the arm of a broken bridge. Mara slows up, steps on to the bridge and stares at what lies beyond – an electric blue ocean of cyberhaze.

Fox? Her voice crackles with static. Are you here?

This is where he promised to be, on the Bridge to Nowhere. But he's not here. There are a hundred reasons why he might not have made it.

Maybe she's too late. Maybe he came earlier and she wasn't here. Maybe he gave up on her. Maybe he fell asleep.

But what if he never made it out of New Mungo? What if he was caught by the sea police? Or drowned in the filthy waters of the netherworld as he tried to swim across to the old university tower?

Fox? Are you safe? Please be safe. Please come.
Panic-stricken, she waits and waits.
But Fox doesn't come.

FOX

The fluttery light of the old woman's lantern illuminates her dark eyes and canyons of wrinkles in a moon-pale face.

She's calm and quiet. It's what Fox needs. He's too estranged to talk and Candleriggs seems to know. Instead of talking, she's given him tasks. *Find eggs*, she told him and sent him searching by lantern-light through the crumbling stone rooms of the old tower, after showing him what an egg is. A nest is such a cleverly crafted thing he can't believe it's made by a bird. He's yet to see a real one of those. In New Mungo, even the birds are fake.

Fox is beginning to understand what Mara tried to tell him: that the birds, the trees, the food and so much else in his city are synthetic versions of what used to exist on the Earth before the seas rose. Down here in the dank ruins of the drowned world, in the shadow of New Mungo's vast towers, life is so raw and harsh it shocks Fox to his core. He can't see how anyone could survive. Yet Candleriggs has, ever since his grandfather, Caledon, threw her out of New Mungo all those years ago. Caledon betrayed her, the woman he loved, abandoning her here so that he could follow his dream.

The tower rooms are crammed with collapsing book-stacks. Even the winding stairway between the floors is strewn with wind-tattered pages covered in feathers, bird mess and spiders' webs. At last, atop a tumbledown book heap, Fox finds an egg. Candleriggs said they are good to eat. Fox cups the hard shell in his hands and wonders how they will eat that.

He finds five eggs in all and breaks two. They're not as hard as they seem and what's inside doesn't look good to eat at all.

The tower rooms are as confusing as a maze but at last Fox finds his way back. Candleriggs is gathering up loose pages from the heaps of books that litter the stone floor. This room is a good place to settle, she says. The windows face South and will catch the sun when it rises over the city walls. In winter, they will have some shelter from the brutal wind that blasts from the North.

Fox thinks of Mara on the ship, heading towards the home of the North Wind.

Candleriggs has taken two stones from the pocket of her cloak and strikes them against each other. Sparks shoot from the stones. Fox watches them fall on the dry pages of the books. One of the sparks smoulders into a tiny flame and the paper begins to burn.

He has never seen fire; not the real thing. In New Mungo fire is an illusion of lumen light. But real fire is made by striking stones on dry paper. It's strong enough to warm you right through to your bones. He never knew.

Candleriggs tends the fire, rubbing her hands in the heat of the crackling flames.

'Aah . . . that's better, isn't it?'

She snuggles inside her cloak. It's made from the strangest material Fox has ever seen and steams gently in the heat of the fire. A strange smell emanates from it.

'Are you on fire?' he asks, bewildered.

Candleriggs frowns then chuckles. 'Just damp.'

Then she explains simply, as if he's a child.

'The fire warms my cloak and the dampness turns to steam. The moss weave of my cloak absorbs the damp air. Stops it seeping into my old bones,' she adds. 'Now, watch. I'm going to cook the eggs.'

She's brisk and kind, but the fact that she has to explain everything means she knows how ill-equipped he is to survive.

Candleriggs cracks the eggs on the stone floor and pours the clear and yellow stuff that's inside on to the hot stone close to the flames. Fox watches the eggs cook. For the first time, he understands how scared and disorientated Mara must have been in New Mungo, having only known the world outside. *This* world.

His heart turns over. How could he have known? Nothing in the gleaming towers of a sky city could ever prepare him for the sheer *earthiness* of the world outside.

Once they have eaten, it's Candleriggs's turn to wonder when Fox takes his godgem from a watertight wallet attached to a belt around his waist.

'Godbox,' he explains. 'Power at my command.'

She peers at the minuscule box as he clips it on to his shirt, close to his heart.

'Headgem. A magnetic mind's eye.'

She stares as he sticks the green gem to the front of his head.

'Godbox, headgem – godgem.'

'This is what computers have become?' The old

47

woman's eyes can't grow any wider. Now they crinkle as she laughs. 'And I thought Mara's cyberwizzard was—' She breaks off and her forehead furrows into deep lines. 'You can speak to Mara with this?'

'Hope so,' says Fox.

He hurtles into the Weave and zips through the electronic boulevards to the Bridge to Nowhere. Mara is not there. He waits, but she doesn't come.

When the exodus of ships fled through the city walls, the pain of losing Mara was shot through with astonishment at the salty sea wind, the fire of the stars, the dark of night and the thunder of the ocean beyond the city walls. Loneliness hit like a hammer blow as he looked up at the vast towers and sky tunnels of the city he abandoned. Then he saw the strange netherworld he'd landed in. Fox peered through the darkness at the dank black sea that lapped around the trunks of New Mungo, at the dark shadow of the high walls that enclose the city's towers. He saw the remains of the drowned city in the water – humps of small islands topped with trees and steeples and ruins. A great black steeple loomed in the darkness – the old university tower.

This was the place his grandfather dreamed up the sky cities that rose out of the waters of a drowned Earth. And this is where Fox hopes to spark a revolution that will break the dark forces that control the New World. Down here is the misery his world is built upon. The vast boat camp and an army of slaves on the sea bridges are just beyond the city walls. How many of those desperate people, he wonders, escaped with Mara on the ships? She begged him to go with her but he stayed here to start his battle with the New World.

Panic swamped him as he stood in the darkness of the

first real night he'd ever known. Thinking he could start a revolution in this grim place seemed a crazy idea. He was a fool not to go with Mara. Yet he can't go back home to New Mungo. He wrecked the city's communications and orchestrated a mass breakout. Now he is a traitor; harsh punishment awaits. Even worse is his family's fury and shame.

A soft light appeared in the darkness. The old woman had come to find him; he wasn't all alone. The other Treenesters were gone with Mara but, like him, Candleriggs had stubbornly chosen to stay.

It was a struggle to steer her raft, Fox swimming alongside, through the flooded halls at the foot of the old tower. The fluttering light of her lantern illuminated the vaulted chambers, pillars and archways of the undercroft.

Once past the undercroft, he dragged the raft through a smashed door then up on to the grand sweep of stairs that led up to the halls of the museum. Walking through the great halls, exhaustion took hold of the old woman. Fox could see she was struggling to go on. So they stopped right there in the middle of a hall, sank down on the floor and slept, wet and shivering, under the shadow of some strange, looming thing.

Fox woke to the sound of a laugh. Stiff and sore, he got up from the floor – and yelled with fright at the long-nosed beast that was staring him in the face.

Keep calm, it's long dead, Candleriggs chuckled.

What is it? he asked, stunned.

An elephant, she said. *No elephants, eh, in your brave New World?*

It took them much of the day to search for the book rooms at the top of the tower. Mara said they were so hard to find they'd be an ideal hideout. At last they found

49

the small door to the tower. Through the door, said Mara, was the climb of a thousand and more tight-winding stairs.

How would he ever get old Candleriggs up a thousand stairs?

And when he did, how would they live, way up there in the tower?

They had to stop many times but they got there. The stamina of such a bent and gnarled old woman amazed Fox.

Now he sits by the fire beside this strange old woman who looks as if she is made of the same cracked stone as the tower walls.

'Did you ever come here with my grandfather,' he asks, 'when you were young?'

She drops her eyes from his face and nods.

Fox gets up and walks over to the smashed tower window. He leans his head against the cold stone wall.

'You're very like him.' Candleriggs's voice creaks like the ancient wood door of the room. 'You look just like he did at your age.'

'I'm nothing like him. I could never do what he's done.'

'What he did was amazing,' says Candleriggs softly. 'The sky cities are wonders of the Earth. But Caledon's dream ruled his heart and made him believe that all kinds of cruelty were necessary to build his New World. You've a better heart, I think. But you've got his spirit and I'm glad about that. You're going to need it.'

It's not just the old woman's words that spook him. He can hear the whoop of the windspires that whirl on New Mungo's towers. Fox draws back from the window. The sound unnerves him though he knows the spiregyres only turn wind into energy, and there's nothing spooky about that. Now Candleriggs's odd lantern is giving him the creeps. Its light is a strange fluttering thing.

'What *is* that?'

'Moonmoths,' says Candleriggs.

He crouches to peer at the huge moths fluttering inside the twig lantern. Now he looks closer, they're not spooky at all. They have the same mesmeric glow as the bedside motherlights in New Mungo.

'Candleriggs,' he says, after watching a while.

She doesn't answer. He turns around in a panic. But she's not gone, just rolled up in her thick, mossy cloak on the stone floor, fast asleep. She has made a nest of sorts from the heaps of wrecked books.

Fox lifts the lantern and looks around him. *Library.* That's what these tower rooms used to be. In the New World there are no libraries or books. There is the Noos.

The Noos is the brain of the New World, a stunning cyber-universe bursting with the information and ideas that are traded between sky cities all across the Earth. Everything you could ever want to know, and wonders beyond dreams, exists in the ever-expanding Noos.

Or so Fox used to think.

Once upon a time, libraries and books were where people stored knowledge and ideas. Later, they used the electronic towers of the Weave too. This wrecked library in the old university tower is where Mara found the book that gave her the idea of finding land at the top of the world. Maybe here Fox will find what he needs.

He sets down the lantern and the light of the moon-moths flutters across Candleriggs's face. His grandfather is just as old, yet his face has not been ravaged like hers. Caledon lives in luxury. A lifetime's struggle to survive is written on Candleriggs's face. And it was Caledon who made that her fate when he threw her out of his world.

That's the kind of man his grandfather is. Merciless. Cruel. And that's the kind of empire he has built as the Grand Father of All the New World.

Now, when Fox looks out of the smashed tower window and up at the sky city that was his home, he feels as angry as the red sunrise that's begun to rip up the night.

It feels better. That's what he needs, that anger, if he is to succeed.

Soon, the mass of workers will start to arrive in the city's cybercathedral where the business of the New World is done. The rooks, the secret police of the Noos, will have been working furiously to fix the systems he crashed.

The thought of all that industry above his head focuses Fox on his own task. He sits against the cold tower wall, prods the fire with the toe of his shoe, but it's almost dead and he doesn't know what to do to bring it back to life. For an instant, he wishes himself back up in his safe, selfish world. At least he knows how to function there.

I'll learn how to spark a fire.

The sun breaks over the city wall. It finds a gap in the trunks of the sky towers and streams through the gloom of the netherworld. A tablet of light lands on the stone floor. Fox stares at it in wonder. In New Mungo, even the sun is a lumen light, a bland imitation of this astonishingly real thing.

He stands in the sunbeam and feels its power on his skin. It's the shot of energy he needs to fire him into action and take his first, tentative steps in the battle he means to begin with the powers of the New World. Fox grabs his godgem and makes a cyberleap into the universe of the Noos.

52

THE FLOATING CITY

The northern ocean is still deep in night, but a slab of sunrise gleams in the East. Someone speaks to Mara and she turns away from the sun, but it takes a moment for the glare to fade from her eyes before she can see the tall young woman who has joined her at the front of the ship. Molendinar's face is half hidden by the fall of hair that almost touches the ground, but a blast of wind and the eastern light reveal a cut and swollen mouth.

Mara stares. 'Mol, what happened?'

Molendinar shakes her head, angry tears in her eyes. 'It's madness down there. People fighting over food and water. Not just those savage little urchins of yours, Mara, it's everyone. Everyone's out of control.'

'But there's plenty, isn't there?' Mara is suddenly uncertain. She has been so caught up in her own turmoil that she hasn't thought to check supplies. 'And they're not *my* urchins,' she mutters. 'They're from *your* world. My people would never abandon little children to the sea—'

Mara stops, stricken with shame. No, it was the old ones her people abandoned to the sea because there wasn't enough room on the boats.

'There's enough to eat and drink for now,' agrees Molendinar, overlooking her mutters. 'But we don't know how long this journey will last. How long, Mara?'

Fox tried to estimate, but he couldn't be sure. The old map of Greenland in Mara's book shows an immense island. It's impossible to know, if they reach it safely, how far along its vast coast they might go. Fox has programmed the ship to sail due North until they hit that coastline. Then, they will have to steer the ship themselves. Mara is counting on Rowan's boat skills for that, though she hasn't told him yet.

'Days,' says Mara nervously. 'Maybe a week.'

'Even if we do find land soon,' Molendinar rushes on, 'the first thing we must do is make shelter, build homes. We don't know what kind of land or food we'll find at the top of the world.'

'We'll fish,' says Mara. She's an island girl; she knows how to survive. 'We'll stay close to the sea and fish. And there'll be bird eggs, seaweed. We won't starve.'

Broomielaw, who has been listening in, nods, but she looks uncertain. 'There are so many of us, lots of children, and we're heading into winter.'

And winter in the Far North will be dark and deep, Mara knows; even darker and deeper than winter on her island home. Molendinar is right, they need to make supplies last.

'A lot of people are sick and don't want to eat, the others eat and fight all day long because there's nothing else to do. The sick will grow weak and the greedy will be slugs, none of them any use. We need everyone strong and good for work if we're going to survive.' Molendinar throws a long rope of hair over a shoulder and glares at a group of urchins who barge past, stuffing their mouths with food. 'It'll take a summer at least to grow my crop.'

'Crop?'

Mara stares at Molendinar's hair, wondering what she means. But Molendinar unfastens a deep pocket in her clothing and shows Mara and Broomielaw the seeds she grabbed before they fled the city.

Broomielaw gives a sigh. 'All I managed to grab was Clayslaps. I left all my inventions behind.'

'Well, you'd rather have him, wouldn't you?' says Molendinar, unusually sharp.

'Mol, you're a wonder,' says Mara. Her mood lifts. Somehow, the tiny seed crop has given her hope.

'It's not just me,' Molendinar protests. 'We can't seem to stop being Treenesters. Ibrox came with his firebox and pockets filled with fire-making stones.'

The Treenesters have as many waterproof pockets as anyone could ever need in their odd but practical clothing made from a knot-weave of the plastic bags they dredged up out of the litter of the netherworld sea.

'Ibrox is making fires?' Mara imagines the ship going up in flames.

'No.' A smile flickers across Molendinar's bruised mouth. 'But he'll start one as soon as he sets foot on land. And I'll start planting my seeds. Possil and Pollock will hunt and Gorbals will make a story of our lives. Just as we always did.'

They're holding on to being Treenesters, Mara understands, to keep a grip of who they are in the world.

Not poor Gorbals though. He's too seasick to be a poet right now.

Mara follows Broomielaw and Molendinar down below deck. The stench in the hold is terrible, getting

55

worse by the hour. Several hundred sick and dirty people, crammed together with no fresh air and few toilets, have made a midden of the place. They've thrown litter everywhere, gorging on whatever they find.

'Speak to them,' says Molendinar.

'Why me?' Mara looks around. Tension frets the stale air. Would they listen? So many of the refugees are adults, much older than she is. Shouldn't one of them take charge?

'You're the one who saved them,' urges Broomielaw. 'If it wasn't for you they'd still be trapped in that horrific boat camp. We'd be left to drown in the ruins. All of us were shut out of the world without a chance. You brought us here so you should lead us. Speak up, Mara, don't be scared.'

Mara steps forward. She doesn't know these people; she *is* scared. Her voice barely makes a dent in the noise. She swallows, tries again. 'Listen, everyone. We need to be careful with the food. We need to share it and make it last. We don't know how long we'll be on this ship. We should be fishing. There's no shortage of fish out there.'

As her voice grows stronger, heads turn and people quieten.

'There must be netting or rope – something that we can use to fish.' Mara looks over at Possil and Pollock, the hunters, thinking on her feet. 'We need to organize.'

A tall woman stands up. 'You're this Mara girl, eh?'

Steely eyes in a pinched face appraise her in a way that makes Mara's cheeks burn. The woman's face and voice take her back to the day she entered the horror of the boat camp outside the sky city's walls. It's the same hostile woman, she's sure, who tried to turn away their boat.

'You're the one who's trailing us all across the ocean?'

56

The woman sets her hands on her hips. 'But you don't know where to, or so I've heard.'

The woman makes Mara feel small and childish, but a little knife-edge of anger is sharpening inside.

'We're headed for the top of the world.' Mara raises her chin and meets the woman's eyes with her best don't-mess-with-me stare. 'To *Kalaallit Nunaat*, the land of the people.'

'Never heard of it.' The woman looks around her. 'Anyone else ever heard of such a place?'

'Its other name is Greenland,' Mara persists, 'though it's been frozen for thousands of years. If the ice cap has melted, it might really be a green land now – somewhere we can maybe make a home.'

'Maybe, eh?' The woman raises an eyebrow and addresses the others. 'That's a whole lot of ifs and maybes.'

Mara rummages in her backpack and finds the book on Greenland. She holds it up in a shaking hand and tries to tell people more, but the tall woman is talking over her, contemptuously blocking out her voice.

'So we have a slip of a girl in charge of this ship who has no real idea of what she's doing.'

Molendinar steps in and challenges. 'Do you know any better? It was Mara who rescued you – did you want to stay and die in that boat camp outside the city walls?'

'Maybe she did.' The woman glances around for support. 'The point is we need adults in charge now.'

There's a muttering among the refugees. Whether they agree or not, Mara can't tell.

And suddenly Mara finds she doesn't care. She is so tired. She never wanted to be in charge of a ship full of refugees. *Let* an adult take charge.

But all around her friends have risen to their feet in

outrage. An elderly woman steps forward and touches Mara's arm. There's something in her shrewd eyes that Mara instantly warms towards. She turns to Mara's challenger.

'Now, Ruby.'

There's a grace and authority about this woman that makes Ruby shrug, ungraciously, and sit down.

'Ruby's very strong-headed,' says the older woman. 'But I see you are too.'

'That one is *wrong*-headed,' mutters Ibrox. He leans over and squeezes Mara's arm.

The old woman doesn't argue. Instead, she introduces herself as Merien. 'You're too tired right now to lead your own shadow,' she tells Mara. 'You need to sleep.'

Mara yawns. She should be in the control cabin, checking the ship's progress. There's a whole day to live through until she can try to connect with Fox tonight. She lies down, puts her head in her arms and escapes into uneasy sleep.

She wakens with a sharp pain in her shoulder. She has slammed hard against a pile of crates.

The ship gives a great lurch backward. Mara is thrown across the hold, feels bone crunching on bone, head cracking against head. The refugees are tossed about like sticks in a storm.

The lights flicker into darkness. There's a vacuum of shock and pain.

'My baby! Where's my baby?'

Mara hears Broomielaw among the aftershock of screams. She feels about in the dark for little Clayslaps. She finds arms, legs, feet, handfuls of hair, but no baby. The ship lurches again. Mara is frantic to find the baby but she must get to the ship's control cabin, at once. She struggles through flailing arms and legs, feels herself step on something soft, hears a child's wail and steps back, reaching down to search the darkness. Her hands are crushed by a stampede of feet.

The child is gone, rolled out of reach.

She feels sick. Was that little Clay?

Shaking, she makes for the stairs. Her legs throb with bruises. Her feet and fingers are crushed. She wipes the taste of blood from her lips, keeps going, feels her way up the stairs, clinging to each rung to stop the lurching ship flinging her back down.

Mara stumbles out of the dark hold into the shock of daylight. A raw sunrise streaks the eastern sky.

'What's happening? What have we hit?'

There's no answer. The impact has scattered people all over the deck. The ship is still shuddering so violently that Mara gets down on her hands and knees and crawls to the edge of the deck. She pulls herself to her feet and stares.

There is no ocean.

Just a vast chaos of flotsam, all around the ship.

Her mind scrambles to catch up with her eyes. She can't make sense of what she sees. From her vantage point she has a broad view and Mara seems to see glinting metal bridges, shimmering channels of sea that run through the flotsam like winding rivers. But it's not flotsam at all, not junk. It's an immense clutter of barges and boats.

The ship must have crashed into a seaport.

The urgent clangour of bells echoes across the boats, amid a rising siren wail – no, the wail is human. It's the sound of terror. A mass of voices, raised in alarm.

What land is this?

Mara can't think.

There's a distant glint of ocean to the North of the

port. Mara frowns as she looks East and sees a glinting line of it there, and reflecting far to the West too.

The sea is all around. And in between the boats.

Now she understands.

This city is not made of buildings, but boats.

This is not land. The ship has smashed into a floating city. And horribly, the ship's engines are still driving forward, smashing the city's bridges and boats.

Now Mara sees the people. They race across the bridges, a great tide of them, running towards the ship to help another, smaller rush of people in nearby barges and boats who are trying to get away. The ship rips through another bridge. Stranded people are screaming, clinging to wreckage. Those with no other option jump into the violent sea.

Behind the ship, an old barge groans; a deathly sound that almost drowns out the screams of the people on its deck. It keels sideways, sinking fast.

Mara grips the ship's rail as the barge goes down. Eyes tight shut, she wills it to be over. The awful sound of it shudders through her bones. With a great roar, the ocean sucks the barge down to its depths.

That was what they hit when she was down in the hold.

A barge full of people.

The ship rocks back and forth. Mara pushes through people, trips over them, stumbles into the ship's control cabin.

This was not supposed to happen. A floating city was not in the navigation plans.

The ship grinds on, further into the city. Mara stares at the controls and doesn't know what to do.

THE SINKING OF *THE GRIMBY GRAY*

Tuck looks up, puzzled. The gulls are going crazy this morning. Beyond the frantic shrieks is a noise that makes his blood run cold though he has no idea what it is.

Tuck stares at the lagoon. The water is still dark, keeping grip of the night. A moment ago it was calm, rising and falling in a drowsy pulse, but now a great shudder rips across the smooth waves.

Tuck watches, puzzled. All around the lagoon the stockholders, busy loading goods on to their gondolas, freeze as the strange shudder vibrates across the city. The gondolas begin to crash into each other as the shudder on the lagoon builds into rolling waves.

There are shouts from the Middle Bridges. A scream rips through Tuck's bewildered daze and he races up on to an arm of the bridge.

A great white ship has entered the city.

It's much bigger than any vessel in Pomperoy.

At first, Tuck thinks it has docked in one of the sea paths. Then he sees that the ship is still moving, faster than his stunned mind. As he stares open-mouthed, the ship smashes into one of Doycha's largest bridges. In that moment, Tuck registers several things. The screams he thought were gulls are not. It's people, screaming for their lives. And the ship has not entered by any seaway. It is ploughing straight into Pomperoy.

The bridge seems to explode. Debris juts into the air, in exclamations of shock that scatter across Doycha. Tuck's stomach lurches. Not all of it is debris. Scattered people, broken bodies, are among the wreckage; early risers on their way to market.

A bone-chilling sound splices the air. Tuck covers his ears.

The ship seems to be reversing.

Tuck peers at the patch of city beyond the maze of Doycha's boats and bridges to where the barges should be. The murky light makes it hard to see but he spots the dark bulks of *Troon* and *Crossness*, the neighbouring barges. One of them is wounded and listing to one side, but it's there. Why can't he see *The Grimby Gray*? Tuck runs from one side of the bridge to the other to get a better view, but it's no good. For some reason, he can't see his own barge.

His heart slumps into his stomach. A taste of metal in the air makes him feel sick. His limbs are suddenly heavy, as if his clothes are weighted with sea. He can't move.

And then he does. He's racing off the Middle Bridge, down into Doycha, leaping across boat roofs and bridges, the pain in his ankle numbed by shock.

He runs on to a bridge alongside the white ship then stops. What can he do?

He grabs the arm of an old man beside him. 'What's happening? What is it?'

The old man is shock-white, shaking with fear.

'*Arkiel*,' he mutters blankly.

62

'What?'

The old man points to the bold nameplate on the ship. '*Arkiel*. It's taken my wife.'

Tuck stares helplessly at the mass of people crowding the *Arkiel*'s decks. Their screams mingle with those in the boats and barges the ship is ploughing into.

'*Stop!*'

Tuck yells at the ship until his throat hurts. What else can he do? There's no way anyone can board the ship; its sides are too sheer, too steep, with no grip, no footholds. His cries merge with a multitude of frantic voices, as if the gypseas of Pomperoy are trying to halt the *Arkiel* with a wall of noise.

A girl has climbed up on to the roof of the ship's control cabin. She is caught in a shot of sunlight and throws an arm across her eyes, blinded by the glare. A great shudder shakes the *Arkiel* as it demolishes a swathe of Doycha and the girl is thrown to her knees.

Another impact hurls the girl right off the cabin roof. The last Tuck sees of her is the scatter of her hair, like a splash of oil, as she tumbles into the crowd on the ship's deck.

Tuck stares around him, dizzy and disorientated, as if he's taken a hard fall himself. Where's *The Grimby Gray*? He rubs his eyes, searching frantically for the familiar rusty wreck of his own barge. *This* is where it should be. Tuck doesn't understand. And then he does.

The ship is where his barge should be.

Tuck feels sick to his stomach, as if he's swallowed mouthfuls of sea. He makes himself look down, and he sees it.

Under the water, *The Grimby Gray* has sunk like a rusted tin can.

There are bodies, pale ghosts in the darkness of the ocean. Half-drowned people are being pulled on to boats. Tuck panics. *Ma? Where's Ma?* A horrible feeling, as if he's been sliced open and gutted like a fish, makes him wrap his arms around himself. He can't see her. And the sharp, empty feeling tells him he won't.

She couldn't swim. If she tried, the panic and struggle would bring on an attack of wheezing. She wouldn't stand a chance. That's if she woke up at all. More likely, the barge would have sunk before Ma, deep in beer-glazed slumber, even knew what was happening. The only chance she'd have had is if he'd been there.

But he wasn't.

Tuck looks back across the city at The Man.

He can just about make out the white-bearded face up on the bridge, beaming his relentless smile. Tuck crosses his fingers, but instead of raising them in the good-luck sign, he makes the reverse sign, the malevolent one. He jabs his crossed fingers straight at The Man's plastic face.

Why Ma? Why old Arthus and all the others? Why not me? I was the one going to steal you. I was the one that didn't believe in you. Never even laid a finger on you though, did I? You never gave me a chance.

Grumpa was wrong about The Man. He's not just a bit of junk. His eyes can look into the dark corners of your mind. He might grant you the miracle you need or punish you without mercy if he doesn't like what he sees.

What else does he see? What else has he planned?

The *Arkiel* keeps ploughing through the city in reverse, making a catastrophically clumsy exit.

Up high on the rig, The Man watches and smiles.

PENDICLE PRENDER

Tuck wanders the city, blank and numb. He ends up back at the lagoon and slumps down on the damp wooden walkways, exhausted. He doesn't know how long he's been there, shivering, when a hand on his shoulder makes him jump.

'You're alive then.'

Pendicle sits down beside him with a sigh of relief.

'Ma's gone,' says Tuck. He has to force the words out; he still doesn't believe it. 'She went down with *The Grimby Gray*.'

'*Urth*,' Pendicle curses softly. He bites his lip and clearly doesn't know what else to say. They sit together awhile, just staring out at the waves on the lagoon. All of a sudden Pendicle gets to his feet. He punches Tuck softly on the shoulder, in place of soft words.

'There's a family meeting,' says Pendicle, with the faint edge of self-importance in his voice that, lately, Tuck has begun to hear. 'Something's happening.'

Tuck gives a small, hard laugh. 'It already *happened*.'

Pendicle's eyes are on his home-boat, one of the Prenders' fleet of masted mega-yachts, anchored alongside the family's market gondolas on the lagoon. A group of people, their windwraps bearing the Prender emblem, are gathered on its deck. Men and woman flock to Pendicle's home-boat from grand yachts and schooners all around the lagoon. Their windwraps are emblazoned with the various emblems of Pomperoy's oil families. Tuck realizes the reason for Pendicle's self-important tone. It's not an everyday family meeting, but an extraordinary summit of the powerful families that rule Pomperoy.

Pendicle shoves something into a pocket of Tuck's windwrap. Tuck hears the rattle of pearls.

'Enough to get you bed and board somewhere, get you sorted,' says Pendicle. 'I'd better go.'

Once upon a time, Pendicle would have taken him back to his boat for a hot meal and a bunk. But he's changing, Tuck senses, from his old mate Pendicle into a fully fledged Prender, becoming part of the powerful engine of the oil families, no longer the carefree wildhead he used to be. Even if Pendicle would harbour Tuck, his Ma won't. She's the kind of woman you cross once if you dare; never twice. That's how the Prenders got to be who they are. She'll be heart-sorry about what's happened to his Ma, she'll even put Tuck in her prayers to The Man, but she'll never have him near her precious boat again.

Tuck watches Pendicle walk round the lagoon to his yacht, tall and proud, with his beautiful windwrap flapping in the wind. It's the walk of a Prender man. Tuck looks down at his own faded blue windwrap, a worn castoff of his Da's. His hair whips across his face, as light and unkempt as Pendicle's is sleekly plaited and dark.

Their differences never mattered when Da was alive.

It's only once Pendicle has gone that Tuck remembers the tattered object he has been carrying about in a pocket of his windwrap; something he stole from a shelf in Pendicle's yacht a while ago. He's been meaning to give it back as a peace offering. It's no use to him anyway. He took the thing all around the market with the rest of his loot, but all it earned him was shrugs. At last he came across an old scavenger in a leaky gondola that looked close to sinking under the weight of its sea spoil. The scavenger was so weathered he seemed to be made out of one of his rescued leather boots. He squinted sunken eyes at the stained and tatty object Tuck handed him and gave it back, saying his eyes were no good for books now. He didn't know anyone else who had any use for a such a thing; he was one of the last who still knew how to read words.

So Tuck's still got the book in a pocket of his windwrap. He should run after Pendicle and give it back. But Pendicle's already gone, his dark head and windwrap merged with the other Prenders on the boat.

Pendicle's left him with a pocketful of pearls, the hard tears of the ocean, and it's Tuck's own fault.

CITY OF A
THOUSAND SAILS

Already, the city is knitting back together. The great tear made by the *Arkiel* is disappearing fast. Tuck stands on a bridge and stares at the spot where his home used to be.

The air rings and clatters with the noise of boat chains and hammers. Wood and metal strain, mixed with human groans, as the boats and bridges are heaved into a new pattern, and chained together again.

By sundown, the city is mended. It's as if all the sunken boats and bridgeways were never there.

Tuck can't bear it. They should have left the hole in the city. There should be some mark, some scar of what's happened. Urth knows how many people are drowned, Ma among them, yet already Pomperoy seems to want to heal the awful scar and get on with the usual business of life. Ma will hardly have fallen to rest on the seabed, where she'll end up as fish food, like the rest of his family and all the other dead.

A sob shakes him. He swallows it down and wipes his nose with the tail of his windwrap, wipes his leaky eyes too. He tugs the windwrap tight around him, secures it with his belt, and stands up to walk the bridgeways back to the lagoon. He doesn't even think about jumping the boat roofs as he usually does. Couldn't anyway; he can't see clear for his blurry eyes. It takes all his energy to put one foot in front of the other. When he reaches the lagoon, he's engulfed by people. They pack the walkways around the lagoon and the arms of the Middle Bridges. The crowd is so huge the whole of Pomperoy must be out.

What's happened? Is it another ship?

But there's no panic in the crowd. They are expectant, quiet, still.

Tuck elbows his way to the edge of the lagoon. *Why is everyone staring out at the water?*

When he sees, his heart skips a beat.

It's the Steer Master's ship. *The Discovery* has un-chained from the cluster of tall ships at the North side of the lagoon. It sweeps across the water, aglow with lanterns, its sails billowing in the evening wind.

Until he saw the *Arkiel*, Tuck would have sworn the Steer Master's ship was the greatest vessel upon the seas. Now the three-masted ship seems a much lesser thing. For the first time Tuck sees how wrecked it is, how the bent masts creak wearily with bedraggled sails.

Still, the sight of it lifts his spirits. The citizens of Pomperoy cheer as *The Discovery* sails into the heart of the lagoon. The ship drops anchor. Expectation buzzes in the crowd.

Tuck pushes to get a clear view. When he reaches the front of the crowd he sees the figure of the Steer Master himself; it's the first time he's glimpsed him since he was small enough to sit on the shoulders of his Da. Even then, the Steer Master was old and feeble, though there was an energy about him still. Now he seems lifeless, slumped in the seat of an old world Land vessel, an ancient car recovered from the sea. A team of attendants hauls the Steer Master's car to the front of the ship. It's a Rover, Tuck knows, because Grumpa liked to gloat that Tuck's own Landcestors once owned just such a car; one as sleek and shiny and speedy as the wind. It's hard to believe that the Steer Master's Rover was ever anything other than a rusty ocean-battered wreck, encrusted with limpet shells.

'We are wounded.'

It's not the real voice of the Steer Master. The Pilot of Pomperoy, a tall and commanding man, nicknamed The Pomp on account of his pompous demeanor, is the Steer Master's vigorous right arm. Nowadays, his voice too. The Pomp relays the Steer Master's message through the long spiralling tusk of a narwhal horn.

'Wounded but still strong. Pomperoy, are we strong?'

The crowd pushes against Tuck, almost landing him in the lagoon. He loses track of The Pomp's words but the voice has the rising rhythm of a gathering storm. The crowd rouses and Tuck realizes he was wrong. Anger is simmering all about him. Pomperoy has not forgotten about the *Arkiel*.

The Pomp continues. 'We will not forget what we are. We gypseas are masters of our ocean.'

An attendant reaches through the empty frame of the Rover's front window and raises the frail arm of the Steer Master. For a moment, Tuck wonders if the Steer Master is even awake. Does he know what is being said in his name? But the rapt faces in the crowd around Tuck tell him it's a lone doubt. The crowd is hushed, tense, fixed on every word.

'This attack on us is a test. Pomperoy will rise to the test,' continues The Pomp. He puts the narwhal horn to his lips and blows out a deep bellow, an alien sound that sends a shudder to Tuck's heart. Pomperoy seems to hold its breath.

The Pomp raises the horn above his head. He aims the tip of the horn past a cluster of stars in the shape of a long-handled salt basket towards the small salt scoop twinkling above it. At the very tip of the salt scoop's handle is the Star of the North. Its light is still a faint pinprick in the salmon-streaked twilight. Tuck knows the map of the sky better than his own face. A gypsea child learns the patterns of the stars in its cradle; the pictures in the stars are glittering bedtime tales. And now he knows why Pomperoy hasn't shown its rage sooner. Gypseas sail by the stars. The city was only waiting till the first stars came out.

In The Pomp's other hand is the long wing of a Great Skua, the ravaging pirate bird of the northern seas. The Pomp holds the wing up towards the rig, pointing it at the face of The Man. The citizens of Pomperoy watch the wing shiver and bend. The Pomp looks at the slumbersome face of the Steer Master and nods.

'The world's wind is with us. Attend to all masts. In the name of The Man, on the wing of the Great Skua and the command of the Steer Master, we will avenge our dead and salvage our pride. Pomperoy will set sail on the tail of the *Arkiel* tonight!'

The crowd erupts. Moments after the cheering dies, before Tuck has gathered his thoughts, the walkways around the lagoon begin to empty. He tries to grab someone to ask what he should do but everyone is rushing off; they all seem to know.

There's a shout behind him. Gypseas are yelling at him to move.

71

Tuck panics. *Where to?*

The city fills with the rattling and clanking of the boat chains unlocking.

A mighty BOOM almost scares Tuck out of his skin. BOOM-BOOM-BOOM! Tuck ducks for cover and pulls his windwrap over him like a tent as a storm of booms erupts. In his seventeen years, Tuck has never heard such a noise, but all of a sudden he knows what it is. He looks up.

The big ships are launching their skysails! Tuck stares open-mouthed at the glorious billows high in the sky. Crowds of fluttering shadows have massed below the skysails as the rest of the city unfurls the boat sails from its masts.

All around the lagoon bridges are heaved on to ships and boats. The great arms of the Middle Bridges that link to the rig crash into the lagoon. The clang of unfastened boat chains is deafening. Now a great groaning fills the city.

The anchors, thinks Tuck, and falls flat on his face as the walkways are hauled up, right under his feet.

Wind fills the masts and skysails. The rigging creaks and whines. Pomperoy heaves into motion like a great beast stretching limbs that have been chained too long.

In the second before the walkway he is standing on disappears, Tuck makes a leap for an abandoned gondola left behind in what was the market, moments ago. There's a coil of rope. He throws it to a passing boat in the hope that someone might catch it, but the rope whacks back down on his head.

In front, the sea is being churned into froth by a steam ship. The *Waverley*'s old body is armoured against the ocean with layers of metal and rubber tyres. Its defunct steam funnels now support thick branches of masts. Tuck whirls the rope around his head, yelling for help.

'Hey, lad, throw it up!'

A woman on board the *Waverley* has spotted him. Tuck throws up the rope, she catches it, knots it around the boat rail. Tuck knots the other end of the rope to the anchor on the floor of the gondola, and he's hitched a ride.

As he hangs on, blasted by wind and surf, there's a fleeting memory of the dark-haired girl on the *Arkiel*, knocked to her knees by the movement of the ship. A mirror image of himself, sprawled here, now, in the gondola, caught in the thrust of the vast, motley fleet that his city has just become.

Pomperoy is set for North, for revenge, chasing the *Arkiel*.

And Tuck is hanging on for his life.

WHAT IS AND WHAT MIGHT BE

Mara opens her eyes. Broomielaw is shaking her out of sleep. She looks panicky and scared. Mara sits up, dizzy and sick. Her head is fuzzy and her tongue is stuck to the roof of her mouth.

'The baby,' she croaks. 'Clay, is he—'

'He's safe, remember? Mol was holding him when the ship crashed.'

Mara lets out a breath. 'I forgot. I was dreaming about him – a horrible dream. But he's safe.'

'You're not safe here, Mara. People are fighting over the water tanks.' Broomielaw nods to a noisy brawl on the far side of the ship's hold. 'You must be exhausted to sleep through that. Quick, come up on deck. We've been gathering rain in empty tins and packets so we don't have to fight over it with that lot.'

Broomielaw pulls her to her feet. Up on deck, mouthfuls of rainwater start to clear Mara's head. But a clear head brings flashbacks of the sinking barge. Mara

74

splashes her face with cold water, trying to wash away the sickening images and sounds.

'She's trouble,' mutters Broomielaw. She squeezes Mara's arm. 'We know it wasn't your fault.'

Ruby, the tall, stern woman who challenged Mara before, stands in the centre of a crowd of refugees.

'So what do *you* think we should do?' another woman argues. 'The girl seems sure there's land in the North. At least she has a plan. What's yours?'

'What plan does she have?' Ruby scorns. 'To smash through more ships and kill more people? To head to the ends of the Earth on a whim?'

'There's the girl over there. Ask her,' says a man. He points to Mara and a hundred faces turn.

Mara wipes the streaming rainwater from her face. Still foggy-headed, she faces the crowd.

'It's not a whim,' she says. She clears her throat but even to herself her voice sounds cracked with doubt. 'There's a book I found in the drowned city. It's in my backpack. It says Greenland is a huge island of mountains at the top of the world. Once the weight of all the ice is gone, it could bob up like a cork.'

'Bob up like a cork? A huge land of mountains would *bob up like a cork*?' Ruby couldn't be more scathing.

'The ice has melted, the seas have risen so—'

'Yes, we've noticed,' Ruby interrupts. 'But how do you know Greenland hasn't drowned? Everywhere else has.'

Mara glares at the sarcastic woman, trying to keep the tremble out of her voice. 'It's written in my book. I found it in the university – that was the old place of learning, so it must be—'

Mara halts, unsure now.

'*Must* be true? Why? That other book I've seen you reading – did you find that in the university too? Is everything *it* says true?'

Ruby holds up *A Tale of Two Cities*. People stare at the unfamiliar object with gold lettering on its cracked leather cover. Shocked, Mara pushes through the crowd.

'That's mine. Give it back!'

'You were asleep and it was lying beside you. I borrowed it. I had good reason to.'

'Give it back.'

Mara is no longer trembling, she's shaking with anger. This woman is treating her like a silly child. Ruby has no idea what she has been through – an immense struggle, unbearable losses. All, in the end, to save someone like Ruby. And now she has to live with another burden of guilt: the bargeful of deaths in the floating city.

'Ruby,' a cool voice warns. 'Let it be.'

Ruby doesn't even blink.

'This book is full of lies,' she tells the other refugees. 'It's just a made-up story about people who never existed. This book is full of things that aren't true.'

'Yes, but – but *some* books—'

'How do we know,' Ruby cuts in, 'what's true and what's not? How do we know that what it says in an old book about an island bobbing up is true? What if it's just a story? Someone's silly idea? What if it's all wrong?'

The faces around her are doubtful; even those of Mara's friends, though they try to hide it.

'I *know* it's true.'

But Mara doesn't. What *is* her proof? She has believed the book because she needed to. It was her one hope. If it's wrong, what will they do? Being wrong about land at the top of the world will turn the ship from a floating village into a floating coffin, once they run out of water and food.

And she has been wrong before, so wrong it cost the lives of the people most precious to her.

Rowan has pushed to the front of the crowd. Mara can't look at him. Gail, his twin and her best friend, died because Mara believed, wrongly, that they'd find refuge in the New World.

Ruby is holding up another book.

The book on Greenland!

Mara lunges at the woman to snatch back the book, just as the ship dips into a valley of sea. As it lurches back up over the rise of a wave, Mara loses her balance. There's a flutter like wings above her head. Mara hurls herself into the air with a yell.

Too late. The wind whips her precious book over the side of the ship. The fragile pages rip and scatter, then vanish among flecks of ocean spray.

Mara turns around.

'You *threw* it – you—'

'Of course I didn't.' Ruby is patronizingly calm. 'The wind took it. But it would never have happened if you hadn't tried to snatch. Anyway, it's time an adult took charge.'

With that, Ruby marches into the control cabin of the ship. Mara stares after her, dizzy with rage. The crowd melts away, avoiding her eyes. Only her Treenester friends remain. Even Rowan has turned away with a frown.

A Tale of Two Cities lies broken-backed on the deck. Mara picks it up and smoothes the book's damp and crumpled pages with trembling hands. Anger seeps away, leaving her shaken and weak.

I've had enough.

Broomielaw puts a hand on her shoulder. Mara lets out a shuddering breath. She will go below deck, curl up and escape into *A Tale of Two Cities* until it's time to go cyber-wizzing. Then she'll zoom into the Weave and wait for Fox to meet her at midnight on the broken bridge.

He'll be there tonight, she tells herself. He must be. He promised.

Ruby and the other adults can see to everything else.

CORRIDOR IN THE SKY

Was the book the only proof of land you ever had?

Rowan's question hangs in the stale air and even with her eyes shut it won't go away.

'It's not safe down here, Mara.'

Mara knows it's not. Tight shut eyes can't block out what is going on in the hold of the ship. It has turned into a brawling, violent, hellish place. She didn't dare take out her cyberwizz in case someone snatched it. She has kept it in her backpack, tucked under her head.

'You're coming up on deck with me. Now,' says Rowan.

Mara turns on him.

'You're the one who always goes on and on about books. Every winter on the island, when we were stuck inside, you *lived* books and stories.'

'I never said it was all real. I never believed everything I read.' Rowan shoots a nervous glance over his shoulder. A man is yelling abuse at a group of urchins. 'Never mind that now. Stop sulking and come with me. That guy has a bad look in his eye.'

Mara gets to her feet.

'Don't look around, just get to the stairs,' Rowan warns her as screaming erupts.

'Rowan, what's happening?' But he grabs her by the arm and yanks her up the stairs before she can see.

'The urchins—'

'Those kids can look after themselves. The other lot,' says Rowan, meaning the refugees from the boat camp, 'have been trapped in hell for too long.' He draws a big breath of air as they burst out on to the deck. 'Now they're trapped here and they're going crazy. The barrels of beer don't help.'

Mara staggers over to the edge of the deck and stares at the wilderness of ocean, willing land to appear before the tension in the ship's hold explodes.

'Look.'

She spins around, wondering what bedlam is erupting now.

'No, *look*.'

Rowan takes her chin in his hand as if she's a child and tilts her face to the evening sky.

Pearls are scattered over the clouds. They catch the sunlight as they move across the sky in unfolding patterns of such grace and power that the pattern itself seems to be a living thing.

The September geese.

The flight of the snow geese always marked the turn of the season. The geese would fill the skies above Wing, following an invisible corridor in the sky. Each September, time out of mind, the corridor led them from the lands in the Far North to a warm winter home in the South and back again in the spring.

'If they're still flying from the North, then – then—'

'Then there must be land in the North.'

Rowan's taut, thin face creases into a sheepish smile.

'And the South. Because they're flying south. There's still land in the world, then. The geese know there is.'

'Yeah.' Rowan's blue eyes meet hers. 'Sorry.'

'In the netherworld,' Mara tells him, 'I learned to read what was left of the world, anything I could find. The sky, birds, trees, books. I learned to read every echo from New Mungo, every scrap of the old world. That's how I survived. That's what we have to do now – read whatever comes our way.' She grins at Rowan. 'And you're the best reader I know.'

The snow geese have given her necessary hope, but there's a snag in that hope that she cannot ignore. Once the North Wind coughs the geese out of their summer home and those pearly white flocks fill the skies, that's when winter begins to finger the days.

Her book on Greenland said that winter at the very top of the world is one long, dark season of night.

Time is against them. That's the message the September geese are writing on the sky.

FOX TAILS

The sky crackles.

A curtain opens in the darkness and a great chasm gapes in the night. The chasm widens, seems to fill with blood. The bloodlight drains and the sky is shot with lilac and indigo. Now golden pillars tumble, a rainbow wall rises, falls. A whole theatre of colour and swirling shapes erupts, crackling and whistling with static.

'There's a land in the sky!' Gorbals points. 'I can see towers, the great arch of a bridge, pillars and the noise – what's the noise? Guns! We're under attack.'

'No, no,' laughs Mara, then bites her lip, seeing the panic on the faces around her.

'The – the sea—' stutters Ibrox, as the waves reflect the cascade of green and pink now streaking the sky.

Even the urchins are hushed, hanging over the ship's rail, entranced by the spectacle in the sky and its weird reflections in the sea.

It's the Northern Lights, Mara explains. The memory of the last time she saw them is so vivid it prickles her scalp. She was standing on the doorstep of the farm cottage with Dad and her little brother Corey. The skies over

Wing were crowded with peaceful ghostlights that suddenly whirled into demon green. *Dancing dragons!* cried Corey, *slithery snakes!* Dad put Corey on his shoulders, telling him all about the lights. *Roaring Boris*, Corey called it because he couldn't say the real name. Mara thinks hard. The *aurora borealis*, wasn't that what Dad said? She was too busy staring at the sky, dreaming, to listen properly. There was so much that Granny Mary and Tain and her parents told her about the world, but half the time she wasn't listening. It didn't seem important, then.

Now, she could kick herself. With so much lost under the ocean, knowledge is the most precious thing in the world.

'It's – um, it's just something that happens in the northern sky,' she falters. 'It's a good sign, it means we're close to the North.'

And she remembers something else; the old Norse name for the lights.

Skauf.

Fox fire.

The lights were said to look like the brush of fiery fox tails in the sky. Mara gazes up at the fox fire with her heart in her mouth.

'Look, Clayslaps.' Broomielaw holds her baby up to see. He wriggles with excitement, his fingers opening and closing like sea anemones, trying to catch a tail of light.

Then he gives a wail. As suddenly as they appeared, the night sky closes its curtain and the lights are gone.

Mara sits down on deck. She doesn't know how close to midnight it is and she doesn't care. The fox fire in the sky has lit a touchpaper inside her. She needs to see *her*

Fox. She pulls out the cyberwizz globe, halo and wand, powers it up and falls, fast as the flash of a skauf . . .

. . . *into the heart of the Weave. The ether crick-crackles as she whizzes down the boulevards until she finds the broken bridge.*

Fox!

Her cry rips through the static like a jag of lightning.

A cyber-fox slinks along the bridge towards her. He's here. The Weave-lights glitter in the fox's eyes. They shimmer in the smooth coat and the brush of its tail.

Can't you be yourself? she murmurs. It's the real, human Fox she needs, though she knows she can't have that, not here in cyberspace. With Fox, Mara has always been a cyber-mirror of her real self.

The tremble in her voice sends a ripple through the ether. The fox blinks. Vanishes. Mara could bite out her tongue for giving him such a cold greeting. She's been so worried he might never make it here at all. Her heart thuds as she stands alone on the empty arm of the broken bridge.

Here. Best I can do.

His voice. Husky, edgy, skin-prickling. She spins around and he's there – an electronic version of Fox stands within arm's reach. His tawny hair shimmers in the ether light, just as messy with static as his real tousle-head, and the eyes that lock with hers are so unnervingly his own they send a hot lightning-bolt down her spine. Mara steps forward to kiss him, reaches out to touch his face–

NO!

Sparks fly. Electrons sizzle. Cyber-cinders fall fizzling at their feet. There's a scorch mark where she touched his cheek. And a rip in the ether between them.

We can talk, but not touch, says Fox.

Oh. Right, I forgot.

No way around it, he shrugs. Dumb old world technology, this Weave.

He kicks the broken bridge and scuffs up a shower of electronic grit.

You're safe? she asks. You got down to the netherworld all right?

He nods.

Candleriggs is here.

Mara lets out a long breath. Candleriggs will look after him. That's something.

Where are you?

The top of the university tower, says Fox.

In her mind's eye, Mara sees the vast gothic steeple that tops the tower and looks like a great black wizard hat floating on the dank netherworld sea.

You? he says.

Oh, me, says Mara. Somewhere in the middle of the ocean.

Her head droops.

We were stupid, she blurts out. This is too hard. You should've come with me . . .

Misery darkens his face and haunts his beautiful eyes. She can't go on at him like this, she shouldn't. It's all too late anyway. She's already an ocean away.

I know, he begins. He stops and sighs. Who said we had to save the world?

That was you, she reminds him, with a bleak grin.

It breaks the awkward distance between them.

He lets out a laugh.

Could have sworn it was you, he retorts.

Well, we're not saving the world, says Mara, just the little bit we can.

That's all, he agrees, catching her smile. We can do that.

*His face drops again. I feel lost here, Mara. You have
people. Here, it's just me and Candleriggs. I can't go back
home. I feel stuck.*

*But what about all your plans? Mara steps closer, is care-
ful not to touch.*

*Fox shrugs. Since I crashed the system the rooks have
put security blocks everywhere. Haven't found a way around
them yet. Can't start anything until I do.*

*You're the best Noosrunner in New Mungo, Mara
reminds him. You can outwit the rooks. You'll find a way.*

He just looks at her.

I should have stayed with you, she thinks.

*She is about to tell him about the fox fire in the sky, to
let him know that she still feels close to him in her world, but
his face freezes. He looks over his shoulder, frowning.*

What?

It's just—

What?

Sirens. I hear sirens.

*It's in his world, Mara realizes; the ether around them is
abuzz and a-crackle but calm. No sign of cyberdogs or haz-
ard spiders anywhere near the bridge.*

*Sea police, Mara warns him. Put out all light and fire.
They come in fleets with the ships to guard them from the
people in the boat camp. Sometimes they raid the netherworld. That's how they got Gorbals. Be careful.*

I need to go.

*One last glance and he's gone. And she's alone again on
the Bridge to Nowhere.*

*She waits a while, stomach churning with fear. When he
doesn't return, she retracks back through the Weave, deso-
late, as suddenly she knows that it's always going to be like*

this. Every time they part, they'll never know if the other will stay safe until they next meet on the bridge.

Each moment together is a gift from time. Just staying alive and meeting here is all they can hope to do.

PINBALL AND
ICE-SOUP SEA

The wind has grown bitter. It's been gnawing at her face while she's been cyberwizzing, ripping tears from her eyes; a wind full of star crusts and the memory of ice.

Mara hugs herself, chilled to the bone in flimsy New World clothes that are not designed for a world so harsh. Maybe all that's left of the Arctic ice is in the wind, just as all she has left of Fox is in the ether.

But she's wrong about the ice. At first she thinks the change in the ocean is just a trail of fox fire, or the glint of starlight on the waves. It's only when a terrible groan echoes across the waves that she sees a sinister thickening of the ocean and the hulking phantoms that loom out of the dark.

There is an instant of hope when she thinks the white phantoms might be the other ships that escaped the city with theirs.

'What is it?' Ruby shoves past to see.

Mara runs towards the control cabin. This time she'll be ready. There will be no more accidents, no more deaths.

'Rowan, there's something – a city, I don't know what.'
She's so panicked she can hardly speak.

A sharp scent cuts through the salty air. Rowan's eyes
are fixed on the white fleet.

'Icebergs,' he says.

They seem to float between sea and sky; strange, wrecked
castles of an icy realm.

Their collapsed towers, spires and arches are an
uncanny echo of the drowned city's ruined cathedral and
the university tower. The death moan as a whole iceberg
topples into the sea is heart-stopping. An end-of-the-
world sound. The salty ocean digests the ancient ice with
a dyspeptic fizzle and gulp.

There's no turning back. The boreal wind wraps
around the ship and hurls them onward into the Far
North.

'Wasn't this in your book either?' says Ruby, sarcasm
icing every word.

It was, but Mara had been sure the rising ocean meant
that all the Arctic ice had melted – though she remembers
the island fishermen would often return from long trips
with tales of an iceberg blitz. Small enough to look like
the crests of waves from a distance, each iceberg, they
said, was big enough below the surface to sink a fishing
boat. Mara remembers her mother calling her out of bed
one night, *Quick, come quick and see*, when an iceberg
passed the island, luminous under the stars. A spectral,
unearthly thing, Mara thought a chunk of the moon had
fallen into the sea.

'Turn back,' orders Ruby.

Rowan's breath is warm against Mara's ear.

'Pinball,' he murmurs. 'Remember?'

Of course she does.

On the island they had a game called pinball wizard, named after a twentieth-century treasure Rowan's dad kept in the cellar among the junk. On long days of winter dim, they'd spend hours playing each other on the pinball-wizard machine. In summer, they recreated the game in the sea. Rowan and Gail and Mara would sneak skiffs out into a small cove along the coast from Longhope Bay. There, they'd practise lethal manoeuvres, pinballing between the rocks and surfing the rolling waves that smashed to the shore. It was a deadly game the adults would have banned outright, if they'd known.

'Just play it as pinball,' says Rowan.

'Your call then,' says Mara. 'You're pinball king.'

Rowan groans, laughs and heads for the control cabin. There's a glint of fear in his eyes, but Mara pretends not to see.

She follows him into the cabin, bolts the door against Ruby and crosses her freezing fingers. There's a rescue rope looped on the cabin wall and Mara is suddenly tempted to make a lucky wind-knot, like the fishermen on Wing would do when caught in hard seas. They need all the luck they can get.

She closes down the navigation program and switches the ship to manual steering.

'Here we go.' Rowan frowns as he stares at the mass of controls and the radar screen. 'I thought you said the ice is all melted.'

'Most of it must be or the world wouldn't have flooded, would it? The book on Greenland said icebergs are like small mountains and these are just hills. Maybe this is all that's left of the ice – baby icebergs and ice-soup sea.'

'Let's just hope there isn't a daddy one lurking,' says Rowan, without a hint of a smile.

'Remember what you see above the surface is—'

'—the tip of the iceberg. I'm the son of a fisherman, Mara, I know.'

He's snapping at her because he's too weak to take on this fleet of icebergs, and he knows it. Rowan is used to being strong. Mara has an idea and opens her backpack.

She pulls out a bottle of bright-orange liquid. *Irn-Bru, energy drink*, says the label.

She unscrews the cap. Candleriggs gave her the bottle. It's something the old Treenester kept from before the world's drowning and Mara promised she would drink to her when they reached the North lands; but they'll never get there if Rowan can't outwit the icebergs.

The drink gushes out in an orange froth. Mara puts the bottle to Rowan's mouth. He looks at it suspiciously but glugs it, splutters, then grins.

'More.'

The Irn-Bru gives him a spark of his old self back. His cheeks are less grey, his hands steadier. Mara takes the chance to slip back out on deck. She has to push through a noisy crowd. Ruby has gathered followers around her. Mara doesn't stop to listen, but pops her head back into the control cabin.

'Lock the door. Trouble's brewing out here,' she tells Rowan, before bolting past Ruby's crowd to the bow of the ship.

Queen Cass's crown of stars sparkles high in the night sky. Her fallen jewel, the Star of the North, glistens behind a blur of cloud. At the top of the world, the North Star would be directly overhead; that's what Granny said. So they are on track, but how much further is there to go?

There is no moon but the sprinkle of starlight picks out a dazzling mosaic of ice that is so fragile it shifts with the movement of the sea. And there is something else. A long, silver point is sticking up out of the thin crust of ice.

Mara screws up her eyes. It looks like a *sword*.

The silver sword vanishes then reappears further in front, breaking a path through the icy waves. Another sword rises out of the ocean, surges towards the first and crosses it. Mara gasps as the swords clash then vanish.

Narwhals.

That's what they are. She only saw them once on Wing. Great, shell-encrusted whales, far out in Longhope Bay. Island folk legend said a speck of ground narwhal tusk a day would make you live a hundred years or more, just as the narwhals do.

A narwhal horn always points to the North Star.

That was another thing the folk legends said. Mara looks, and catches her breath. Amazingly, the narwhals are tracking a route through the icebergs, their spiralling tusks pointing straight to the Star of the North. And the narwhals know what Mara doesn't: where the hulking mass of icebergs lurk under the waves.

Between the radar, the narwhals and Rowan's pinball skills, maybe, just maybe, they can make it through.

Mara rushes below deck. The hoard of objects the urchins looted from the netherworld museum is stashed behind a pile of crates in a corner of the hold, watched over by urchins and Scarwell's model apeman.

'Telescope,' says Mara, but the urchins have no intention of letting anyone get their hands on their loot. She mimes the act of putting a telescope to her eyes, pleading, but it's no use. The urchins are fierce guards. Snarling, they bare teeth, more feral than child-like.

'The telescope!' she commands. 'Wing? Where's Wing?'

A small, wiry, filthy creature jumps down from a crate, gives her a wide smile and holds out his hand.

'I don't have any presents, Wing. Listen, I *need* the telescope.' She does the telescope mime again. 'Please?'

There is a wordless, stubborn calculation in his eyes.

'Oh, you!'

Mara yanks off her backpack and rummages until she finds her own precious loot, a pencil. She scribbles on a crate then rubs out the mark with the rubber. Wing watches, fascinated.

'Deal?' says Mara.

Wing grabs the pencil. He pulls out a telescope from the plastic bag that is tied around his waist and replaces it with his new toy.

At last.

Mara trips over a crumple of plastic bags in her rush to get back on deck. There's a howl of pain.

A head emerges from the plastic bags. It's Gorbals, huddled in a ball of seasick misery.

Mara kneels down beside him. 'What are you doing down here on your own? It's not safe. Come up on deck. The sea is a lot calmer now.'

'Grooo,' he grunts.

'Come on,' she urges. 'I'll show you something amazing.'

He follows her unsteadily and trips over a jumbled heap. Mara helps him up, then sees that the jumble is clothing. She picks up one of the garments. It's an embroidered coat, tough and weatherproof, with a fur hood and lining. She sniffs the garment and knows the material, though she can't tell what the fur is. The people of her island made winter boots and jackets from this.

93

'Sealskin! Where did these come from?'

'The ratkins stole it all from the museum.' Gorbals glares at the urchins. 'They bite if you try to take any of their stuff.' He shows her teeth marks on his arm.

Mara turns to the urchins. 'Wing!'

The child peeks out from behind a crate. Mara rummages in her backpack and takes out the crumpled sheets of blank paper she stole from Fox's grandfather. She folds them into paper birds as she used to do for her little brother, Corey, with the pages of an old book.

Mara fires the paper planes at the urchins who yelp and scrabble to catch one.

'Now I'm taking these clothes.'

Wing only grins as he sends a paper bird flying through the air.

Mara pulls an embroidered sealskin coat over her thin New World clothes. There are skin mitts in the pocket too.

Gorbals is pulling a sealskin jacket over his bedraggled tatters. The arms are much too short and his tattered plastic clothes hang out of the sleeves. He only just manages to pull the hood over his head. But he doesn't care. A skimpy sealskin is warmer than any amount of ragged plastic clothing. 'The ratkins have rat skins anyway. They don't need clothes.'

'Lucky them,' says Mara. She grabs the heap of skins and takes them up on deck.

'Treenester clothes are too thin for the wide world,' says Broomielaw, close to tears as she and Clayslaps snuggle inside a warm heavyweight of animal skin.

'Favouring your friends?' snipes Ruby, recoiling as a passing urchin bumps into her. She stares in disgust at the child's thick-downed, weather-toughened skin.

'Yup,' Mara snaps back.

She hands coats to the Treenesters but not to Ruby, and heads for the the control cabin where Rowan is so numb with cold that Mara has to pull the coat over his head.

'We have guides in the sea,' Mara tells him. He looks at her with weary blankness. 'Narwhals.' She gives him a hug and the sealskin coat crackles. 'Remember what I said about reading signs in the world? If we follow the narwhals, they'll help us through.'

She rushes out to the bow of the ship and scans the dark sea with the telescope. At last she picks out the glint of a horn.

'Look.' She hands the telescope to Gorbals.

'*Risings of fire and risings of sea*,' he chants and lowers the telescope in a shaky fist. 'A war in the sky, now ghosts and swords in the sea.'

'You *have* been reading my book.'

Gorbals nods and hands the telescope back to Mara.

'What are narwhals?' he whispers.

'Huge sea creatures, much bigger than a man, with long tusks like swords.'

The glimmering tusks of the narwhals surge northward as Mara tells Gorbals the folk legends of these ancient lords of the sea. If the sword-like horns disappear or veer off in another direction, they'll alert Rowan. But as long as they can keep the narwhals in sight, keep on their track, they might just stay safe.

There's so much in the world that's impossible to trust, that misleads and betrays: people, maps, books, weather, sea and land. But some things hold true. There are the September geese, flocking through hidden corridors in the sky. And the narwhals, navigating the icebergs, horns thrust at the North Star.

THE DARK WAVE

A tentacle of light lifts the lid of the night and a path through the icebergs becomes clearer. Now Mara can locate each one at a distance, instead of them looming with lethal suddenness out of the night. The twilight has softened them into milky castles that drop lumps of ice like clots of cream into the ice-soup sea.

Sometimes a trick of the light will set an iceberg ablaze with sunset amber or turn it a shimmering greeny blue, as if they are ice cathedrals lit by coloured lamps. Most are no more than the size of small skiffs now, on the surface at least. Mara yawns and stretches. Her body aches from the strain of the long night's watch.

Gorbals has gathered a crowd around him on deck. The northern chill has numbed the muscles of the waves, slowing up the ship. Gorbals is coping with the sea at last. He is telling the Treenesters' legend of the stone-telling and how Mara's arrival in the netherworld fulfilled it because she is the face that's cast in the stone of the sunken city below New Mungo.

'We're still living our story,' he finishes. 'We don't know how it'll end. But the story set in the stones came true.

Mara saved us and we're not Treenesters trapped in the netherworld any more. You,' he speaks to the refugees from the boat camp, 'are not shut out of the world, dying outside the city wall. And you're not ratkins any more.' He winks at the urchins. 'We are all people now. People of the free world on the way to our home. I dreamed about it last night.'

Everyone leans closer, eager to catch a glint of Gorbals's dream.

'The sun was low and orange over the sea. The wind had a voice full of secrets. We had lived in this land more than ten thousand days. My hair was silver and thin, but there was still more of it than now.' He rubs his shaven head and everyone laughs. Baby Clayslaps joins in with throaty gurgles. Gorbals turns to the baby. 'And little Clayslaps here . . .' He hesitates for a moment, 'Yes, I think I remember, he was a strong and handsome man.' He tickles the baby and Clayslaps gurgles again. 'It was a good place to live and it had a good name. We called our land Mara.'

The crowd is hushed. Gorbals smiles across at Mara, hiding in the shadows at the back of the crowd. 'The land of Mara was our home.'

Tears spring to Mara's eyes. Their faith in her is such a weighty and precious thing.

'Fairy tales and nonsense.' Ruby's brisk voice breaks the moment.

The elderly woman, Merien, speaks up. 'There's often hidden treasure tucked away in the corners of a fairy tale,' she says. 'I enjoyed your story,' she tells Gorbals. 'I hope it comes true.'

She is a woman in the mould of her own Granny Mary,

97

Mara senses. Maybe that kindred spirit is what draws her to Merien.

'*I see a beautiful city and a brilliant people rising from this abyss,*' Gorbals announces to the back of Ruby's head.

Mara smiles. The words are from *A Tale of Two Cities.*

The iceberg blitz begins to thin at last and now the ship splices through ice floes with a crunch and hiss. When Mara returns to the control cabin, Rowan is grey, exhausted, beyond the help of Irn-Bru.

She makes a snug from some blankets, on the floor, and makes him lie down to rest.

'Yell if you need me,' he mutters, asleep in seconds, but Mara is glad just to have him there. Rowan grounds her. His familiar presence reminds her of a time when life was happy and simple and ordinary. She can hardly remember how that felt.

When sun breaks across the ocean, Mara begins to relax. Now she can see clear ahead. But what she sees makes her heart stop. Beyond the glittering patchwork of ice floes is a dark and terrible thing.

Mara runs out on to the deck. The deep shadow of a wave stretches all across the horizon. It is massive, as dark as the icebergs were luminous. And deadlier by far. It's possible to outwit a sea of icebergs, but even the biggest ship is at the mercy of a tidal wave. Mara knows all about the giant wave that hit Wing and swept away whole villages, in the Century of Storm when Granny Mary was young.

Anything is possible, she tries to tell herself. She thought there was no way through New Mungo's vast city wall, yet there was. There seemed to be no way into the sky city, yet there was. Escaping the New World seemed impossible, yet they did. Leaving Fox behind seemed the most impossible thing of all, yet she did that too. But this deadly shadow of a wave stretching across the northern horizon has risen like a wall against the future and she can't see a way through.

During those mad games of pinball, Mara learned it was best to ride right into the most ferocious waves. You held steady and steered straight ahead, up and over the wave. It was the only way. But a wave as vast as this?

In a corner of the deck, Merien has shared out scraps of breakfast among a group of urchins. Mara can hear her softly chanting *one, two, three* to the urchins, teaching them to count out the food. Mara cries out something wordless, and Merien looks over. Terror is buzzing inside her head and Mara can't hear Merien's reply. In a moment, the older woman is at her side and Mara sees her own stricken look reflected in Merien's face. Mara stutters, can't find her voice. She points to the wave and shoves the telescope into Merien's hands.

Merien takes the telescope and peers through it for a long moment. She lowers it, her eyes still on the horizon, and puts the telescope back into Mara's shaking hands.

'Look again now, look hard. That's no wave, my dear.' There's a glint in Merien's shrewd eyes; a puckish smile on her mouth. 'It's land.'

A FISH-HOOK MOON

The eastern sky is mother of pearl, the inside of a mussel shell.

Sun is prising open the night. It steals across the ocean and nips the jostling topsails of Pomperoy. The city has travelled leagues of sea under darkness, the thunder of the masts and skysails and the shouts of the gypsea sailors making an invisible, ghostly rabble in the dense ocean night.

Tuck has clung to the gondola all night long, chilled to numbness, willing the rope that attaches him to the *Waverley* not to snap. There was nothing else to do. By a sliver of moonlight, they tried again and again to haul him on board, but the wind was too hard, the sea too rough. Tuck would have smashed like a piece of driftwood off the side of the ship. When cloud swallowed up the moon, the gypseas couldn't see him any more; the glow of their lanterns couldn't reach him, so all he could do was hang on as the gondola whacked and crashed through the froth of the *Waverley*'s wake.

Now, someone is shouting down at him though it's hard to hear through the blast and roar of the ocean.

Tuck wipes spray from his eyes and sees a wind-leathered gypsea face peering down at him from the side of the ship. He yells back as loud as he can, and the old man cries out in surprise.

'Great Skua, it's Jack Culpy's lad! Hang on down there, we'll have you on board in a finflick.'

The old greybeard with long wisps of silver hair streaming out of his windwrap looks like a hundred other gypseas. But something in his salt-rasped voice strikes a memory. It's Charlie, an old bridge-master mate of his Da. Tuck last saw him the night of Da's sea burial.

A knobbly knot of rope strikes him on the forehead. Tuck grabs it, close to sobbing with relief as he's hauled up through bales of wind and spray on to the *Waverley*.

Charlie grabs Tuck in wiry arms and sets him on his feet, but Tuck reels and crashes on to the floor.

'Easy, lad, easy. Take time to find your boat legs again.'

Charlie steers him across the deck, under the masts and past the fat funnels that once upon a time pumped steam, and takes him below deck.

It's a long time since Tuck has seen such a homely place. Pendicle's home-boat was spick and span, the wooden decks and walls all scrubbed and polished, cushions plumped and porthole curtains neatly tied; it was sheer luxury compared to his sparse shack on *The Grimby Gray*. But the bridgers live in the cosy clutter that Tuck's family enjoyed when Da was alive. The bunks overflow with feather-filled quilts; hanging racks are crammed with pots and pans, drying fish and wet windwraps; huge baskets spill with sea spoil and bridging tools. It's such a comfortable mess it gives Tuck a homesick feeling that he can't understand because it's not his old shack he's homesick for, it's this ramshackle place he's never set eyes on till

101

now, that reminds him of his real home-boat, the one the Salters took.

Tuck is made to sit down and sup a steamy bowl of oyster broth. The bridger-women fuss over him and the minute he yawns he's snuggled into a feather quilt that's as cosy as a warm cloud. Tuck falls into a doze, half-listening to the bridger-women's chatter.

'Time we got the wind back in our sails,' an old bridger-granny grunts, puffing clouds of pungent smoke from a seaweed pipe. 'We'd grown stagnant as algae stuck to that rig.'

'Mother, all those years of bridgework, lost—'

'I just hope we're not off on some wild gull chase across the ocean,' says a woman who has just burst in from the upper deck, bringing an icy chill of sea blast with her.

'We've got the bridges all packed up. We can bridge up again any old place we like.' The bridger-granny puffs happily then pulls her pipe from her mouth and points to her feet with its stem. 'Water, Joss!'

Joss groans and grabs a mop and bucket and hurries over to the small puddle of water that's seeped up through the floor at the bridger-granny's feet.

'This leaky old boat's not sea-hardy enough for a wild gull chase,' Joss grumbles as she slops the sodden mop into the bucket. 'We'll all drown.'

Through half-shut eyes, Tuck watches the newly arrived bridger-woman loosen her windwrap from around her head and a mane of hair the colour of sea foam spills out. It's Charlie's wife, Cath. 'I'd rather be a clump of sea algae, slick with oil,' she declares, 'than fall off the edge of the world in a storm or circle the world for evermore. What do we do when our oil tanks run out and we're a hundred leagues from the rig? Has the Steer Master thought of that?'

'It's not the only rig in the ocean,' puffs the bridger-granny. 'We'll find another.' She points the stem of her pipe to the floor beside the stove. 'Water!'

Joss drags the mop and bucket over to the stove, spitting curses.

'Plenty rigs, Gran, but most are pumped dry of oil,' Cath retorts.

'It's not the Steer Master,' says a young woman with a toddler on her hip, stirring a huge pot on the stove. 'He's aged back into dribbling babyhood. It's The Pomp who's steering us. He's taken his chance to make sure the masts are set *his* way. He'll tie himself in windknots over this, wait and see. Where will it all end up? It's no good saying war and piracy's in our blood. I've never killed a soul, and neither have any of you. Neither have most of our men.'

Tuck sits up.

'Maybe,' says Cath, 'but you go up on deck and look at them all. They're like sharks on the trail of blood.'

'Are we at war?' Tuck asks, but the women are too busy clattering and chattering to bother with him.

'You know what this is really all about?' Cath prods a finger in the air. 'It's nothing to do with avenging the dead or salvaging our pride. We need more boats, that's what. It's as cut and dried as salt cod. The whole of Pomperoy's all crammed up tight with nowhere left to spread. Driftwood's as precious as stardust, and there's been no passing boats in ages, except those toxic ghost ships. The Pomp is after that big white ship and I'll bet he thinks there'll be more boats wherever it's headed. Can't you imagine the glint in those cold fish eyes of his when he saw such a ship?'

The other bridger-women nod and mutter.

'*That's* what this is all about,' Cath declares. '*The Discovery* is old and druxy and The Pomp wants the *Arkiel* for the launch of his Steer Mastership.'

'That's on the horizon soon enough,' says a small, stout bridger-woman who is slitting open a pile of oysters that's almost as big as herself. 'The old Steer Master's sun's setting fast by the looks of him.'

'We should've slept on our anger,' sighs Cath. 'We should've stayed our masts a while, not set sail in a temper. The Man only knows where it'll all end up.'

'What kind of gypsea talk is that?' The bridger-granny spits a mouthful of seaweed ash on to the stove and it hisses.

'Mother!'

'Cath's right,' says the woman with the baby on her hip, her face flushed and fearful. 'Some of us want our babes to grow up safe and sound. Some of us liked being bridged up and anchored to the rig. Some of us don't want to ravage and rampage across the ocean like a scavenging flock of Great Skuas.'

'When fear flocks round your head, don't let it nest in your hair,' the bridger-granny grunts. Her eye lands on Tuck's face. 'What's Jack Culpy doing skulking down here with the women?'

'It's Tuck, mother, Jack's *son*. Jack's been dead a while.'

The bridger-granny looks befuddled for a moment. 'Whoever he is, he should be up on deck, not cosied up down here like an old woman. Water, Joss, water!'

Joss heaves the bucket yet again and clatters it down, looking as if she'd like to stuff the mop head in the bridger-granny's mouth.

'You stay where you are, Tuck,' says Cath, with a

friendly wink. 'You can help out once you're rested and had a bit of looking after. Haven't had much of that, have you, for a while?'

The dig is at Ma. Tuck is surprised by a pang of anger on his Ma's behalf, though he's thought and said much worse to her face, himself.

These are his own people, they've made that clear, and they won't cast him out, especially not if they're headed into a pirate war. There's nowhere to cast him *to*, anyway, except ocean. Bridgers are like one big family, though since Da died he hasn't so much as looked their way. They never forgot him though. Who else left sacks of fish and seaweed outside the shack door after Da died? Who tried to get their boat back from the Salter thugs? The bridgers offered him and Ma bunks on bridger boats but Ma's fierce pride, then her drinking, stuck them in the barge shack. Still, when Ma was ill with grief over little Beth, it was the bridger-women who'd come and sit with her, every day, for weeks on end, while Tuck wandered the city all night and crashed out in his bunk all day.

His Da always said there's something in a bridger's nature that makes them want to mend every broken wire they spot. The bridgers saved Pomperoy, forging bonds between gypseas as they bridged up the boats.

It was the bridgers, claimed Da, that made Pomperoy a great city. They rescued it from itself. They'd linked up a thousand bridges, even as rival pirate gangs threatened to smash every last boat into flotsam. On the day the great Middle Bridges were raised, there came a lull. Gypseas stopped fighting each other and came to see the great sight. The bridgers had engineered a miracle, said Da, and every gypsea seemed to take a deep breath that day as they looked at the wonder of the five radiating bridges that now secured them to the rig. Pomperoy saw the great city it could become and the fighting stopped.

The bridgers know about Tuck's looting. It's a shameful throwback to that pirate past. They've rescued him from the city's prison barge more than once. The bridgers know he's broken the bond with his Da's trade, yet he's still the son of a bridger – and not just any old bridger; one of the best bridge-masters Pomperoy's ever known.

After a while, Tuck can't take much more of the bridger-women's fussing. He's too used to Ma's narking. He even misses it. Misses *her*, he suddenly knows, with a horrible lurch inside. Tuck throws off the fuggy warmth of the quilt. He needs to get out, needs space, but there's nowhere to go except the deck and that'll mean work on the masts. He *flumps* back under the quilt and escapes into his head, imagines himself leaping and racing through Pomperoy until he reaches the calm black glass of the lagoon and falls asleep at last.

When Tuck wakens, he realizes he's slept away the day and maybe even most of the night. All around him, bridgers are bunked down. The smell of leftover fish soup and the sound of snoring fill the air. It's so cold his breath makes white puffs like the bridger-granny's pipe.

Tuck tugs his windwrap tight around him and tiptoes between the bunks, pushing through cold strands of sea tangle drying on a line of rope. He's creaking open the door that leads up on deck when a gleam catches his eye. It's a little silver box in one of the overflowing baskets of sea spoil. He hasn't a clue what it is, but a looter's force of habit makes him grab it.

Outside, the wind is brittle with shavings of ice. The bridgers on deck are yelling about something and they don't see him; they're focused on the ocean. Tuck slips

106

under the shadows of the masts and wonders where he can hide. He climbs on to the upper deck and stows himself in one of the lifeboats, burrowing down between piles of nets and ropes.

The little silver box he's looted gleams like pearly fish-skin or a slab of moonshine on sea. Tuck turns it over in his hand, trying to prise it open, fiddling with buttons, but the bitter cold makes his fingers clumsy and numb. A tiny window blinks open at the top of the box and Tuck blinks back in surprise. He puts his eye to the window to see what's inside, and yelps.

Inside the box is the world outside.

Tuck takes his eye from the window and looks out at the night. With his own, weak eyes the moon is a blurred silver fish-hook above a herring-skin sea. A sea that wraps the boats of Pomperoy in clinging mist. At the eastern edge of the sky, day nibbles at the horizon. Tuck puts his eye back to the little window – and there's the fish-hook moon, sharp as the curved blade of a cutlass, and there's the nibbling dawn, he can see every streak and ribbon of it, clear as day. All inside the box!

Tuck studies the world with his new, sharp eyebox and spots a strange, ghostly rock trailing clouds of mist. A strange, sharp scent carries on the sea wind.

Iceberg!

The shout echoes across the boats and brings the other bridgers running up on deck. Tuck sits where he is and keeps the little eyebox pointed at the iceberg, trapping it safe inside. His trembling fingers touch a small button. There's a buzz and a long nose shoots out of the box. Tuck jumps and stares at it, puts his eye back to the window and yelps again – now the iceberg is so close he could reach out and touch it.

107

He tries to trick the little silver box. He points it up at the masts, at the moon, pressing the button that shoots the nose in and out, but each time the box catches whatever he points at, zooming it large, shrinking it small. Tuck is about to smash the box on the side of the lifeboat, to crack it open like a shell to see what's really inside, when it catches a darkness beyond the icebergs. He focuses the box on the jagged crust of darkness that, he now sees, lies all along the northern horizon. A glint of daylight touches it and now the very tips of the darkness look like a shoal of silver fish heads nosing out of the sea, baited by the bright hook of the moon. Tuck presses the button that shoots out the box's funnel-nose and the shoal of glinting fish heads zooms up large.

Every nerve in his body is a-jangle as the little silver box shows that the silver-tipped shadow is not a shoal of fish heads, neither is it a leftover crust of night.

It's *Land*.

He just knows it is by the tremble that runs up his legs.

He can hardly believe his eyebox.

For the first time in his life, Tuck is looking at *Land*.

THE STONES SPEAK

The great wave of land rumbles with thunder.

Yet all across the northern horizon the ragged peaks rip into clear blue sky. Sunlight lashes off mountainsides that look like crushed metal.

Mara is so fogged with exhaustion she feels unreal. Her body is a dense and dragging weight, as if it's no longer part of herself. Every now and then panic spikes her fogginess and spooks her with the thought that Merien could be wrong – that what seems to be a vast mountain range really *is* a wall of water. She scans the glinting peaks but the telescope assures her that it's mountain rock all right; but even the telescope can't fathom the source of the strange, invisible thunder.

All day, as the ship moves closer to the coast, the thunder roar grows. At last the telescope reveals what it is. The mountains are punctured with waterfalls. Chutes and cascades of water pelt down, thumping off ledges and rocks, crashing down with so much force that the air froths and fizzles with rainbows and the sea along the coastline churns with whirlpools.

'Like a worm-eaten apple,' says Merien, wonderingly. 'Worms made of ice.'

Mara looks close, sees what she means.

Over aeons of time, the ice must have bored tunnels through the rock like worms into an apple. Now melted, the immense ice cap that was once cupped by the mountains pours through the punctured peaks.

Greenland is not green at all. It's a land of silver mountains and thunder-water. There *is* still ice at the top of the world, but only a little, Mara can only suppose, of what there was once. Ice frosts the mountain peaks. The sea is sludgy with icy floes and the North Wind carries tiny, sharp splinters. The coastal whirlpools fling out a skin-stinging froth of salt and ice and legions of dwarf icebergs emerge from endless chasms that cut deep into the land.

Every drop of water on the ship has been guzzled. Throats are parched and sore and all they have, now that the rain clouds have cleared, is the salty ice they catch on their tongues from the biting wind.

But we have found land.

Mara gazes at the endless shining peaks. Greenland seems to stretch ever onward, as far as she can see.

Pollock spots something with his hunter's eyes.

'What's that?'

He points warily. Mara looks up. High on a mountain-side, a strange figure seems to want to catch the rays of the rising sun. It's too enormous and still to be human, yet there's something heart-rending in the way its open arms reach out to an empty world.

Only once Mara fixes the telescope on it does she see what it is.

'It's a stone man. Big as a giant.'

She lowers the telescope and passes it to Pollock, but

he shakes his head. He'll use his own good eyes. Pollock frowns up at the stone welcome, suspicious of anything that hasn't been examined by his own hand.

The telescope is passed around the ship.

'It's probably an ancient thing,' says Rowan, once he has studied the stone creature for a long moment. Mara knows he's thinking of the circle of standing stones on their island, remnants of another world lost in distant time.

'He points that way,' says Gorbals, staring uneasily at the stone giant.

'North-East,' nods Rowan.

Mara says nothing. Following signs in the ether and messages set in stone has brought them all here, for good or ill, to the ends of the Earth.

'There's another one!'

Possil points to the next mountain. True enough, perched precariously high on a stab of rock, outlined against the sky, is another stone man.

Even without the telescope, Mara can see this one is different. There is no open-armed welcome. This one – she grabs the telescope in ice-pained hands, peers through – this one has an arm raised, pointing along the coast of the land.

Mara lowers the telescope and looks at the people she trusts. Rowan, Broomielaw, Molendinar, Gorbals – and she searches beyond them until she finds Merien.

'What do you think?'

'It *seems* to be pointing the way,' Merien murmurs.

Mara thinks of all the times she has made the wrong choice. All she can do is try to read whatever signs she finds in the world but it's often hard to know what things mean.

'Go the other way,' says Pollock.

'The *other*—'

'Why?' asks Merien.

'Why does it want us to go that way?' Pollock squints up at the stone creature. 'What does it mean? It could be a trap.'

Gorbals looks scornful but Mara can't help smiling. 'Pollock, you think the whole world's a hunter's trap.'

Pollock raises an eyebrow. 'Uhuh.'

'It means we're not alone. People are here,' says Molendinar.

'Or *have* been,' adds Rowan.

Mara nods. 'If there are people and they wanted us to go away, wouldn't they use something more threatening?'

'Not if they're trappers,' says Pollock. 'A trap's a trick.'

He looks at Mara and the others as if they are fools.

'Oh, Pollock.' Broomielaw raises her eyes skywards. 'Why would someone want to trap us? They don't even know we're here.'

'We're a *ship*. Maybe we're the catch they're waiting for.'

'We're a great *big* ship, so what could anyone do to us?'

Pollock stares hard at the stone man, trying to divine his purpose, but he can't.

'It – it's a message left in the stones,' Gorbals cries. 'Of course it is! Look at it. This must be part of our stone-telling legend. A part we didn't know.'

Mara could kick him. The Treenesters' owl-eyes settle on her with an expectant, trusting stare that makes her want to run and hide.

'It's another sign,' Gorbals rushes on, 'like the stories our ancestors left in the city stones about Mara saving us and—'

'There was no sign,' Mara cuts in. 'It was just a statue.'

She doesn't need to look at Ruby; she can feel her sneer. But others, who were listening in to Gorbals's storytelling the previous night, look curious.

'We'll vote on it,' says Mara briskly, eager to divert attention from herself.

'There's another one! Two!' someone yells.

Another stone man is pointing resolutely East. On the next mountain a stone friend gives an open-armed welcome.

That seems to settle things. The overwhelming vote is with the stones.

Pollock watches the land, a deep scowl on his face.

WRECKERS

A sickle moon hangs like a lopsided smile. Its thin, sharp light casts a cold armour over the stone giants that have been the ship's guides all day. Even when night closed in, even now, as a patch of fog swallows up the ship and the rest of the world vanishes, the refugees refuse to lose heart. The stone giants are rock-solid messages of hope.

Only Pollock, headstrong and thrawn as ever, refuses to trust the signs set in stone.

The snow geese and the narwhals led the way, Mara tries to reassure him, and now the stones.

'Animals can't lie,' says Pollock, 'but men can.'

'Even stone men?' Mara teases. She makes a funny face at baby Clayslaps who is trying to wriggle out of Pollock's arms.

'Who made the stone men?' is Pollock's gruff reply. He frowns. 'Why is the thunder suddenly far away?'

Clayslaps gives a gull-like shriek and kicks his legs. The child points excitedly at something.

'Lights!' cries Broomielaw.

Mara gasps. They have burst through the thick fog as

fast as they entered it. Rising out of the sea right in front is a heap of twinkling lights.

'Slow down!' she yells at Rowan in the control cabin. 'We're going to crash.'

There's a great pull and the ship heaves and shudders as Rowan cuts speed. Broomielaw grabs baby Clayslaps from his father's arms.

The lights of what must be a village blaze out of the dark. The thin moon makes it hard to see whether there is a harbour.

'There!' Ibrox the firekeeper has tracked the patterns of light and points to a line of blazing torches that reaches out into the sea and ends in a wide curve.

Mara races into the control cabin. 'Keep slow but steer to the harbour lights,' she tells Rowan.

His forehead is damp with sweat and his hands grip the steering wheel. His eyes are fixed on a screen full of tumbling numbers. 'Still way too fast,' he grunts.

'No, steer away!' Pollock bursts in. He stares at the ship's controls, looking frantic. 'This is wrong. There's no harbour. The stone men, the lights—'

'Pollock, don't be a dolt—'

'We're in a trap. I'm a hunter, I set traps, I *know*—' Pollock yells.

The ship gives a huge jolt that sends them all crashing against the cabin wall. There's a metallic screech and groan, a horrible sound, and screaming from the deck.

Mara struggles to her feet and peers out the cabin window. The harbour lights are all gone.

What happened? Where are they?

She rushes into the uproar on deck and stares out at black sea. A moment ago there was a clear line of lights. Now there is only dark.

115

A horrendous banging erupts, deep in the ship's bowels.

'Rocks!' Rowan yells. 'We've hit rocks!'

The world lurches. Mara is flung off her feet and is sent rolling across the deck. She crashes into the ship's rail, tries to grab it, but it's gone. There's a long, dark moment of freezing wind, tumbling stars. *The stars are falling*, she thinks, bewildered, feeling them rush past her head as she plunges into blackness.

The moment stretches. She can't breathe, can't see, can't find her way out. Where are the stars, the ship, where's the sea? She's suffocating, alone, in freezing black space.

Sea.

It's more instinct than thought, an instant knowing that electrifies her. This frozen blackness *is* sea. Mara thrashes around in terror. *Which way, which way?* The darkness is too deep; she can't see where the surface is. Her head and lungs ache with the weight of the sea. The impulse to breathe is overpowering. She can't resist, must, *can't*. Thoughts tumble, fragments of consciousness scatter like smashed stars.

Someone help me, I'm lost . . . Fox . . .

Light, light . . . there . . .

A light hangs in the darkness. Mara reaches for it, claws and kicks away the blackness that has begun to drag like a stone weight. The thin curve of light bobs out of reach, there are too many smashed stars inside her head, she's too weighed down.

Can't see, must breathe . . .

Air hits her lungs. She breaks through the surface, raking in painful, barbed breaths. A wave fills her mouth with sea and she's choking. Salt water stings her eyes. A sharp shadow that must be the ship's hull juts into the froth of the stars. But there's something wrong. It's listing sideways, at a precarious angle. The ship is groaning like a dying iceberg.

Mara's stunned mind clicks into gear. The lights went out. The ship hit the rocks. It has capsized, it's sinking. And she is close to freezing in this icy sea.

Keep moving. Swim to the rocks, find a rock.

Lights flash in front of her. Someone shouts. Mara looks up and sees a lantern on a long stick looming out of the dark.

A loop of rope dangles from the lantern stick. Mara lunges for it but her freezing fingers cannot grip. She forces her hand to make a claw, lunges again, feels the hot burn of rope in her hands, and is pulled into shore. Rocks rake her skin but pain is numbed by shock and cold. Mara lies where she's been dragged on to a slab of rock.

Unable to get up, she turns her head. The sickle moon hangs above the silhouette of an open-armed stone giant like a glinting fish-hook, or a sly smile.

PEEKABOO MOON

Fox rips up books and feeds them to the fire. The cold stone of the university tower has seeped into his bones and he can't sleep. Every time he shuts his eyes he sees Mara trapped in the arms of the wind, separated from him by a wall of sea.

She didn't make it to the bridge again tonight. *Is she safe?* Fox puts on his godgem once more and zips into the Weave, but the electronic boulevards zing with loneliness. The Bridge to Nowhere is empty, the ether undisturbed.

Realworld zings with emptiness too. Unseen presences of bats, cats and rats haunt the tower. The ghoulish screams of owls echo across the netherworld sea. The only signs of life are the white cargo ships that slip through the gate in the great wall. In their wake comes a blast of sea-police sirens and a tide of rank sewage from the boat camp outside the wall.

Fox's only company is the fire and the luminous moon-moths in the twig lantern. Candleriggs is fast asleep. The old woman sleeps a lot; she's missing her Treenester people badly. Awake, she dedicates all her dwindling energy to teaching Fox survival skills, as if she's thinking the same as he is: that she is increasingly frail and winter is on its way.

There's a lot to learn. Weather is a shock after the sky city's mellow air. In summer, says Candleriggs, the netherworld bakes under the metal grill of New Mungo but winter is cold and stormy and they need to prepare. Now Fox knows how to make fire, where to find food and fresh water. It takes so much time and effort to survive, he's often too exhausted to make any progress in the Noos. No wonder his battle with the New World has stalled.

Yet tonight, when he can't sleep and could be working, he wanders the tower room, wondering what's happened to Mara and restlessly flicking through books before feeding them to the hungry fire.

A page flutters on to his lap. In the instant before he tosses it into the flames, some words catch his eye.

I am come into deep waters, where the floods overflow me.

Fox saves the page and stares dumbfounded. He finds the book it belongs to: a little black book that just fits the clasp of his fingers.

Pocket Psalter.

He puzzles over the title, picked out in faded gold. Pocket Psalter? What's that? Sounds like a pocket of salt. Fox opens the first page.

A pocketbook of sacred songs.

He opens the book at random and his heart skips a beat.

let me not sink
neither let the deep swallow me up

And suddenly, in his mind's eye, he sees Mara's ship on a heaving ocean, in the blast of the North Wind. '*Let her not sink, neither let the deep swallow her up,*' he murmurs. There's a gentle power in the words, like the rise and fall of a calm wave.

A gnarled hand appears on his arm.

'Books are good for feeding fire. But some have fire tucked away in their pages. Be careful.'

Fox shakes off her hand and slouches over to the window. He's suddenly sick of the old woman, always at his elbow, telling him what to do, what to eat, how to think.

Outside, the netherworld sea is as black as oil. Fox tenses and stares. Something glints in the sea between his tower and the shadow of a small hump of land topped by trees. What *is* that in the water? A lumen light? Down here? Wind ripples the dark sea and touches his face. The lumen shivers. So does Fox. A glint catches the corner of his eye and he looks up. Another one! A crescent lumen, just like the one in the water except it's sharp and steady, not fretted by the waves. It can't be the moon because the moon is round. Fox shivers again, but this time it's not the chill of the wind, it's because the shining crescent reminds him of the halo of Mara's cyberwizz.

The crescent in the sky illuminates something that sits on the tip of one of the spires of the drowned buildings that spike the netherworld sea. Fox peers at the glinting thing. It's a ship with masted sails. The ship sits upon a globe and turns slowly in the wind, catching the light of the strange halo in the sky.

'Candleriggs?'

She's huddled down by the fire, yawning, but his urgent whisper brings her to his side.

Candleriggs follows his puzzled gaze at the lumen-like lights in the sea and sky.

'It's only the moon,' she says, 'and its reflection in the water.'

Fox shakes his head. 'The moon's round.'

'Only when it's full. The crescent moon grows into a full moon every month.'

Now Fox feels stupid. 'The New World only has a full moon.'

'Ah, but everything's plentiful up there, isn't it?' Candleriggs squeezes his arm. 'The netherworld moon is thin and hungry, eh? But it'll soon grow fat and strong.'

Fox points to the slow-whirling ship. 'Why is the ship on the globe?'

'That's a weathervane,' says Candleriggs. 'Tells you which way the wind blows. Look, there are lots more on the drowned roofs and spires. This was a trading city, long ago. Once upon a time ships sailed all across the oceans from here, all over the world. Well, they still do.'

They watch a white cargo ship steal across the netherworld sea. It steers a careful path between the small islands and rooftops of the drowned city and docks at the foot of one of New Mungo's vast towers. Candleriggs hugs her cloak around her and glances at the weathervane. 'A bitter North Wind. It'll be a hard night out on the ocean.'

Let her not sink, Fox prays.

There is no point in pretending any more. Candleriggs is as worried as he is. She knows when he has met Mara and when he hasn't. She can tell by his mood.

'She didn't come again tonight,' he says quietly.

'Ah.'

Candleriggs's face sets like stone as she turns back to the fire.

The crescent moon and the sailing ships blur as unwanted tears burn in his eyes. Fox scrubs them away.

The whole world carries echoes of Mara. He is beginning to feel haunted by her in this lonely place. She's there in the crescent-moon halo that peeks through the towers and the ships on the weathervanes. Her presence ghosts the bookstacks. Sometimes he thinks he hears her sigh or whisper as she leafs through a book, though he knows it's only the wind and the birds. The white ships that dock in New Mungo remind him of her. She even called to him through the words of the book he almost burned.

Something tugs at his memory.

Fox unseals the waterproof wallet attached to his belt. He takes out a piece of thick, pulpy paper he almost forgot he had. Just before she left, Mara gave him Gorbals's netherworld poems. He picks up the lantern. The clumsy charcoal scribbles are hard to make out in the flickering moonmoth light.

THE STARS ARE NIGHT DAISIES
TRAPPED IN HIGH BRANCHES

Fox looks up through New Mungo's sky tunnels to the sparkling heavens above. A smile breaks on his face as he sees what the Treenester poet saw. The writing is rubbed and faded in places but three words jump out at him:

PLAY PEEKABOO MOON

Fox stares at the words, breathless. Then glances up at the moon playing peekaboo between the sky city's towers. It has given him the glimmering of an idea. Has Mara left him the very clue he needs to kickstart his plans?

Watch over her, he begs the moon. His heart beats hot and fast as he puts on his godgem and leaps into the Noos.

ARKIEL

Thin moonlight lands on a battered sign wedged between two rocks. Mara can only just read the faded letters. *Tikerak.* She sounds out the strange word under her breath. Even whispered, it has the same harsh crack as her captors' whips.

Her hands are bound tight, her feet tied just loose enough to let her walk. If she doesn't move fast enough, if she stumbles, the sting of the whip lands on her back.

They walk in a hobbling army of threes then they are made to sit on the ground for what feels like hours. Ruby is on one side of her, Molendinar on the other. The dark lifts at last but a cold blind fog has engulfed them and Mara still can't see where they are. All she knows is that there are rocks and pebbles, strands of frozen seaweed, underfoot. The thunder of the waterfalls is a faraway growl. She can't make sense of what is happening.

'Pollock was right,' murmurs Molendinar. 'The lights were a trap.'

Now Mara understands. The stone giants lured them to the false harbour lights and the lights lured them on to the rocks. The ship was wrecked and they've been captured by their wreckers.

Is everyone safe?

She searches for Rowan's shaved blond head and finds him. Gorbals's darker head sticks out above the rest. She tries to make out heads and faces in the fog, mentally ticking a list of who is here, safe, if not sound. Caddie, Fir and Tron are bunched together. She can't see the urchins, but she can hear Hoy yelling an indignant 'oy!' every time a whip lands on him. What about Wing, her own special urchin? Is he safe? Little Wing, who once saved her. Wing is a wiry survivor, as all the urchins are. Surely he'll be all right? She can hear Pollock muttering frantically behind her and Possil whispering back. Mara scans the mass of heads yet again. Where's Broomielaw and baby Clay?

Mara earns a whip sting as she looks over her shoulder.

'Broomielaw?' she whispers to Molendinar.

The answer is a sob.

The ice wind is bitter. Mara shivers, gripped by a deeper chill. Broomielaw must be safe. She would have saved little Clay if it took her last breath.

'Pollock?' Mara hisses over her shoulder, not caring if it earns her another crack of the whip. 'Broomie and Clay?'

The whip stings her ear but she hardly feels it; she cannot believe what Pollock is saying.

Lost.

Pollock's eyes look bruised. His mouth is set hard. He can't mean it. But his face tells Mara he does.

Broomielaw and Clayslaps, Pollock's baby son, are lost.

Mara could lie down on the ground and weep, but there's no chance of that. She is hauled to her feet, bound to the march of this bedraggled army. Even if she stopped, the others would pull her along whether she liked it or not.

Molendinar gives another sob. She and Broomielaw are as close as sisters. Mol helped deliver little Clayslaps into the world.

'We'll find her,' Mara whispers. 'Broomie would never let anything happen to Clayslaps. They'll be all right. They'll have washed up somewhere.'

'She can't swim.' Molendinar forces the words through chattering teeth. 'Candleriggs made us all learn but Broomielaw wouldn't, refused to get in the dirty water.' Mol gives a hard laugh. 'You know what a fusspot she is, everything has to be spick and sp—'

A deer clatters across the pebbled shore.

'No tok!'

The deer rears up as it pulls on its harness and a whip cracks over Molendinar's head. Mara turns and sees the stocky, hard-faced herder on the deer is a woman.

'Our friend—' she begins, hoping that a woman might be kind, but she's wrong. The woman kicks her so hard she falls, almost pulling Mol and Ruby down with her. Ruby yanks her to her feet as they are herded on to a fleet of long, narrow skin boats.

'Merien?' croaks Mara. She's crammed hard against Ruby. 'Is she——?'

Ruby nods to a boat that has already pushed out from the shore. 'I thought I saw her. I'm not sure.' Her mouth twitches and Mara realizes with a shock that Ruby is close to tears.

'She took me under her wing. All my family died,' Ruby murmurs.

Mara hesitates. 'So did mine.'

For the first time, Ruby glances at Mara without her usual sneer.

Mara returns the glance with surprise. It's a truce of a kind. And something more. Mara is sure she saw a softening of Ruby's sharp eyes. Being human, thinks Mara, is maybe all they have left.

An oar lands on Mara's lap and she obeys the signal to row almost without thinking, as the others do. As the boat pulls away from the shore they pass the bruised white hull of their ship, keeled over on the rocks. It looks almost peaceful, as if it's only resting awhile. As they leave it behind, Mara glimpses its name for the first time.

Arkiel

How many others from the *Arkiel* are lost? Mara looks over at the other boats, feeling sick. Lost, she tells herself. That means they could have washed up somewhere. Her mind reels back from the word *drowned*.

They row in and out of fog drifts. Suddenly they enter a clear patch and Mara can see where they are.

It's a vast fjord. Mountains loom high on either side and far in front, enclosing the channel of sea. The boats make a winding route through ice floes, islets and skerries, the rocky humps of land that clutter the fjord. Their precarious journey through the fjord is like a giant pinball game, thinks Mara, and she glances across at the back of Rowan's head. Her arms are aching from the oars, but Rowan was grey and trembling with exhaustion on the ship. What state is he in now?

Beside her, Molendinar is scanning every islet and skerry, desperate for a sign of Broomielaw and baby Clay. Alongside them, a long boat is heaped with booty plundered from the *Arkiel* – all the stuff the urchins looted from the museum in the drowned city. There are swords,

126

spears, shields and axes, bits of armour, musical instruments, jewellery, engines, cogs and wheels and microscopes and compasses, jars of pickled brains and, sitting atop the huge pile with a crown on his head, Scarwell's stolen apeman.

The waterfall thunder grows louder, so loud it seems to thrum in the bones. The boats slow up as they approach a wide, rocky bay.

Mara stares around her, sullen and furious. No one knows where these people are taking them, why they've wrecked and captured them or what they intend to do with them, yet everyone is mindlessly doing what they're told.

There must be thirty refugees in this boat alone. The handful of whip-cracking wreckers are well outnumbered. Surely, even with tied hands and feet, if all the refugees act in a surge . . .

Mara spots a gun in the belt of a wrecker. But do they all have guns? She glances at each one in turn, but can't be sure. How many bullets does a gun hold? If they overpowered their captors quickly enough, they could turn the guns on them.

They are close enough to struggle ashore. All Mara needs to do is shout at the top of her voice and rouse the others, command them to fight.

But they won't trust me. Not after I've landed them here in this mess.

She looks around and catches the eye of one of the men from the *Arkiel*, tries to hold his glance but he looks away. Mara takes a breath, opens her mouth.

'Don't you dare.' Ruby's voice is murderous.

'Mara,' Molendinar whispers on her other side. 'Have you lost it?'

127

'I'd say so,' grunts Ruby, and kicks Mara so hard she almost yelps.

Mara kicks back. 'There are a lot more of us than them,' she hisses. 'Why are we acting like lambs?'

Molendinar looks puzzled. 'Your backpack,' she whispers.

Mara feels as if she is falling through the floor of the boat. *My backpack.* It's not here. How could she not have noticed? She's kept it with her ever since she left her own island.

'All your precious things,' murmurs Molendinar.

Mara can't speak. *Where is it?* She tries to remember when she last had it. It must have been wrenched off her when the ship went down, when she was thrashing about, struggling to reach the surface of the sea. Her arms follow the movements of the oar, though she feels ill with shock. Her backpack has the cyberwizz zipped inside, safe and watertight, though what good is that if it's lost on the seabed, along with the wrecked ship?

It's her only connection with Fox and it's gone. Mara feels sick to her soul.

Mol squeezes her hand, hard. 'It'll wash up somewhere. So will Broomielaw and Clayslaps.'

Guilt stings Mara. The loss of two precious people is much worse than the loss of her cyberwizz, she knows it is. Yet deep down she knows she can survive their loss because she has survived even worse, the worst there is: the deaths of the people closest to her in the whole world. Losing Broomielaw and baby Clay and even Fox is not worse than that. And Fox is still alive; it's only her connection with him that's lost. But to lose him and know he's not dead; to know he's out there, forever unreachable – how will she bear that? She has imagined them an ocean apart yet together always, meeting on the Bridge to Nowhere, no matter what the future may hold.

'Mol, I can't bear—'

'No tok!'

The wire whip cracks across her back but Mara hardly notices. Hopelessness has fallen upon her like a rock.

They have steered into a rocky enclosure, a rough harbour cluttered with boats. The wreckers begin to mass the refugees on to a shore stacked with boulders. Mara sees Molendinar mouth something at Gorbals as they are herded across the shore.

Gorbals stares, stumbles, almost falls.

'*Broomielaw? No . . .*'

The words hang frozen in the air. Mara closes her eyes but not quick enough. Gorbals looks as if he's just stepped off the edge of a cliff.

Torrents of icy water crash from the mountains, frothing the sea in the bay. Some waterfalls are so high their beginnings are lost in cloud. A ray of sun shoots through the mist and lands with a flash among the waterfalls. Another breaks through, then another. The rays merge into one broad, strong sunbeam that begins to burn away the mist.

Mara stares at the flashing mountain that looms above. Peaks jut into the sky in violent exclamations of rock.

She hears Rowan behind her, a crack of amazement in his voice. 'Up there, are those – they can't be . . . doors?'

Doors? Mara looks up and blinks.

The mountain is studded with them. She studies those nearest the ground. Their cracked and faded colours have a metallic sheen. And now, as the blur of mist burns away, she can make out what seems to be stone dwellings, each one fronted by a door, carved out of the rock face. There are more doors set into mounds of rock, stone-built versions of the igloos pictured in her Greenland book, perched precariously on ledges all over the mountain. Mara screws up her eyes and sees that each stone mound is wrapped in chains. The stone igloos are fastened to the mountain by chains.

Near the heel of the mountain there's a metallic flash as an opening door catches the sun. Someone steps out and there's another flash as the door shuts. The person ties a rope around their middle and swings expertly down a sheer mountain rockway. The figure reaches a ledge and disappears into the open mouth of a cave. A moment later a doleful bell clangs in the cave and echoes all across the bay.

The bell detonates an explosion of flashes and bangs across the foot of the mountain, as a multitude of doors open and shut. A moment later the mountain is alive, crawling with movement, as people spill out, swinging down the rockways, attached to ropes.

The people of the mountain reach the ground and unharness their ropes. The bay fills with human noise and the bellow of the sea seems to recede. From caverns and rocks they drag out the apparatus of a marketplace and in the time it has taken for the sun to burn away the last tatters of mist, the empty bay is transformed into a racketing metropolis.

The ship-wrecked refugees are whip-cracked into a raggedy line and bullied along the shore towards the metropolis at the foot of the mountain.

The gang of wreckers halt on the shore in front of a stone giant. The giant's arms are wide open in greeting. Dangling from them is a motley collection of litter and driftwood signs.

One of the wreckers points to the stone man, grinning. He cracks his whip on the ground.

'TAMASSA!' he announces and the others laugh. They stand in front of their captives, hissing the word, *tamassa! tamassa!* whips flicking like the tongues of a nest of snakes.

Mara stares at the stone giant's signs. The word TAMASSA is hung around the stone man's neck and dangling from his right arm on a slab of cracked driftwood are the only words she understands.

WELCOME TO ILIRA
PLACE OF FEARFUL AWE

One of the wreckers shouts and the rest fall into a sudden hush. They're tense now, whips flicking nervously on the pebble shore. '*Scutpak*,' they mutter, and the word crackles among them like the rock lichen underfoot.

Scutpak? What's that? Heart thumping, Mara stares around, but can't see why the wreckers are so fraught.

Something bright up on the mountain catches her eye. Mara looks up and sees a huge clock face with no hands. Instead, a pattern of fiery words radiates from the clock like sun rays. The word-rays are the same gleaming amber as the bottle of Irn-Bru she gave Rowan on the ship. Like the welcome sign, the words are strange and unknown but reaching up to the sky at the point of midnight, Mara spots the word ILIRA again.

Ilira.

A place of fearful awe, said the scrawled sign. Mara's spine prickles. *Fearful awe?* It sounds like somewhere out of a fairy tale, not this bleak, harsh place.

Above the clock a great broken bird with smashed

wings and tail is wedged between the mountain and a great thumb of rock.

'What *is* that?' Mara murmurs over her shoulder.

'A plane,' Rowan whispers back. 'A real plane. Remember? They were in Tain's *World Encyclopedia*. They used to fly through the skies like giant birds, all over the world. This one must have crashed way back . . .'

Mara stares at the smashed plane. It looks nothing like the pictures in Tain's book, more like one of the crumpled paper birds she made to amuse the urchins on the ship. A great lassitude engulfs her. The mountains might be full of giant birds, giant men, fiery clocks, strange signs, flashing doors and windows, all kinds of miracles and wonders. Mara doesn't care.

She has made it to the top of the world and it doesn't seem to matter.

Broomielaw and baby Clay are lost. They might be lying at the bottom of the sea. She has lost her cyberwizz and she's lost Fox.

It feels like the end of the world.

ARMADA

The Steer Master's horn sounds a long, ominous bellow.

Tuck shivers and knots his windwrap tighter. Another boat lost to an iceberg. Since the berg blitz hit, it has been every boat for itself, but the seafaring skills of the steerers are blunt and rusty; Pomperoy was anchored to the rig for so long. Now the sea is clearing and it's more perilous to go back than to go on. They'd better find the *Arkiel* soon, Tuck reckons. He can smell gypsea temper in the air.

Sunlight swords the fog and Tuck is dazzled by a mad sparkle of sea and ice floes. He feels dizzy and breathless as if he's been leaping bridges and boats, but he's still huddled in the lifeboat on the upper deck as the *Waverley* hurtles across the ocean with fists of wind in its sails.

Land rises out of the ocean like a giant, petrified wave. Tuck lowers the silver box from his eyes and presses the button that retracts the long zoom nose. He no longer needs it. The Land is close enough now.

The Steer Master's horn bellows across the Pomperoy fleet once again. This time it's a continuous blast. Tuck points the eye of his silver box at the Steer Master's ship and almost drops the box with fright as he finds himself eye to eye with The Man. Now he looks with his own eyes and sees that The Man has been hung high on *The Discovery*'s middle mast. He's still The Man in the Middle then and still spying on Tuck.

The bridgers are arming themselves, though there's still no sign of the *Arkiel*. But the Steer Master's ship has a long eyescope on its deck that, it's said, can see the faces of the stars so maybe it can see the great white ship.

'Ah, there you are, Tuck, lad. Grab yourself a cutlass, you'll be needing one.'

On the deck below, Charlie beckons him. Tuck clambers out of the lifeboat and jumps down. Charlie hands him a curved sword that's as wide as his arm and almost as long. Tuck swallows, throat tight, as he takes the cutlass. He has never felt less ready for a fight. There's an ache in the pit of his stomach, as if he's eaten bad fish, but it's not that. He can't stop thinking about his family. He wanted them so bad in that strange, lonely moment when he looked for the first time at the world of his Landcestors, at the miracle of Land.

There's another signal from the Steer Master, a melodic horn blast that Tuck doesn't know. But the bridgers next to him do. Their gypsea eyes narrow and glint, just like the curved cutlass blades in their belts. There's a sudden brash swagger about these men that should make him laugh, but makes him wary instead. The women, some of them, have it too. Others disappear below deck with the children, looking grim, as the ragged fleet of boats manoeuvres, with the instinct of a flock of birds or a shoal of fish, into the shape of an arrowhead. Tuck watches, wondering what's happening. Then he hears the Land's thunder, a noise like the warrior roar of an enemy fleet. And as they draw close, his eyebox shows

134

him what the Steer Master's powerful eyescope must have seen when the warning horn bellowed: the giant stone men that guard the Land.

The day wanes and the sun falls behind the thundering mountains. The vast arrowhead of boats still follows the jagged line of land, every vessel spiked with swords and spears.

Armada.

That's the word Tuck hears, shouted from boat to boat. The Steer Master's ship sets up a soft, predatory drumbeat that spreads from boat to boat like a footstep. Soon the whole fleet is a-throb with the march. Pomperoy is no longer a city, it's a dense arrowhead, an armada on attack, heading for the great wall in the ocean that is Land.

Up against a wall, you can hurtle onward or retreat. Pomperoy does both. It hurtles forward and turns back into what it once was.

Tuck remembers the words Grumpa would growl whenever his temper was roused.

Time to turn pirate again.

SNAKE ON A STICK

The female wrecker is yelling into a black box that crackles with white noise. A man's voice shouts out of the crackling. The woman puts it to her ear as she scans the shoreline, screwing up eyes that are so deep-set they almost disappear among the folds of her weathered face.

'Tok-tok,' she nods, and clicks a switch that kills the noise of the box. She glances at the captives and frowns, shoves them into tidier lines and surveys them with a satisfied smile.

The other wreckers stop picking through the litter the sea has junked on the shore. To focus her mind beyond the horror of what seems to be happening, Mara scans the litter. Plastic bags and bottles, tins and cans, a small metal disc full of rainbow lights, a scatter of bones, a bashed thing that must once have been a wheel and the eyeless head of a doll. Her heart turns over when she sees a green welly and a branch of bare, bent spokes that was once an umbrella. When she was little Mum used to let her stand in the rain in too-big green wellies with an old daisy-covered umbrella, as long as the wind wasn't too high.

Faraway hooves clatter on the rocky shore. In the distance, four deer gallop towards them, the riders dressed in a ferocious drama of feathers, wings, bird heads and fur tails, beaks, claws and strings of teeth. The riders look more unnervingly animal than the deer.

'Scutpak!' the wreckers announce, a warning in their eyes.

Sand and pebbles scatter as the deer clatter to a halt. One of the gang the wreckers call *scutpak* jumps down from his saddle. His entire tunic is covered in teeth and claws. He scans the crowd of captives with a quick, keen eye.

'Ah, yaaaa,' he drawls. 'Yup, yup, yup.' He begins to select some of the men. 'Nup, nup, nup, ah, yup.'

Mara turns her head and catches Rowan's eye.

'Like the Pickings,' she whispers and he nods, his gaunt face grim and scared. He was 'picked' before in the boat camp outside New Mungo and ended up a New World slave.

The picked men are cut free, Pollock and Possil among them, but there's no chance of escape; a noose is immediately looped around their necks. If they try to run, they'll yank the noose tight.

The scutpak leader is making his way along the lines of captives. 'Yup-yup. Pffff! Nup, old bones.'

The chosen are cut from their bonds, noosed and led across the shore. The tooth-and-claw man reaches Gorbals and Rowan, and frowns. 'Dud. Skinny-scrawny, see!' He pinches their arms, peers at their eyes. 'Young, huh . . . mibbe, mibbe.' His frown lifts and he claps his hands. 'Ok*ay*!' His frown returns at the sight of the tiny, scrawny urchins. 'Nup, nup.' He waves them away, then changes his mind. 'Yup, yup. Un, doo, tree. Tree for un. No sale then junk 'em all.'

137

He makes a cut-throat sign.

Now he's yupping at Molendinar, Mara, Ruby too. As they are noosed and led away, Ruby gives a cry.

'Merien!'

Mara looks back. Merien has been left behind on the shore, her hands and feet still bound.

But there's nothing to do except go where the noose pulls. In front of her, there's an outburst of screams. Now Molendinar screams, right in front. The noose is yanked hard around Mara's neck, and someone rips the clothes off her shoulder. Mara screams too as a metal pole jabs her arm and red-hot pain flashes through her.

The top of her arm sizzles. The skin is black and burned. The smell of her own cooked flesh makes her sick and faint. She can't believe what is happening. They are being branded like cattle.

The noose is yanked hard again. Mara chokes, goes where she's led. She is hauled with the others into the middle of the market, and stands confused, in a daze of pain, among the busy stalls. A crowd gathers and the scut-pak gang begin to sell their noosed captives.

The clock with no hands and the crashed plane on the mountain, the sky and the noisy crowd reel around her. Mara feels unreal, as if she's been shocked out of her own self. '*Mara.*' She murmurs her own name because for a petrifying moment she can't remember who she is. She has lost herself in the herd. '*Mara,*' she repeats, and concentrates on the pain of her arm. The pain is the only thing that feels real. Mara eases the clothes from her shoulder to let the icy air cool her burned skin, and sees the symbol that's been branded on her arm.

A snake coiled on a stick.

There's a hot graze on her neck as the rope is pulled,

the flash of a blade, and she is cut free of the others. One of the scutpak pushes her in front of the gathering crowd. He lifts her arms to show her muscles, turns her around to show her straight back.

'Young, ha? Strong and *stark*, yup?' he prattles.

There's a mutter of interest in the crowd. Mara stares at her prospective buyers. A man in a hooded skin tunic that reaches the ground, the hood so deep, his black and silver beard so bush-like, that all she can see of his face is a long nose. A woman draped from head to foot in furs that are fastened and knotted as intricately as Broomielaw's woven plastic clothes. The woman wrinkles her wind-scoured face, weighing up Mara as if she were a cut of meat.

The scutpaker is rummaging in a bag. With a flourish he pulls something out.

Mara gasps.

Candleriggs' red shoes!

The scutpaker waves the shoes under the nose of the be-furred woman and pushes Mara towards her with a prattle of sales patter that Mara can't follow. The woman's face crinkles into a mean smile and as she moves forward to grab the red shoes, Mara catches sight of the bag in the scutpaker's hands.

My backpack!

She *did* have it strapped to her when the ship sank. She was sure she did. Now she remembers she had to swim against the weight of the backpack. She almost didn't make it, risked drowning rather than take it off. She was lying on the rock, choking on seawater, but the backpack was still safe. The wreckers took it when they found her, half drowned and exhausted.

She screams so hard the woman drops the shoes in

139

fright. Mara grabs a shoe before it hits the ground, just as the scutpaker reaches for the tail of rope round her neck. Before he can yank the rope, Mara slams the small, sharp heel of the shoe into his nose. She drops the shoe, grabs her backpack and runs.

She's forgotten all about Rowan and Mol and the others. She hasn't a clue where she's running to. All she knows is she's got her backpack with her precious cyber-wizz and she *must run*.

The pebble shore shifts under every scrambling step. The stones seem to drag her backward; it takes twice the effort to run, but she *is* running. If she can make it across the shore and through the market stalls to the foot of the mountain, there might be a cave or a rockway she can hide in . . .

Her foot catches on a rock.

Mara crashes face down on to stones, but she's still got her backpack gripped in one hand. Scutpakers and wreckers crash across the stones, close behind. Something punches her in the back and her chin smashes into the stones. She can't get up. Someone is trying to rip the backpack from her fingers. She holds on tight, even as they stamp on her hand.

A point of freezing cold metal stings her forehead. There's drumming in her ears. Mara raises her bleeding chin from the ground and stares into the barrel of a gun.

EARTHLANDER AGAIN

Just being alive has never felt so good. Tuck stares around him as if he's seeing the world for the first time.

Everything about Land is a surprise. It's so much more than he ever imagined. The mountains are vast and beautiful, the thunderwater that pelts down them so loud it shakes his bones. But what entrances him most of all is the fact that Land does not move. Not at all. Tuck's never known what stillness is because he has never felt it before in his life.

He takes the little silver box from the belt of his windwrap and zooms in on such a violent pelt of waterfall that he recoils with a yell.

'Tuck, lad! What you goggling at like a gormless gull? You armed and ready? From here on, you be ready for anything.'

Tuck waves his cutlass at Charlie and catches a crescent of first morning light on the curved pirate blade.

'Well, stop playing with that camera and get down here!'

Tuck looks at the little silver box in his hand. *Camera.* He tries the strange word on his tongue.

'TUCK!'

A gypsea roar shatters his reverie. The almighty BOOM of the Steer Master's cannon shocks him into the moment. The armada has entered a gap in the land: a wide, curving channel of ocean that winds between the mountains. Vast arms of rock enclose the fleet on either side while right in front jagged peaks rise out of the fog.

'Urth!'

'Eyes of The Man!'

'Great Skua help us!'

Yells and curses erupt from the steerers and lookouts as they suddenly spot the rocky humps and islets that litter the fjord. There's a sickening crunch of wood and the moan of metal on rock as the gypsea boats hit the land traps in the sea. The *Waverley*'s lookout boy screams as an island looms out of a fog drift. Tuck hangs on to the rail as the steerer heaves the ship clear, almost smashing into one of the ferries. Behind them, the wrecked hulls of sunken boats circle the whaleback island like shark fins.

Chancing another yell from Charlie, Tuck grabs his camera and zooms the eye on to the mountain at the head of the fjord. At first, all he gets is a blank windowful of fog. He sweeps the mountain, zooms in on a flash of sunlight, and finds himself face to face with a sleepy-eyed child who stands open-mouthed in front of a door on a ledge of rock watching the armada appear out of the fog. The sun bounces off the door again as the child yanks it open and disappears inside. Tuck has a moment's glimpse of the cave that lies behind the door. He stays fixed on the door, jolted with emotion, once it slams shut for it's so like the door in his sunken shack on *The Grimby Gray*. A yellow car door, battered and scraped by rocks and

142

waves. The camera reveals a mass of car doors set into the rock face.

Tuck feels a tug inside.

The pirate roar of the armada is like nothing he has ever heard. An order from the Steer Master's ship cuts it dead. But the drumbeat rolls on. Tuck stares at the sudden industry that fills every ship, as the oil tanks, catapults and cannons that each ship hoards in case of sudden sea attack are hauled up on to the decks.

For long moments he stands there, shifting from foot to foot as if the deck is on fire. An idea is swirling like fog in his head.

Tuck tightens his windwrap and secures the camera in his belt. He races along the deck to the back of the ship. The gondola he was rescued in lies among a pile of ropes, nets and driftwood. He selects two long sticks of driftwood for oars, wraps the gondola in a wide, thick rope-weave of netting, the kind used to catch dolphins and seals, and lowers the boat until it's almost touching the surge of the waves. He knots the end of the netting to the *Waverley*'s metal rail then he begins to climb down it like a rope ladder, finding footholds in its wide weave. When he reaches the gondola he makes a slash in the netting with his cutlass and climbs inside.

Now he sits in the gondola and waits.

He waits until he is close enough to Land to see the people on the shore. Then he hacks at the netting that cradles the gondola, just above the sea, and slices the boat free with his blade. The gondola crashes sideways into the waves and Tuck has to struggle with every ounce of his strength to set it upright, turn it around and stop it being churned to pieces in the *Waverley*'s wake.

143

No one seems to notice he is gone. The pirate storm consumes the armada, head, heart and soul.

Someone yells his name as a fleet of yachts surges past. *Pendicle?* Tuck scans the decks but sea spume blinds him and by the time he's wiped his eyes the yachts are way in front. He oars frantically through the wake from the angry fleet. All the time he is aware of the enclosing shadow of the unknown Land they are invading. But these are *my* people too, he suddenly knows, and he doesn't mean the gypsea pirates, but the EarthLanders with their sea-scavenged car doors. Tuck is a motley mix of gypsea, pirate and bridger. But now he senses, deep inside, that there's something Lander in him too, though he's never set foot on Earth.

But his Landcestors have and they must have left strong, Earthy footprints on his soul.

His last blood bond with Pomperoy sank with Ma on *The Grimby Gray* and a strange tug inside now pulls him to Land.

TARTOQ darkness

Midnight comes; kings are clay; men are earth.

The Play of Gilgamesh by Edwin Morgan

PIRATE AGAIN

Night fled in a panic when dawn revealed what was burrowed in the dark. A drumbeat sneaks behind the march of the ocean. Hidden in fog and helped by the tide, the terror creeps up the winding channel of the great fjord.

The people of Ilira are still rubbing the sleep from their eyes, shocking themselves awake with the icy spray of the waterfalls, grabbing new-laid eggs from the mountain ledges, roping down the rockways to market where the scutpakers sell shipwreck booty and branded slaves.

A faded red skysail punctures the fog.

Ilira is entranced by the playful red dash that billows above the fjord. Sails begin to bloom all across the sky. A motley patchwork of masts bursts from the fog like a tattered army of spears. The Steer Master's horn bellows and the sneaky drumbeat rouses into a gypsea storm.

If the wall of mountains behind Ilira cracked open to reveal a flaming dragon, the shock would be just as deep.

The armada of boats erupts from the fog with a petrifying roar as Pomperoy turns pirate again.

THE STAIRWAY AND
THE BLUE WISP

Mara doesn't dare stop. She stumbles up a steep, narrow rockway until it forms into rough steps. The stone stairway might have been hacked out of the mountain by aeons of grinding ice or human hands, she can't tell, but it climbs so high she can't see where it ends because the rockway disappears into a shelf of fog. Soaked by spray from waterfalls that hiss and thunder from crevices all across the mountain, Mara prays she doesn't lose her footing on the drenched rock. If she does – she looks behind her to the base of the mountain where the waterfalls smash into fizzling rainbows – she'll crash all the way back down.

She had one second to escape the gun pointed at her head, a moment when the world around her erupted and the cold metal of the gun barrel trembled then lifted from her forehead. She took her chance and raced across the rocky beach, faster than wind, until she found herself at the bottom of the mountain in a maze of rockways that brought her to the mountain steps.

A hundred more slithering steps take her underneath a massive waterfall that drenches her in icy spray. Here, the rock is so lethal with iced slime she hardly dares move. Then she sees the rope. She's been so intent on keeping her footing that she hasn't seen the thick rope stapled as a handrail into the mountainside. Mara grabs it, glancing behind her for the umpteenth time, but still there is no one on her tail.

Up through yet another waterfall, the stepped rockway splits. She can either climb up into the fog clouds or take the descending way. Upward is cold and terrifyingly blank, so she takes the way down, though these steps are so steep and twisting her head spins and the world reels. Mara grips the mountain rope so tightly her freezing hands burn.

The steps wind down around a knuckle of mountain and Mara finds herself on a wide ledge in the middle of a crowd. A shrieking woman yanks on ropes knotted like harnesses around the squat, fur-wrapped bundles of two small children. Mara stares at the doors set haphazardly across the cave-pitted face of the mountain. *Car doors.* There was such excitement on those rare occasions when one washed up on Wing. Mara remembers the scramble to claim such scarce scrap metal.

The car doors are bashed and ill-fitting for the uneven cave mouths. The scraped, motley colours couldn't look more out of place. Yet somehow they give the bleak mountain face the homely look of a village. As the shrieking mother drags her children inside, Mara glimpses a cavernous darkness made snug with candles, furs and skins, and feels a jolt of wanting. She wipes a stream of water from her drenched face and tries to catch her breath. The crowd of weathered-looking people stare out to the ocean.

Mara sees the stricken faces. She follows their eyes.

A vast tide of boats fills the fjord.

What she thought was the roar of the mountain waterfalls was only partly that; the rest is the battle roar of an invading fleet.

All the way up the mountain, escape was Mara's only thought. She grabbed the chance to save her backpack, and her life. Only now, as she watches the horror erupting in the bay below, does she remember what she's left behind: her friends, abandoned on the shore.

Slamming erupts all around her. The mountain vibrates with the metallic percussion of car doors. People armed with guns and spears are racing out of the caves and hurling themselves down the rockways, harnessed to ropes. Others drag their children inside.

Which way? Which way? Should she escape further up the mountain to who knows where, stay here, or join the people rushing down to the battle on the shore?

The snake burned into her arm throbs, reminding her that this race of people had her bound and branded as a slave. Escape is the only sensible thing to do. But her friends are down there on the shore.

A firebomb catapults from a ship and explodes in one of the boats on the bay, scattering blazing debris on to the shore. Gripping the rope rail, Mara begins to run down the mountain steps, as fast as the slippery rock allows. She reaches a lower ledge crowded with stone igloos. Mara uses the wall of an igloo to brace herself against the ice-chipped hurl of the wind. She looks down the mountain, trying to figure out what's happening, trying to see which way to go.

Ma-ra-ra-raah . . .

She scans the mountain. Are her ears playing tricks? Is it the shriek of the wind in the rockways or is someone really calling her name? It's hard to tell amid the uproar in the bay. A stone cracks against the mighty slab of granite that forms the ledge and bounces close to her foot. Mara picks it up. She peers at the ground below.

A mass of people are rushing on to the firebombed shore. Smoke and flames now fill the fjord. Mountain people have taken cover behind rocks to return fire at their attackers, but the invading fleet is out of reach of short-range guns and spears. Firebombs are devastating the anchored boats in the bay while the counter-fire of the mountain people lands in the sea.

Ma-ra-ra-ra . . .

Her name, again, she's sure. Another stone cracks against the rocky ledge. Mara scans the mountain slopes and the shore below her. Where are they? Where? Far below, a cluster of people are out on the open shore. Mara thinks she sees Rowan's dark blond head, Mol's stream of hair whipped up in the wind, the ragged scarecrow that is Gorbals. The wind clears a gap in the smoke and now she's sure it's them – there's Pollock, wiry and dark-headed, his arm raised to throw another stone. Mara waves frantically, then screams as she sees what they can't because they're looking up at her: a firebomb flying across the bay towards them.

Mara shuts her eyes as the firebomb explodes. When she opens them, her friends have been thrown to the ground but a large rock seems to have sheltered them from the worst of the blast. One of them – in the confusion she's not sure who – staggers up and begins racing to the sea, flames streaming from an arm. A spark from the firebomb has caught the raggedy plastic clothing that hangs in tatters from the sealskin coat. The figure trips over a rock and crashes into the sea.

Gorbals.

He flails about in the water. The others try to reach him but a hail of gunfire from the shore halts them in their tracks. Gorbals is struggling against the waves but the others can't make it through a line of gunfire, and there's nothing Mara can do. She is about to look away, unable to watch, when her eye is caught by a blue wisp, racing towards Gorbals. The wind whips the tail of the blue wisp high into the air. Mara screws up her eyes. What in the world is *that*?

The telescope.

Does she still have it? Mara rips open her sodden backpack, rummages, and it's there. She grabs a thick handful of her hair and scrubs the lens clean, then leans as far as she can over the rocky ledge and focuses the telescope with shaking hands.

The blue wisp is a boy or a man in a garment that's wound round his head and body and flutters into a long, wind-frittered tail. He runs into the sea, unwinding his garment and flings its long tail into the waves. Gorbals disappears under a wave, but when he resurfaces the blue tail is thrown once again. He grabs it and the wisp, now soaked to a deep blue, hauls him out of the sea.

They disappear among the smoke of the firebombs. When the wind shifts the smoke there's no sign of them, only the shell of an overturned boat.

Mara looks all across the shore to the spot where she last saw the others. They're gone too.

She scans the whole of the eastern shore, the rocks and the foot of the mountain. *Where are they?* Shoving the telescope in the pocket of her sealskin coat, she hurries down the mountain steps, towards the battle that rages in the bay.

EARTHED

Tuck lifts up the edge of the upturned gondola and peeps out.

The gondola is the only thing protecting him and the half-drowned ragbag he's just rescued. Not that a wooden gondola will be any good if it takes a direct hit from a firebomb. Behind those car doors in the mountain, that's the place to be.

But Tuck can't make his legs move towards the mountain even though he knows that he'll be safe there. Pomperoy will loot and steal every boat it can, and burn and sink every one it can't. What a true gypsea will never do is set foot on Land.

But the Landers don't know that.

Up close and underfoot, Land has turned out to be such an overwhelming thing that Tuck only dares look at it in glimpses from under cover of the boat. When he and the gondola crashed on to the shore, he tried to get up and staggered so much he fell over, his head swimming as if he'd been gluggeting seagrape beer all night.

Only the gangly man-boy rushing into the sea, flames streaming from his arm, brought him back to his senses.

He didn't mean to rescue anyone, it's not his kind of thing at all, but someone screaming and drowning right in front of him made him think of Ma in her last moments on *The Grimby Gray*. Almost without thinking, Tuck found himself in the ocean, yanking the drowning ragbag back on to shore and under the shelter of the upturned gondola.

All around him Land rises up in mountainous waves that seem to surge and swell, threatening to break like gigantic sea rollers upon his head. Tuck knows the Land is not moving and neither is he, for the first time ever in his life. What if his gypsea heart is so wired to the beat of the ocean he's not meant to be still? What if the sea-swell in his head never settles and calms? What if he's stuck forever here on Earth but never finds his Land legs?

Ocean is a moving, live thing but Earth's so still and solid it doesn't seem right. Maybe it's dead. What if that's why the Land sunk down into the sea – because it died? Tuck picks up a pebble and feels the deathly cold of the stone, with no beat of life in it at all.

'Th-thank you.'

The scraggy one sprawled on the ground beside him grabs Tuck's hand and, though his grasp is almost as cold as the stone, Tuck is grateful for the touch of another moving, live thing. He finds a strand of wet seaweed and wraps it around the boy's burned hand.

'My name's Gorbals,' the ragbag winces.

'I'm Tuck,' says Tuck.

A firebomb explodes nearby and a hard rain of stones falls upon the gondola.

'Is that a place?'

'Is what a place?'

'Tuck.'

Tuck narrows his eyes.

157

'Oh, never mind.' Warily, Gorbals lifts the boat and points to the mountain with his good hand. 'See, there's a cave. I think that's where my people are. If we make the boat our shell and run—'

Tuck sees the crack of darkness at the foot of the mountain.

His heart hammers.

'Safer in there than out here,' says Gorbals. He rises to a half-crouch, balancing the boat over his head as if he's a human snail. His burned arm makes him wince again.

'Give a hand,' he urges.

Tuck stands up on shaking legs. He should have ignored that impulse on the *Waverley*, when he felt the first roots of Earthiness stirring inside. Now look what's happened to him.

Instead of pirate, he's turned *Lander*.

The world reels and spins but he grips the gondola hard over his head and runs with the raggedy stranger across the rubbish-strewn shore like a fast, four-legged snail, towards the terrifying crack of darkness that will take him to a place he's never imagined in his wildest gypsea dreams.

The inside of Earth.

THE FACE IN THE STONES

Mara reaches ground at last and is hit by a pelt of hot stones as a firebomb explodes on the shore. All she can do is crouch and put her arms over her head, while the stones rain on her back. She stands up, shaken and bruised. Every large rock has been commandeered by the mountain people to launch their counter-attack, so there is no shelter. She runs away from the battle towards the far end of the bay. The rockways down the mountain were so winding she's lost her bearings. The overturned boat, her one landmark on the shore, has vanished so she can only guess at the spot where she last saw the others.

The sun is low, without the energy to rise any higher. It's hard to tell what time it is. So much has happened it seems like an endless day. The smoke from the firebombs has cast its own gloom but Mara is sure daylight is beginning to fade. She must find the others before night falls. There's a lull in the firebombs and Mara pauses, shivering in the icy wind. Winter comes early in the Far North. Her own island, Wing, only had a few hours of daylight in deep winter. Here, at the top of the world, the sun disappears below the horizon until spring. All too soon, they will plunge into a season of endless night.

Mara looks up at all the cave doors, at the sheer steps and rockways of the precarious metropolis the people have made of the mountain. *They've found a way to survive. But will we?*

It's not the homeland she hoped for, this harsh, barren place.

The war in the bay is ferocious again. We'll be lucky, thinks Mara, to survive to the end of the day.

Something trips her up and sends her sprawling on to the pebble shore. Mara curses and rubs her raw knee, then sees it's not a rock or driftwood but a child crouched on the ground.

'Wing!'

He's alive, if not safe. Wing smiles but squirms away from her frantic hug, more interested in the great heap of shiny pebbles he is piling up. A rabble of urchins comes running out of a fold in the mountain. Mara sees Hoy and opens her arms to hug him too, but like Wing he only throws a quick smile at her and rushes to add his armful of pebbles on to the growing pile.

There's a tug on her arm. It's Scarwell, the urchin girl who once ripped Mara's face in a fight. They gauge each other warily, then Scarwell breaks into a grin as she points to the lifesize plastic apeman, lying on the shore.

Mara has to laugh. Somehow, Scarwell has stolen back her beloved apeman from the wreckers.

Another explosion, followed by screams, reminds Mara that they are an easy target here in the open. Used to the siren squads of sea police in the drowned city, the urchins seem unperturbed by the noise of the battle in the bay.

Mara grabs little Hoy and points towards the mountain. 'We need to hide. Come with me, come on.'

'Oy,' grunts Hoy, wriggling free. He puts his handful of coloured pebbles on the heap.

'Hoy, it's dangerous—' Mara blinks as the sun flashes on the pile of pebbles. Blood-red, sea-green and sunset-amber, the stones are gem-like, polished by ice and sea and time.

Yet another explosion, far too close, rains a painful hail of stones on their heads.

'Quick! Follow me.'

She grabs Hoy again and stops. The whole world seems to stop as Mara sees a face in the stones.

Wing is picking gems from the heap they've made, gently placing them upon the almost-buried face.

Mara grabs hold of Wing. 'What are you doing?'

He looks up at her and smiles.

Mara sinks to her knees and forces herself to claw the gems and pebbles off the ashen face. Then reels back in shock when she sees who it is, sees the garish splash of blood on the stones.

Merien.

Mara lets out a wail. She can't speak. The urchins could not have done this, they couldn't. These children are wild but surely they couldn't *kill* . . .

But *she* killed a man, didn't she?

Wing crouches down beside her. He points a finger at the face and imitates the sound of a gunshot, then points back at the battle.

Of *course*. It wasn't the urchins. Abandoned here on the open shore, still bound by the wreckers' ropes, Merien was trapped in the blast of the battle.

Mara feels shamed. Merien was the urchins' friend.

161

How could she think they would harm her? But it's hard to keep trust in anyone or anything any more. The world has become so strange, everything so precarious, shifting and unreal that it's hard to gauge what anyone will do, including herself.

When the gun was at her head, her only thought was to save herself and her cyberwizz. In that instant and in the fear rush that followed, she never gave a thought to her friends.

Wing and Hoy begin to replace the stones that Mara has clawed off Merien's face, pebble by pebble, gem by gem, chanting under their breath. Mara kneels down beside them and listens, wondering what it is these wordless children are saying. The rest of the urchins join in, all chanting together.

They're counting.

Death, smoke and fire fill the bay. The wind howls around them, full of ice. Still, the urchins keep counting, *one, two, three, four, five,* over and over, just as Merien taught them to on the ship. Except now they are burying her gently beneath the Earth's beautiful stones.

INSIDE EARTH

The mountain has swallowed them whole.

Tuck looks back at the cave mouth, at the grey sky and familiar roll of the ocean and his legs twitch, eager to run him back to the world outside. Suddenly, he'd rather take his chances in the battle than face this terrifying darkness that is Earth.

The cave walls lean too close; they bump against his shoulders and his head so that he has to walk bent and stooped as his old Grumpa. He seems to feel the pressing weight of the mountain overhead. The only thing Tuck ever has over his head is his windwrap, the roof of a boat or the sky.

'Aah.' Gorbals stands up straight and stretches his long limbs. 'That's better.'

Wary, Tuck raises his head. The low roof of the cave has suddenly opened up. Now they stand in a rock hall so large the Steer Master's ship could almost fit inside. But it's a cold, dark miserable place, with only a glimmer of daylight penetrating the gloom. A place to end your days, not begin anew.

Tuck tries to go back.

'Ooof!'

A spike of rock sticking out of the cave floor stabs him in the ribs.

'They're everywhere.' Gorbals puts a hand on Tuck's shoulder and points. 'See, on the roof, all over the floor.'

Tuck can only just make out the spiky shapes. 'What are they?'

Gorbals shrugs. 'Rock spears. This is a brutal land,' he mutters. 'Even the rocks. *Mol! Ibrox!*'

Tuck jumps as Gorbals bellows.

Ox-ox-ox-ox!

His voice ricochets echoes off the cave walls. An answering shout crashes off the rocks.

Ere-ere-ere . . .

'They're here!' cries Gorbals. 'Where?'

'Look up-*up-up-up*!'

Gorbals looks up and yells again.

The echoes merge into confusion. Tuck puts his hands over his ears and closes his eyes. The noise and the dark, his spinning head and spiked stomach are too much. He thinks of the *Waverley* in the thick of the battle out in the fjord, and though he'd rather be there than here, there's no pirate beat in his blood. None. Tuck no longer knows what he is. But Gorbals has grabbed his arm and is pulling him further into the Earth. They climb, feeling their way in the deepening darkness towards the guiding voice.

'Keep your shoulder to the wall,' the voice urges.

On one side is the cave wall, on the other there's nothing, just the dark. Tuck tries out each step warily, expecting the cave floor to fall away at any moment, but the rock stays solid underfoot.

'Through here!'

The cave has closed in tight on both sides. They

squeeze through the narrow rockway, then burst into light. Tuck blinks in the relief of daylight. He draws fresh, cold wind into his lungs. Then jumps in fright as shadows spring from the cave walls. Tuck draws his cutlass blade but Gorbals cries out.

'Wait! It's my friends. Molendinar, Ibrox . . . my people.'

Tuck slides the cutlass back in its scabbard as the friends hug each other. With a stab of shock it strikes Tuck that turning Lander means he'll never see his own people again.

'This is Tuck.' Gorbals pulls him forward. 'He pulled me from the sea.'

'We saw,' says the young woman, Molendinar, who has hair that falls to her feet. Hair like a mountain waterfall, thinks Tuck, shifting from one foot to another as the girl seems to drink in his face with her huge, dark eyes.

Ibrox, a sturdy older man, shakes Tuck's hand. 'You risked your life for this clumsy clump. The last person who needed to catch fire is Gorbals. Now if it had been me . . .'

'Ibrox is our firekeeper,' Gorbals explains. 'He's good with fire; I'm only good with words.'

Ibrox leads them away from the windy cave mouth to a crackling fire in the shelter of a large rock.

'Aah, that's good! My bones are cold as stone. Here, Tuck, grab some heat.'

Tuck almost groans with relief as Ibrox settles him on a rock beside the fire. The warmth is bliss.

'Move over, Clyde.' Gorbals nudges a flame-faced boy out of the way.

His eyes search the cave. 'Did you find Mara?'

The others shake their heads. Gorbals looks sick. 'First we lose Broomielaw and the baby, now Mara.'

'This higher cave is a better lookout than the one below,' says Molendinar. 'That's why we climbed, to keep watch for them.'

There's a moment of silence, a lull in the battle outside, when the only sounds in the cave are the crackle of the fire and the rumble of waterfalls.

'Who is here?' Gorbals peers around the cave. 'Mol and Ibrox, Caddie and Clyde, Fir and Tron, Partick . . . is that all?'

Mol points to a heap of bodies curled up asleep on the cave floor.

'Gallow and Spring and Park. And Rowan, Mara's island friend. Lots of people are missing. All those people on the *Arkiel*, where are they? And the urchins.'

'The *Arkiel*?' says Tuck.

'Pollock and Possil?' says Gorbals.

'Gone fishing.'

'Fishing?' The word hisses off the cave walls. '*Fishing? Haven't they noticed there's a war on?*'

'Keep your head, Gorbals,' says Ibrox. 'These caves seem to worm deep into the mountains. There's a stream that runs right through here – see?' He points to the trickle of water that runs along the floor of the cave. 'Possil and Pollock said they'd follow the water and see if they could track down a pool where there might be fish. We need to eat.'

'Pollock didn't think he should look for Broomielaw and his child first? No, he had to go *fishing*.' Gorbals spits the words as if they taste of acid. He jumps to his feet.'Well, *I'll* look for them if he won't.'

Molendinar and Ibrox exchange a glance.

'Broomie and Clay could be anywhere,' says Ibrox firmly. 'Maybe they're safe in a cave just like this, worrying about us, or washed up on one of the little islands or—'

'–blown to bits in the middle of the battle or lying at the bottom of the ocean.'

'Gorbals, *don't.*' Mol's face crumples and she turns away.

Gorbals slumps down on a rock and hangs his head between his knees. His burned arm trembles.

'Let's – let's do our sundown.' Ibrox tries to sound matter-of-fact, but his voice wavers. 'The sun's falling fast.'

'Let the sun die. I don't care,' says Gorbals into his knees.

Ibrox shakes him by the shoulder. 'Stop it. We can't forget who we are or all this will have been for nothing. Come on, Gorbals. Lift up your chin and do something useful. That's all Pollock's doing. No one's giving up on Broomielaw or Clayslaps or Mara. You know that.'

'*Pollock.*'

Gorbals grinds the name between his teeth. But he lifts his head and looks out the cave mouth at the sun that is about to settle among the mountain peaks. 'All right. I'll do it for Broomie and Clay and Mara.'

Those who are awake gather around the fire as Gorbals begins the Treenesters' sundown ritual. He chants a faltering beat of words that build into a grim rhythm as, one by one, the people who were once Treenesters stand and shout their names into the fire.

Squashed among them, Tuck watches.

'Anyone can join in,' says Ibrox. 'Just shout out your name to tell the world you're here.'

Tuck feels his shifty legs twitch and gives into the impulse. He jumps to his feet.

'Tuck,' he bursts out. 'Tuck Culpy. Landed on Earth!'

He sits down again, burning with embarrassment. Ibrox claps him on the back and Molendinar gives him a shy smile through her hair, but Gorbals drops his head back on to his knees and says nothing.

Tuck rises from the sundown fire and goes over to the mouth of the cave. The falling sun means the darkness at the back of the cave is creeping towards him. He doesn't mind the true dark of the night. He's used to that. But this darkness inside Earth seems an unnatural, monstrous thing. The cave mouth is high above shore and sea, as high as the mast of a tall ship. Here on the eastern curve of the wide bay, the last beams of the sun fall on Tuck's face – and on the carnage his people have brought to the fjord.

He feels nothing as he looks at the blur of boat wrecks in the harbour and the bodies on the shore. Too much has happened; things don't feel real any more. Tuck takes the little silver box from the pocket of his windwrap. He looks into the tiny window, presses the button and the zoom nose pops out. He scans the fjord, trying to find the masts of the Steer Master's ship or the fat funnels of the *Waverley*, but the fading light and the smoke in the bay has made a ghost of the pirate fleet, though firebombs still flare across the bay.

'What is this?'

Molendinar's large dark eyes are on the little silver box in his hand.

'It's a—'

Tuck struggles to remember the name, the sound of rolling hills of ocean. Mareca? Carema?

'Camera,' he remembers.

'Ca-mera,' Mol echoes. 'Can I look?'

He puts the little window to Mol's eye. She looks through it and jumps back. Looks at the world outside. Then puts the camera to her eye again and breaks into a wondering smile.

'Does it put the world inside its box or does it take you over there?' she demands.

Tuck shrugs, smiling. 'It's a kind of magic eye.'

Mol gives a shriek and shoves the camera back at him. 'There's a face . . . a giant face . . . in the fog.'

Tuck scans the fog and jumps with fright as he finds himself eye to eye with the face. A drift of fog blanks him out. Tuck lowers the camera and looks at Mol's scared face.

'It's only The Man,' he tells her.

'What man?' Tentatively, Mol takes back the camera.

Tuck shrugs again. 'The Man in the Middle. He watches. He sees.' Tuck chews his lip as he thinks of his silly plan to steal The Man. 'He makes things happen, I think.'

A shiver runs from his head to his toes as he realizes that the camera gives him a power to match The Man's all-seeing, all-knowing eyes.

'Mara has a magic machine too. It takes her to another world,' says Mol, sweeping the camera eye all across the mountains, 'but she keeps it to herself.'

Tuck has trouble following the girl's quick tongue though they both speak the same words; but hers fall from her lips as fast as rain while his have the rhythm of deep-sea sway.

'The *Arkiel*,' says Tuck. 'I heard you say something about the *Arkiel*.'

But Mol is too excited. 'One moment I'm on a moun-tainside, there's a blue door, now I'm down among the rocks on the shore and – oh.' She jerks the camera to a halt and the colour drains from her voice. 'So many people dead. All the boats burned.' Her mouth is tight. 'Horrible, horrible, why did they – oh.' She falls silent. Her knuckles tighten on the camera.

'Mara?' she whispers. 'Is it . . . ? Mara!'

Tuck has to grab Mol's arm to stop her running out into thin air. The camera has tricked her into thinking she is down on the shore, instead of standing at a cave mouth high in the mountainside. Tuck takes back the camera and zooms on to the cluster of people running along the shore. A bunch of children. Seven, he counts, one of them dragging a creature behind her. And an older girl. All he can see is the swirl of her hair in the wind, hair as dark as night or the inside of Earth. She turns to look at the mountain and he sees her face. And knows he's seen her before.

It's the girl who fell on her knees on the *Arkiel*.

TIREDNESS KILLS

Tuck watches from the shadows of the cave as the dark-haired girl is gathered into the firelight among her friends. His heart clenches as tight as his fist because there's no one, not a soul left in the world, not Pendicle or any of the bridger-people, who would weep over his return like that.

The girl soon slips aside from the others and sits on a rock near Tuck. The light of the fire illuminates her face. Tuck watches as she takes something from her bag. He shifts closer and his narrow eyes widen when he sees the glowing globe in her lap.

The globe opens like an oyster shell. Tuck holds his breath as the girl slips a silvery crescent, like a slice of moon, over her eyes and dips a small silvery stick inside the globe. Her face softens as if she's falling out of the world into a dream.

'That's *her* magic machine,' Mol whispers in Tuck's ear.

She hands him a tiny sliver of fire-smoked fish. Possil and Pollock found a chute of violent thunderwater deep inside the mountain, but with no light to see by, their only catch was a single fish that leaped out of the waterfall and landed at Possil's feet.

171

'What does it do?' Tuck stuffs the fish into his mouth and stares hungrily at the magic globe, his looter's instinct astir.

'It takes her into another world,' says Molendinar, 'but her body stays in this one.'

Tuck swallows the fish in a gulp. 'What world?'

'I don't know. I don't really understand . . . Broomie-law said . . .' Mol hesitates.

'Said what?'

'She goes to a place where she can be with someone she lost.'

The faces of Ma, Pa, Grumpa and little Beth, his own lost ones, flash through Tuck's mind. He feels hollow, as if the wind that haunts the cave has blown a hole right through his heart. He shakes himself like a sail in the wind and tries not to think of Ma, sunk by mountains of sea, tries to rid himself of the panicky feeling of being sunk inside the Earth, Land-locked with strangers.

'Come by the fire, Tuck, and shake off that chill,' Ibrox calls over. The grizzled-looking man livens the embers with a stick. 'Shove along, you lot,' he tells the urchins then brandishes the hot stick at Scarwell, who has just pinched his fish.

Tuck stares at the creature sitting beside Scarwell, the one he saw her dragging along the shore. The hairy beast has a human look about it. Its eyes gleam in the firelight but it doesn't move at all. Tuck decides it might be best to befriend it and offers it the fishbone.

Around him, people burst out laughing. Mol knocks on the creatures head.

'He's not real.'

Feeling a right dubya, Tuck nibbles on the fishbone.

'Broomielaw said that Mara told her something else,'

Mol whispers, squeezing in beside him, her breath almost as hot as the fire on his neck. She fiddles with the long tail of her hair.

'What? What else?' Tuck wants to know.

'She said the cyberwizz holds the secrets of the past.'

Tuck looks into Molendinar's large dark eyes. 'What secrets?'

Mol shivers. 'The secret of what happened there.'

'Where?'

'In the past.'

Tuck takes that in.

The fire is newly fed with sea grass so it's nice and hot. He stares into the flames until his brow burns and his eyes sting. His head feels full of hot light.

The girl's globe holds the past like a hoard of lost treasure? Yet Grumpa always said the past was lost, sunk at the bottom of the sea.

'The *Arkiel*,' he ventures, raising his voice. 'What do you people know about that?'

CLANG!

The noise is so loud the very mountain seems to quake.

CLANG!

Tuck covers his ears with his hands, as the **CLANG** sounds over and over again. When a vast percussion of **BANGS** erupts, Tuck is sure the mountain is about to fall on his head.

'It's inside as well as out,' yells Partick, and it's true. The bangs and clangs echo all across the mountainsides and inside the caves.

'The caves burrow into the mountains like rabbit warrens,' Pollock yells back. 'The people live in them like rabbits.'

173

'Wormholes,' shouts Possil. 'Noise runs through them like worms.'

That's what Merien said on the ship, Mara remembers. That the mountains were like a worm-eaten apple. She tugs Mol's arm, her throat tight. 'I found her on the shore. She's dead.'

'Broomielaw? *No.*' Mol breaks into a wail.

'No, no, I mean Merien.'

Mol quietens and looks blank.

'Ruby's friend. She was left behind by the scutpak. She was a good person, Mol, and she knew things, she would have – would've kept us *right* somehow—' Mara breaks off, drowned out by the banging and clanging, unable to put into words her sense that Merien is a real loss. They need someone like her. Mol is only relieved that it's not Broomielaw Mara found dead.

A hand grabs hers and squeezes it.

'But *you're* OK,' says Rowan.

Mara nods.

'Still got that telescope?'

Mara nods again and pulls the telescope from the deep pocket of her sealskin coat.

Rowan crouches at the cave mouth and scans the mountains.

'That's what I thought,' he calls over his shoulder. 'It's not gunfire, it's the mountain doors banging shut and—' Rowan bursts out laughing.

'What?' Mara crouches beside him and he gives her the telescope. She scans the mountain and sees people rushing up the rockways into the caves and banging the car doors shut.

'Look right above the big clock,' Rowan tells her.

Above the clock with no hands, the last rays of the low,

fiery sun have lit up the words of a large, bashed metal sign that's set into the mountain rock. Mara focuses the telescope on the sign.

TIREDNESS CAN KILL
TAKE A BREAK

She lowers the telescope and laughs too. 'Tiredness can *kill*?'

Rowan half-yawns, half-groans. 'Well, I feel half dead with it.'

Mara turns to the Treenesters. 'It's only their sun-down,' she smiles.

The sun is falling fast and already the sign above the clock is dimming. The last of the car doors bang shut so that by the time the sun has dropped behind the western peaks and the words on the sign have faded, the people of Ilira have shut themselves tight inside the mountain.

Ghosted in fog, the pirate fleet falls silent, as if stunned by the sudden disappearance of their prey. A horn blasts and a final firebomb fizzles in the wrecked and smoking bay.

'The Steer Master's horn says stop.'

Everyone turns to stare at Tuck.

'The what?' says Rowan.

'The Steer Master. He gives the orders.'

'How do you know?' asks Mol.

'I was a gypsea. I just Landed today.'

'You're one of *them*? Those *murderers*?' Mara jerks her head towards the pirate fleet.

Tuck glares at her. Who's *she* calling a murderer? She was on the *Arkiel* that drowned his Ma.

175

'I thought you were one of the mountain people,' says Gorbals.

Tuck shakes his head. '*Was* a gypsea. I'm a Lander now, like all of you.'

Mara stares at the large curved blade in the wire-woven scabbard that hangs from the belt of Tuck's faded blue wrap. The firelight catches at crystals of sea-salt in his sun-bleached hair. The roll of the ocean is in his words, the whinny of sea winds on his breath.

Tuck shakes his hair out of his gypsea eyes. 'The fleet'll rest awhile now the light's gone then start up again at dawn with the Steer Master's horn.'

'What do they want?' asks Rowan.

'Loot, booty and boats. Pomperoy's short of boats.'

'All they'll have is a pile of cinders,' says Mara, 'if they carry on like that.'

'Well, there's two ways to loot,' says Tuck. 'Sneak or storm. They were in a stormy mood.'

Pollock and Possil exchange glances. This is the kind of talk they understand.

'They only fire from the boats,' says Pollock. 'All day, they've fought from the sea and looted the boats but they've not landed. Why?'

'A gypsea won't set a foot on Land.' Tuck stamps on the rock floor and his face cracks into a bleak smile. 'You have to turn Lander for that, like me. They won't. They're raging because—'

'Sounds like they're scared,' Possil interrupts.

Tuck blinks. 'A gypsea's not scared. We've too much pirate in us.' But he's scared, so how much pirate is there in him? 'But Land's not safe. Land sinks and drowns. A gypsea's safest at sea.'

'So why've you turned Lander,' asks Mara, 'if it's not safe?'

Tuck shifts from foot to foot, as if he's ankle-deep on a waterlogged boat.

'Urth knows, I just, just—' His eyes flit around the dark depths of the cave, out to the fog-blanked sea and back, as restless as a wave. 'I just wanted to *see*.'

Mara locks glances with him. She understands that kind of wanting. It's what led her deep into the cyber-world of the Weave, then took her from her island to the sky city, to Fox, and brought her on a journey she could never have imagined, that has ended up right here at the top of the world.

'He saved my life,' Gorbals reminds them all. 'He's not like the others.'

Now Tuck has their attention. 'You,' he stares hard at Mara, 'were on the *Arkiel*.'

Mara wonders why he looks at her like that.

'It was our ship,' says Mol.

Tuck weighs that up. He pulls his cutlass out of its scabbard.

'Your ship. So it wasn't just her. It was all of you.'

Everyone stares at the curved blade glinting in the light of the fire.

'Our ship,' nods Gorbals, looking bewildered at the cutlass blade. 'It sunk. It was wrecked on the rocks – Tuck, what's up? Put your sword aw—'

Tuck jabs the cutlass towards the two sneaky-looking ones, Pollock and Possil.

'*The Grimby Gray* sank,' he yells. 'My Ma sank with it and drowned. It was the *Arkiel* that sank them both – my Ma and my barge home. The *Arkiel*'s why Pomperoy turned pirate, it's why I'm Landed up here . . .' Tuck looks around at the shocked, unfamiliar faces, at the darkness of the cave, and feels more alone than he's ever been. He falters. Urth knows what he's doing here.

What'll he do now? Run them through with his blade and chop them to bits? They deserve it, don't they? If it wasn't for them Ma would still be alive, he'd still have his gypsea home.

He'd still be stuck in a broken-down shack on a wrecked barge with his moaning Ma, wishing she was dead and that he was free.

Hot, sweaty guilt rushes up his legs and all through him, churning his insides. Tuck can't bear it. He clangs the cutlass against one of the rock spears sticking up from the cave floor and an urchin falls off his feet in fright. The impact runs up Tuck's arm, jangling all his nerves. Sparks fly from the blade and he feels the power of a cutlass in his hand.

And for the first time in his life Tuck feels a pirate beat in his blood.

ALL STORMED UP

'It's not their fault, it's mine.'

Mara, the girl he saw on the *Arkiel*, faces him. Her mouth trembles but her eyes are not scared. Just in case his own fear is showing, Tuck swishes the long curve of the blade close to her face, so close he lops off a strand of her hair. Mol screams but Mara's dark eyes only glitter at him. She doesn't flinch.

'I never knew there were boat cities out on the ocean. I never knew your barge was there. I tried to stop the ship as soon as I saw but I couldn't. I'm sorry.'

Tuck remembers her desperation. He saw it, when he glimpsed her on the ship. He hears her voice break over the word *sorry* and knows she means it. But he's not going to let her off that easy. She killed his Ma.

'Sorry's no good,' he tells her, 'not to my drowned Ma. And there's only one gypsea city, that's Pomperoy.'

Though he doesn't know for sure if that's true.

Her eyes drop and she twists her hands together.

'What can I do?' she mutters.

'Well . . .' Tuck pretends to think, but he knows what he wants.

When she looks back up at him, Tuck's heart turns over and the fledgling pirate in him fades. The girl's sorry and scared, white as moonlight. Something about her catches at his heart. The looter instinct in him is alive and strong though.

'If you're sorry, prove it.'

'How?'

'Give me something to make up for the death of my Ma.'

Mara looks aghast. 'What'll make up for that?'

Tuck knows nothing will. He's bluffing. His breath turns greedy. 'You have to lose something that's precious to you. Like that globe thing – your whatsitwizz – your magic machine.'

Mara's eyes have the dark gleam of an ocean night. Now they turn stormy.

'*No.*'

Tuck flashes his cutlass in her face again. He's not really angry any more, but there's something about this Mara girl that dares him to impress her. The cutlass-flashing is just for show.

Mara sways.

Urth, he's scared her. She's looks like she's going to–

Tuck drops the cutlass and catches her as she falls.

She can't believe it. She almost passed out. And now she's thrown up. All over herself and the pirate boy.

He'll probably kill her now. Except his pirate blade is on the ground and he's leaning over her, shaking vomit off the tail of his blue wrap.

Mara takes a deep breath to quell her queasiness. The cave spins, but she has to make sure her backpack and her cyberwizz are safe. She turns her head, sees the bag through someone's feet and lunges for it. She can't reach and the effort makes her sick again, right over Tuck's old cracked boots.

Tuck makes a disgusted noise and grabs the backpack. Mara kicks him as hard as she can, but he hands the bag calmly to her.

Amazed, Mara grabs it and wraps her arms around it.

'Wasn't really going to chop you.' Tuck gives her an apologetic smile. 'I was just all stormed up about my Ma – aah!'

The blue windwrap becomes a noose around his neck. The cutlass glints above his head. Tuck chokes and struggles.

'Pollock, no!' Mol yells. 'He said he wasn't going to hurt her. He's just upset. We killed his *mother*, Pollock! We sank his home. Let him be!'

Mol throws herself at Pollock and sinks her teeth into his fingers until he yells and unloosens his grip on the noose he's made of Tuck's windwrap. Tuck breaks free, choking for breath.

'Foghead!' Mol rages, glaring at Pollock until, reluctantly, he lowers the cutlass. Rowan, with a rock in his fist, lowers his arm too but keeps up a threatening glare.

Mol crouches beside Tuck, now on his knees. 'Water, someone. He's choking, water!'

Tuck unhooks a small wooden flask from his belt. 'Here's water,' he gasps, but hands the bottle to Mara, first.

Mara takes in the look on Mol's face as she sips Tuck's water.

'Oh, yes, of course, you were sick,' mutters Mol, her cheeks flushed.

'I'm fine now,' says Mara.

181

'Maybe it was the fish,' says Gorbals.

'Huh!' Pollock jabs the point of the curved blade at Gorbals's behind. 'The fish was fine. No one else is sick, are they?'

'Give me that.' Ibrox takes the cutlass off Pollock. 'Now, I will melt this blade in the fire,' he declares, 'if there's any more trouble from any of you. Our lives are precarious enough. We need to save our energy for keeping alive, not killing each other. Yes?'

He lays the cutlass beside the fire and glares around him.

'*Yes?*'

Everyone nods.

Mara sits up and leans her head against the cave wall. She hands the water bottle back to Tuck.

'I'd probably have killed me if I was you,' she admits.

Once again, the horrible memory flashes up of her own kill back in the sky city.

Tuck gives her a wobbly grin. 'Lucky I'm me, then.'

Mara returns a thin, wary grin before pulling up the furred hood of her sealskin coat. She lies down on the rock floor, hugging her backpack tight to her chest.

'I'm truly sorry about your Ma,' she whispers. 'I lost mine too, so I know. I lost all my family.'

Tuck leans across the cave floor and grabs his cutlass. He cleans the blade in the ash and embers of the fire and scrapes off the sick on his boot with the tip of it.

'Me too,' he murmurs.

He doesn't need to raise his head to know that, Pollock, Possil and Rowan, and the firekeeper, Ibrox, are watching his every move. Gorbals is pretending he is not. Mol, the one with the hair as long as herself, never stops watching him. Tuck puts the cutlass back in exactly the spot Ibrox placed it, on the stones by the fire. He finds a place to sleep that's not too far from the heat and winds himself tight in his windwrap.

If he decides to stay with them, he'll have to win their trust.

And if he doesn't, well, they don't have the all-seeing eyes of The Man in the Middle. They can't see his thoughts and watch his every move, all night, every night, to see what he will do.

A SHATTER OF DAYS

Half asleep, Mara thinks the silver crescent cutting through the mist is the moon. She sits up, heart thumping, when she sees it's Tuck's curved cutlass. They've been here long enough to see the thin crescent moon grow fat, yet there's something about Tuck that she still doesn't trust. But he's only cutting down the few strands that remain of the tough sea grass that overhangs the side of the cave, to stoke up the fire Ibrox struggles, night and day, to keep alive.

The fog is like a live creature. It creeps round the bends of their doorless cave to the inner caverns they have made their home and curls icy fingers around them as they sleep. Each morning they wake up fog-blind and coughing.

The siege in the bay ended when winter arrived in a shock of cold so deep even the sun seemed to lose the courage to face the day. The pirate fleet panicked as night swallowed day and the sea began to creak. Ice threatened to trap the invaders in the fjord where they would become the prey of the mountain people. They made a clumsy retreat through the hardening waves, grabbing a loot of boats and booty, along with a harvest of bridge-building metal from the wrecked ships at the neck of the fjord.

And left a bay full of ruin behind.

Mara has seen bodies broken and burned, tangled in seaweed on the rocks where the tide has cast them.

The one good thing the battle brought is a fjord full of driftwood from all the bombed boats. But even Ibrox's fire-keeping skills can't quell the cold. In the gloomy light of the dimming days Possil and Pollock and Partick sneak out of the cave to gather whatever eggs and seaweed and driftwood there are to be found among the rocks near the cave mouth. Tuck shows how to dry, weave and knot seaweed into nets and sleeping mats and throws. The urchins are both pests and helpers, but Mol is his most ardent pupil, hanging on the salt-scraped ocean-roll of his voice and the sea-glitter of his eyes in the firelight.

They keep their presence hidden from the people of Ilira. A reminder of their brutality is branded on so many arms. But as winter deepens and hunger grips, Mara has to fight the urge each day to grab more than her fair share of food and fire. She begins to see how survival in such a harsh place might have made the mountain people as brutal as their land.

At the end of each day, when the setting sun illuminates the TIREDNESS CAN KILL sign, the mountain shudders with the noise of the curfew bell and all the cave doors bang shut in a grand slam. Then, the refugees claim the bay and take to the shore with driftwood spears and seaweed nets and fish by starlight or fog-clouded moon. Each day the curfew comes earlier and earlier. The days shorten as the sun's power fades and it cannot seem to find the energy to climb into the sky.

One day, the sun doesn't rise at all.

The mountain is still and silent. The people of Ilira are land-locked inside now that day has become one long winter's night. The North Wind whines across the ocean and up the fjord. It whirls through the mountain rockways, kicks on the shut doors and rampages into the open caves where it hurls around the spears and pillars of rock, spitting ice and shrieking like a demented banshee.

Mara aches to the marrow of her being. Her turns at the fireside fill her ice-bitten limbs with scorching pain. Hunger is a raking agony. She has been sick again and brought up the sliver of fish and sip of seaweed broth she had only just gulped down.

Tuck carries the cut sea grass over to the fire and feeds a bundle to the flames. But it only fizzles, too full of frost to be much use.

Ibrox sighs. 'We'll be lucky if it lasts till morning. Stupid to let the fuel get so low.'

He's angry with himself for falling ill with a bad cold. No one else has Ibrox's nose for driftwood. He goes to the cave mouth and sneezes as he looks out at the stars banked thick and high above the ocean. 'If I could steal some of *that* fire.'

One of the young Treenesters yawns. He ruffles his hair out of his eyes and groans. 'I'll go,' mutters Tron, 'and find some.'

'No,' yelps Fir, from underneath the heap of sea grass and seaweed that is their bed. She tries to pull him back down beside her. 'You're not going alone. It's too dark.'

'The stars are like moonmoths tonight.' Tron shakes her off. 'I'll be fine.'

'No, Tron,' growls Ibrox. 'Fir's right. No one goes out alone. That's how we lost Partick.' He falters and the others fall into a stricken silence. Partick went out alone

186

to gather driftwood from the rocks at the other end of the bay one night when a sudden fog descended. They have searched and searched but there's been no sign of him since. 'Oh, you can curse me as an old fire-fool,' cries Ibrox, 'but we can't afford to lose any more of you strong young ones. And you can't bear to lose one another. You can't tell black ice from rock in the dark.'

Tron gives Fir a nudge. 'You come with me then.'

'Me? In the cold? In the black dark?'

'Someone has to,' snaps Tron.

'I'll go with you.' Ibrox sneezes and hunches down beside his dying fire. 'Just let me warm up first.'

'Such a crowdy sky,' says Gorbals. He spends much of the endless night mapping the patterns of the stars on the cave walls with charcoal embers from the fire. 'Forests of stars. We never saw all this in the netherworld. The lights of the New World were too bright.'

'Where's Pollock and Possil?' Ibrox ignores Gorbals' star rapture and peers into the dark nooks of the cave.

'Gone worming,' says Tron. He frowns at Fir, who has wrapped her arms around him and wrestled him back in their sea-grass snug. 'She didn't want me to do that either.'

'Worming?' asks Gorbals.

'Cave-worming,' says Fir. She prods Tron in the chest. 'And they've been gone an age. We might never see them again.'

'Possil and Pollock could track their way out of any-where.' Young Clyde glares at her. 'They'll be back.'

Tuck rummages in the pockets of his windwrap. He brings out the book he stole from a shelf in Pendicle's boat in what feels like another life, and hands it to Ibrox.

'It's not much, but it's got three hundred and thirty-seven pages so if we tear it and feed it slow, it might keep the fire awake till morning. I've been saving it till the last. Take it.'

Ibrox stares at the book and jumps backward, as if Tuck's tried to hand him a firebomb.

Gorbals, on the other hand, leaps forward. 'A book! Look, Mara.'

But Mara has fallen fast asleep, curled up beside Rowan, and looks so wan and exhausted that Gorbals can't bring himself to waken her, not even for a book.

'We can't burn this.' He takes hold of Tuck's book. 'It's not like our netherworld where the sea was full of book pulp,' he reminds the others, 'and their pages blew about us in the wind. We burned books like litter then, but we can't do that now. I lost my only book when the ship went down. All we have left is *A Tale of Two Cities*. No, Tuck, this book of yours is more precious than fire.'

Gorbals turns the book over in his hands. The cover is stained and tatty but the title is big and bold and clear.

'NATURAL ENGINEERING by C. D. STONE,' he reads, settling down beside the weak ember fire and beginning to flick through pages blurred with water stains.

'*Urth.*'

Tuck curses under his breath. He's been working hard to win back the trust he broke with his cutlass. The pretended sacrifice of something that he doesn't even want was meant to seal that trust, but the only one he's impressed is Gorbals, who trusts him with his life anyway, just because he saved it once.

Gorbals is flicking through the book. 'Is this where you learned all your weaving and knotting, Tuck?'

Tuck nods, though he has hardly glanced at the thing.

'Listen,' Gorbals is muttering. 'It says here that animals are the best builders in the world. Look, termite tunnels and towers, how a beaver builds a bridge, ants, spiders . . . the technology of birds, of a worm . . . ha! Wait till Pollock sees this.'

Tuck stares at the book in astonishment. 'It tells you all this?'

Gorbals reads him out a passage about the drill-like action of a worm in earth.

'And these – these dead insects tell you this?' Tuck stabs a finger at the black words on the page.

Gorbals laughs. 'Yes, that's it. These dead insects are words. When you read them they tell you all sorts of things.'

'How do you know what they say?'

'My mother taught me,' says Gorbals. 'I'm the only Treenester who reads. The others, well, they were brought up to be scared of books. You saw Ibrox just there.'

Tuck nods.

'But Mara has a book.'

'Oh, yes,' agrees Gorbals. 'But she's not one of us.'

'She's not?'

Puzzled, Tuck glances at Mara, deep in sleep. *What is she then?* He remembers a snatch of conversation he over-heard between Mara and Rowan as he dozed by the fire. They were talking about a place called Wing. An image of a Great Skua's wing pops into Tuck's mind and his skin prickles. He always wondered where the flocks of Great Skua go. Could it be a place called Wing? Does Mara come from the place that the Great Skua fly to? Is that what draws him to her like the moon draws the tide?

Yet she treats him warily, like a stranger, and always sits with her Treenester friends and the other one, Rowan, who must be one of her people because he also knows Wing.

Gorbals has thrust another page of the book in his face and Tuck casts aside his thoughts as he looks at a sketch of small creatures who seem to be building a drift-wood bridge across a river.

'My Da was a bridger,' he tells Gorbals. 'One of the best. He built a hundred bridges.'

So Ma said, though Tuck only ever counted seventy-three that were branded with his Da's trademark, the Culpy crescent, the shape of a fish-hook moon or a cut-lass blade.

Tuck takes the book from Gorbals's hands and studies the page on bridge-building.

'Read this to me, Gorbals,' he urges, pointing at the insect-like words that lie in neat lines all across the page. 'Tell me how to build a bridge.'

HUNTING A STAR

'A beaver,' reads Gorbals, 'is the ultimate bridge-builder or *pontifex*. Now, what's that? Ah, see here,' Gorbals taps the page, 'it's an old word for a bridge-builder. Listen to this, Tuck. In ancient times, people thought the making of a bridge was such a miraculous skill that it must be inspired by the gods. A *pontifex* was an almost sacred title. A great bridge-builder was treated like a god.'

Tuck listens, mesmerized, as Gorbals puts down the book and tells him about the vast bridges of the New World. Miraculous, impossible things that stretch across seas.

And as he listens, Tuck begins to think of his own Da in a new way. Not as an ordinary gypsea worker but as a hero with a sacred skill, inspired by the gods. And he *wasn't* an ordinary bridger, Tuck remembers, he was said to be one of the best bridge-masters on Pomperoy. People said you could always tell a Jack Culpy bridge because it wasn't just a way of getting from one place to the next, it was unusual, intricate, a tough and beautiful thing of sea-scavenged wire and rope.

Now Tuck remembers his Da's fascination with spiders'

webs. Weak-sighted like Tuck, with gypsea eyes used to scanning fields of ocean, Da would peer at the tiny patterns like the grain in a block of driftwood or the whorls on a shell. Spiders were rare on a floating city ravaged by ocean winds but if you looked hard, you'd find them scuttling and spinning in the deepest, darkest corners of the boats. Da would spend ages studying the intricate designs of their webs. Tuck used to think he was daft, but now he sees why.

'What was that old word for a bridge-master?' he asks, but Gorbals has jumped up to follow Ibrox. From the depths of the cave comes a rabble of echoes. Tuck hopes it's Pollock and Possil with a catch of waterfall fish. He scans a few pages of the book but none of the dead black insects looks anything like the words that Gorbals read.

He screws up his eyes and tries to remember the ancient word. Something to do with fixing. Pontifix. Wasn't that it?

'Hey! Look at the size of these!' Possil bursts into the cavern swinging a hefty catch of fish over his shoulder. They land with a squelch on the cave floor.

Possil flings the fish one by one on to the hot stones around the fire and kicks away Scarwell before she steals a whole, raw one for herself.

'Fish don't live in waterfalls,' declares Possil, breathless. He seems to gleam with excitement. The fish begin to sizzle on the stones. 'They jump down waterfalls from a *place.*'

'What place? Where's Pollock?' asks Ibrox.

'A place,' says Possil, waving away Ibrox's worry with a grin. 'A *watery* place. Like a sea. But not salty. The water is clear, like rain. You can drink the waterfalls.'

'We know that,' says Gorbals. 'But what are you say-ing? There's a sea up in the mountains?'

Possil taps his head. 'You put words together, Gorbals. Me and Pollock, we put together clues and track them. We found a tree root that's grown through the cave roof. Waterfalls with water that's not salt, and a giant waterfall, deep in the belly of the mountain, full of fish. The wink of a star at the top of a whirling chute of water far, far above us in the roof of the cave. Put all that together.'

People frown, trying to make sense of Possil's clues.

Possil pulls something out of his pocket, with a grin that suggests he's saved the best fish till last. But it's only a small stone. He puts the stone down the neck of Mol's sealskin coat.

'Eeeh, it's hot!' Mol wriggles and bursts out laughing.

Possil grins. 'This stone is from a place deep in the mountain, almost eight thousand steps from here.' He laughs. 'A warm cave with a pool full of bubbling hot water. The cave glows like the moon and the sound of the water bubbling is like a song. If we go there until the sun comes back, we'll have hot water and heat. There's fish and fresh water from the falls and I've marked a trail with fire stones so that we can find our way. We can still come back here to the cave mouth to collect eggs and wood.'

Possil looks at all the ice-pinched faces around him. 'Well?'

'Fire stones, you said?' Ibrox picks up the hot stone Mol dropped on the ground. 'Like this?'

'No, they're cold but they look like chips of fire. See?' Possil digs in the pocket of his skin coat and shows Ibrox a handful of fiery amber stones.

Ibrox takes one and studies it in the light of his fire.

193

'So deep into the Earth,' Tuck murmurs, 'how dark will that be?'

'But where's Pollock?' asks Mol. 'You haven't lost him?'

'He's hunting a star.'

'Hunting a *star*?'

'The one that winked at us from way high up through a swirling water chute in the roof of the cave,' says Possil. 'It's the clue to the place where the waterfalls come from.'

'What place?' Gorbals tuts.

'They fall from the sky, do they, all those waterfalls?' Pollock laughs.

Mara gets up from her sea-grass bed. Wakened by the excitement, she has been listening hard.

'There could be a sea over the other side of the mountains.' She scrapes back the dark fall of hair that sleep has tangled all over her face. 'Let me *think*. My book said the mountains enclose a sea of snow and ice. It fills the interior of the land. Over many thousands of years, the weight of it all made the land sink in the middle, like a basin. Greenland is the biggest island in the world. Now the ice is melted there could be an interior sea.'

'A *sea*?' Rowan puts down the hot fish he has grabbed from the fire.

Mara rakes her hair again, her face lit up.

'Well, it could be a sea now. Couldn't it? I mean, a lake almost as big as a sea. All the melted ice, cupped by the mountains.'

'A freshwater lake like the one in the hills above Wing,' croaks Rowan, scrambling to his feet. His shorn hair stands on end and there's glint of life in him that Mara has rarely seen since they left their own island.

'Maybe that's why this place thunders with waterfalls.'

Mara grabs Rowan's hand. 'They leak down through the mountains from the interior sea, like all the burns and springs ran down from the lake in the hills.'

'Lake Longhope.' Rowan smiles at her. 'That was its name.'

Mara bites her lip. It was the name of her farm.

A spark of hope flits around the cave.

'And you said you saw a tree root?' whispers Mol. She nudges Possil. 'Huh?'

Possil nods as he tears a fish apart and stuffs it in his mouth.

'Tree roots in the cave roof? If there are roots, there must be trees.' Mol looks as if she has stopped breathing. 'We could be Treenesters again.'

'It was an old root,' Possil confesses through a mouth of fish, 'turned to stone.'

'But it *was* a tree root?' Mol persists.

Possil scowls. 'I know a tree root when I see it. I lived in a tree too, remember?'

'And there's heat?' Fir asks. She snuggles up to Tron, teeth chattering.

Possil smiles. 'The air is like a summer's day. I had a bath,' he gloats, 'in the hot pool.'

'If there's a tree root,' Mol insists, 'then there must be trees somewhere.'

'A hot *bath*?' Fir gapes at Possil, her mouth an outraged, envious, fish-filled *O*.

'But why not stay right here?' Tuck's skin is crawling at the thought of moving deeper into the Earth.

'I want heat.'

'I want to *see* those tree roots.'

'I want to see if there's a way through these tunnels into the interior . . .'

'We'll freeze if we stay here. We're hardly into winter. It might get colder yet.'

'We could go to the people in the mountain. Surely they'll help us,' tries Tuck. He'll do anything, anything, but he cannot go deeper into the cave. He just can't. His head aches constantly and he is sure it's the weight of the mountain pressing upon the air. He lies in bed trembling at the thought that at any moment the whole mountain might collapse upon him. *Great Skua, who knows that it won't?*

Tuck stamps on a tiny ember that's fallen out of the fire. And that would be him, smashed into dust, snuffed right out of the world.

'The mountain people wrecked our ship.' Mol's lips tremble. 'They lost us Broomielaw and Clay and Merien and a lot of others too. They tried to sell us as slaves.'

Mara pushes up the sleeve of her sealskin coat and shows Tuck her charred arm. 'See? They branded us with this.'

Tuck stares at the mark on Mara's arm. He knows it. It's the old sign of power and wealth; the oil-black emblem like a wriggly eel on a fish rod that is embroidered on the Prender family windwraps. Gently, he touches the brand on Mara's arm. She flinches and pulls her sleeve back down.

'The mountain people did that. They're brutal and dangerous,' she insists and tells him of the stone giant's sinister sign that welcomed strangers to a place of fearful awe. 'They had a gun to my head,' she continues, 'they'd have killed me if I hadn't run – if your gypsea fleet hadn't attacked.' She stops, confused, realizing that the attack by Tuck's people probably saved her life. 'If that's what the people of Ilira were like *before* the attack, they'd surely kill strangers outright now.' The others are nodding in agreement. Mara stares into the darkness at the back of the cave. 'But the interior. Maybe we can find a safe place there . . .' She turns to Rowan. 'What do you think?'

'I think I'd risk my life for a hot bath,' says Rowan. 'I really would.'

'Oh, me too,' says Fir. 'Even if we starve to death at the back of the cave, I'd rather die *warm*.'

Ibrox is already tidying up the tools of his little firebox and stuffing it securely inside his skin tunic. He breaks into sneezes.

'So we're agreed?' asks Rowan. He glances at the faces around the fire. 'No point hanging about then. Let's go.'

Mara can't help grinning at the sudden resurrection of the old, feisty Rowan, brought back to life by the thought of a hot bath.

GYPSEA HEARTWIND

Stone by fiery stone, Possil's torch flame picks out a glittering amber trail on the floor of the tunnels that worm deep into the mountain. Mara, Rowan, Tuck, the Treenesters and the urchins follow. Each time Possil rounds a curve and the torch disappears, Tuck swallows a panic that makes him want to yell. Touch has replaced sight. His skin is raw-nerved. The hot scrape of the cave wall, an icy blast of waterfall, the stub of his head or toe on rock: every sensation is magnified in the dark.

Tuck touches his nose, feels the familiar bump, but can't see his own hand.

The only thing that calms him is counting, and the only things to count are his footsteps or the beats of his heart. His heart is racing too fast so he counts steps. He's counted nine hundred and three when the person behind grabs his arm.

'Tuck, where's your hand? Give me your hand.'

He turns, can't see anyone. Flails his trembling hand around till Mol finds it.

'You're shaking like a leaf and your breath's fluttering like a moonmoth.'

'It's the dark. It's closing in.'

'It's not,' says Mol. 'It's just the cave walls are narrow here.'

'I can *feel* it.'

'I can *see*.' Mol squeezes his hand. 'My eyes are strong in the dark. I was born into a dark world.'

Tuck puzzles over Mol's words. Survival, and adjusting to the great rift in his life, has taken up so much of his thoughts and energy he hasn't questioned what he thought he knew about these people from the *Arkiel*. He assumed they lived on the ship just as he lived on a barge shack in Pomperoy. He wonders what dark world Mol means, to unstrap his mind from the fact that the tunnel is now so narrow that he has to walk sideways.

'I thought the *Arkiel* was your home.' His forehead scrapes on a sudden lowering of the cave roof. His heart bangs. This is what he feared most, the mountain caving in. Now he has to walk sideways *and* stooped.

'Oh no,' says Mol. 'My home was a scrap of land in a netherworld at the foot of a sky city. We lived on the Hill of Doves, among the trees.'

Mol's voice breaks on the last word. Tuck hears it. Driftwood comes from trees, he's sure, though he doesn't know what a tree is. Mol seems very keen on them though. He knows Mol and her people call themselves Treenesters but he's never thought to ask why. It's just who they are, as he is a gypsea. Or was. What he is now, he doesn't know. A true Lander wouldn't have such a terror of Earth.

'Why did you leave?' he asks Mol, to keep his mind off his terror.

'The water kept rising. We had to leave before our Hill of Doves drowned just like Mara's island in the sea.'

'Mara's from the sea?'

199

'From the island of Wing in the Atlantic Ocean.'

Tuck imagines an island on the world's ocean shaped like a Great Skua's wing.

So Mara has the ocean in her blood too. She lived surrounded by it on an island called Wing. That must be what draws him. *Something gypsea about her*. They have breathed the same salt winds. And she gives Tuck the unnerving sensation he had when he first sighted Land, as if she is a missing piece of something he hadn't ever known he'd lost.

Mol sniffs the air and tugs his hand. 'It's not so cold. The air's turned soft and damp, like the breath above a mushroom bed.'

'What's a mushroom?'

Mol giggles. 'I suppose you don't get mushrooms on the sea. They grow in dark Earth places. They're good to eat.'

Mol's presence is solid and grounded; she settles him down. But Mara, ah, she's like an ocean heartwind. Tuck knows the very one. The heartwind that would come at the far end of winter, in the deepest folds of night, and haunt the lagoon and the boat masts with whispers of summer. The one that unsettled him with its secrets and unknown scents and tucked dreams in the pockets of his windwrap. A wind that made him want.

Tuck bangs into the person in front, who has stopped. He looks up ahead. The torch has stopped too, he can just see it, and Possil's hazy, moon-white face in its flame. The tunnel suddenly opens out and with an intake of breath – as if he's been underwater and just broken to the surface – Tuck steps into a wide cavern.

The air is warm and thick with vapour clouds.

Everything looks hazy and soft. Tuck stares around, amazed.

The roof is as high as a boat mast and when the torch-light flickers up the walls of the cavern they glow like a fogged moon.

'What is it?' he asks Mol. Her hair shivers with the luminous glow.

'A moon cave!' She stares up through the steamy haze at the cavern roof. Crusts and fronds of rock hang down. 'If I half-close my eyes they could almost be the branches of trees in moonlight.'

Tuck looks at up at the dim-glowing fronds of rock. *That's what trees are like?*

There's a crash of water. An explosion of splashes, shrieks and yells. Mol pushes past him, struggling out of her sealskin coat and the crackly layer of knotted plastic she wears underneath. She jumps into a steamy, bubbling pool that's tucked into a nook of the cave.

Tuck's banging heart calms. Each lungful of warm air relaxes him and his Earth terror lifts.

'Come in, Tuck!' Mol shouts. 'It's lovely.'

Mara is already sitting at the side of the pool, her feet in the water, her eyes closed. Rowan crashes in, soaking her and she laughs. The urchins are splashing up a storm. Tuck throws off his fears and his windwrap and under the strange, steamy moonglow, he plunges into the most bliss-ful warmth he's ever known.

WORLD WIND

'Come on then,' says Fox.

His tawny eyes and hair glint in the flickering lights of the Weave.

She follows him off the broken bridge, down the ruined boulevards that stretch as far as she can see. Unravelling carcasses of data-worms slither across great heaps of cyber-junk. Fox takes her past the junk mountains into a wide boulevard stacked on each side with tumbledown tower-stacks – sparking, crumbling Weavesites crammed with the rotting electronic data of the drowned world.

'Don't you remember this place?'

Mara looks around her, at the flickering towerstacks, at the cracked and buzzing street name. After the cold, dark tunnels and the unearthliness of the moon cave, it's a relief to plunge back into the familiar world of the Weave with Fox.

BOULEVARD OF something, says the flickering ice-blue sign. Mara peers hard and sees that the unlit last word is DRE\AMS. A crack runs right through the word and the blue light has died in that part of the sign, as though the dream is dead.

'This is the boulevard where I first saw you,' says Fox.
'It was?'

Mara remembers the creeping Fox presence that haunted her Weave visits when she would zoom down the boulevards for fun, her realworld self safe in her bedroom in Wing. Now, that not-so-distant past seems like someone else's life.

Fox has stopped outside one of the Weavesites.

'In here.'

'WORLD WIND.' Mara reads the faded name that flickers on the the towerstack.

'It's a wind that blows you all around the world.' Fox pauses. 'I found it the other night when you didn't come. Spent half the night just wandering the Weave. Most of this boulevard's rotted or dead, but this site's ace. You ready? Here we go . . .'

The Weavesite crackles and Mara gasps as she's sucked into the whirl of a cyberstream. In the second it takes to yell Fox's name, she has whooshed right through the cyberstream and shoots out into calm black space. She draws a breath, swallows, blinks.

Looming up before her is a vast glowing gem.

'Planet Earth,' says a voice in her ear.

They are floating in black space. Mara wants to grab Fox's hand then remembers she can't. She stares up at the amazing vision.

'This is Earth?'

She can hardly breathe as she takes in the beauty of the glowing, gem-like planet: the stunning blue of the oceans, the brown and green of its lands and ice-crusted mountains and white ice caps, all wrapped in swirls of cloud. It's hard to believe that in realworld she is sitting in a cave deep in the mountains in the dark of winter at the tip of such a vivid world.

203

Fox is watching her, not the planet. The glow of the Earth reflects in his cyber-eyes. But she can feel his real self looking at her. Can he feel her too?

'But – but how is this possible?' she whispers. 'To see the Earth . . . ?'

'Satellite images,' says Fox. 'Remember, the old satellites all round the Earth that hold the Weave? This is an image of the Earth taken from the moon, long ago. Look, there's the date.' Above them, a label hangs in the ether. 'The Earth photographed from the moon, 20 July 1969.'

Mara laughs. 'People went to the moon? And I suppose it was made of cheese?'

'Cheese?' Fox looks at her askance.

'When I was small,' Mara explains, 'my mum used to tell me the moon was made of cheese. People thought it was, once.'

'Once upon a time,' says Fox. 'In a time out of mind.'

They float in space, the bright Earth-gem in front of them, the words tingling between them.

Mara breaks the spell.

'People really did go to the moon?'

'Once upon a time, they did.' Fox's voice drifts. He's staring at Mara, and she knows he's thinking of their once upon a time. He looks away and when he speaks it's with a forced matter-of-factness. 'OK, there's a wind-shuttle here somewhere that we can navigate with and if I can just instruct my godgem—'

The slow-spinning planet and the disorientating whirl of black space have begun to make Mara feel queasy.

'Fox.'

'–we can go for a whirl around the Earth.'

Mara swallows her queasiness as a craft that looks like a shiny beetle with wings zooms towards them. They board the wind-shuttle and begin to orbit the Earth, crossing blue expanses of ocean, surfing the undulating plains and mountains of its lands, speckled with the cluttered mosaics of cities.

Fox zooms in closer and now the occasional shock of noise, an image or a disembodied voice flashes up from the planet below.

'What was that?' gasps Mara, as a rumbling line of tanks appear and vanish.

'Ti-anan-men Square.' Fox reads the sign that flashed up with the tanks. 'It's old message flags. Historical stuff.' He shrugs. 'Don't really know. Wind-shuttlers – people of the old world who used this site – left all sorts of blogs and flags and messages. Wow, did you see that?'

A mushroom cloud billows up. In the distance, a tidal wave crashes on a raft of islands, obliterating the land. Ahead, cracks appear in the mountains and the Earth shudders.

'Nuclear bomb, tsunami, earthquake.' Fox reads the flags at each event. They pass over the bombed ruins of several countries. Mara can't read the messages on the tattered flags but a great wail of despair rises from the smoking remains.

'Fox, stop, this is—'

He veers away. Far beneath the wind-shuttle, a great wall crashes down.

'–horrible.'

A vast continent in the middle of the Earth seems dead. There are no noisy messages from the past here, just a mass of silent flags.

HELP, they say, **SEND AID** and a solitary one, **TOO LATE**.

'Stop,' Mara pleads. 'I've seen enough.'

Fox nods, his mouth set in a grim line. He pulls the wind-shuttle back from the Earth. The planet looks calm and beautiful once more.

'We'll go North,' he says, sounding shaken, and revs the craft to full speed.

The empty blue of the ocean is a relief. Mara's stomach settles a little as they zoom across it. She draws breath as the white-capped top of the world comes into view.

'Is that really what the old world was like?'

'It's not all like that,' says Fox. 'I promise. We must've been at the wrong altitude and picked up all the bad stuff. There are loads of amazing things too. Just wait.'

'. . . ice caps melting twice as fast as feared . . .' A dis-embodied voice crackles in the ether then fades.

'What was that?' Mara almost grabs Fox by the arm. 'Go back.'

Fox pulls the wind-shuttle into reverse and tracks the lone voice.

'. . . we may be on the edge . . . not much time left . . .'

The voice seems to be coming from one of the satellites marked NASA. This one hangs above the northern hemi-sphere.

'. . . all countries must stabilize emissions of carbon dioxide . . . can't wait, must act . . . flooded Earth would be an alien planet . . . armadas of icebergs, rising oceans . . . the end of civilization . . . how long have we got?'

Fox revs the wind-shuttle.

'They knew,' says Mara.

Another surge of nausea hits her.

Fox leans closer. 'It was a hundred years ago, Mara. It's history.'

'But they knew. They could've done something but they

didn't. They knew. They didn't think about the future, did they? They never thought about us.'

The nausea turns violent. Mara doesn't know whether it's Fox's zip-zooming navigation or all those terrible message flags from history, but she needs to get back to realworld, fast.

'Fox. Stop.'

His electronic eyes flash at her.

'I need to go back.'

'Go back? Where?'

'Home. I mean, realworld. Out of here.'

'Why?'

He looks as if he'll grab her if she tries to leave. Then remembers he can't.

'Mara, there's beautiful stuff too – the Grand Canyon and the Great Wall of China. The patterns of the old world cities are stunning. I've seen things that are more amazing than anything in the Noos. The sun rising over the Himalayas. A massive river that slides through a jungle like a silver snake. A land full of castles and towers and forests and lakes. A million pink flamingos sweeping across a lake like a flame. And elephants – Mara, elephants and animals you can't imagine were ever real. A black pool of penguins on an ice shelf at the bottom of the world. And I was going to show you Greenland. We're nearly there.'

'I need to go. I'm sorry.'

He looks at her blankly as she exits the wind-shuttle and spins away through black space into the crackling cyber-stream.

Just in time, Mara yanks the halo from her eyes and crashes back into realworld. And promptly throws up.

'Mara?'

Mol puts a cool hand on Mara's forehead. 'No fever. What's wrong?'

'All this seaweed and fish. Doesn't agree with me,' Mara croaks. She goes over to the hot spring to scrub herself clean. Poor Fox. She remembers the bewilderment in his eyes.

'But you're an island girl,' says Mol. 'You must have eaten lots of seaweed and fish.'

Mara lies down on her seaweed mat. Mol is right, but she's too sick to try to answer. She closes her eyes and tries to quell the queasiness by imagining she has zipped out of realworld and is with Fox again, gazing at the vast, glowing gem that is Earth.

THE WRECK OF
THE WORLD

Mara yawns and stretches, soothed from a long dip in the hot spring after a sleep so deep it might have lasted a month. As she dries herself on one of the scratchy sea-weed mats, she sees Tuck studying a dim nook of the cave by the light of a torch flame. There's an intensity about the way he is peering at the wall that makes Mara go over. For the first time she sees there are carvings etched in the rock.

'There were rock carvings on Wing,' she remembers. 'Circles and spirals all over the standing stones. Ancient stuff – nobody knew what it meant.'

'These are old but not ancient.'

Tuck rubs the words that are carved into the rock and shows her the charcoal stain on his fingertip. Mara hears the tremble on his breath. She looks at the words in the rock.

THE WRECK OF THE WORLD.

Mara takes the torch from Tuck.

The carving shows a vision of the sun beating down on

209

what must have been a great city. There are towering buildings, streets crammed with cars and people, a sky criss-crossed with winged objects and their smoky trails. Mara remembers the broken bird on the mountain. Planes. Beside the city, tall chimneys in a field belch a dirty cloud. Mara moves the torch flame along the wall. The city seems unaware of what is rolling towards it – a wave, seething with people and animals and the debris of a destroyed city. Mara peers into the wave. Carved into the great swirl of water are what look like bits of paper, each one marked with (Mara peers even closer to be sure) the very same sign that is branded on her arm.

The snake on a stick.

Mara tries to think what the sign could mean but she has no idea.

The torch flame flickers on a bus full of people. The luminous cave wall makes them glow like ghosts. Yet the carving is so detailed that Mara can see the open, screaming mouths of the people as the great wave threatens to swallow the bus. She remembers the wrecked bus the urchins played in on the remains of a sunken bridge in the netherworld.

It's as if the world is a wrecked ship and all that is left is the flotsam of the past.

Mara drops the torch and leans her head against the rock wall, nauseous once again. Her imagination reels with the horror of what it must have been like.

A hand pulls up her chin. The wet lip of a bottle touches her lips.

'I'm all right,' she mutters crossly.

Tuck picks up the torch from the floor and blows gently on it to revive the flame. 'You not goin' to sick up on me again?' he teases.

Mara shakes her head and manages a smile. She takes a gulp from Tuck's water bottle, catching his eye as she hands it back.

'What's sickening you?' he asks.

'Nothing,' she retorts. 'There's nothing wrong with me.'

'You're sick a lot.'

'The sea made me sick. Now the food—'

'You've been Landed a while now,' Tuck persists. 'Two, three moons?'

Even the rise and fall of his gypsea voice makes her feel seasick.

'How do I know? It's all this fish and seaweed, it's turning my stomach. And the eggs.'

Mara steers her thoughts back to the carvings on the cave wall. Even they are preferable to the thought of an egg.

But, like Mol, Tuck won't swallow that.

'An ocean girl from an island can't tummy fish and eggs?'

Tears prickle Mara's eyes. 'I don't *know* what it is.' She takes back the torch, scrubs her eyes with her sleeve. 'Let me see the rest of this.'

Beyond the great wave is a carving of a child. The hair suggests it's a girl. Mara peers closer and traces the faint outline of a halo around the child's head.

'It's your magic machine.' There's a crackle of excitement in Tuck's voice as he points. 'See?'

Mara stares at the cave wall, unnerved. The child is cradling a globe. Ah, but it's not *her* globe. Mara touches the intricate patterns carved into the child's globe and knows what it is.

'It's the Earth.'

'The Earth?' Tuck's eyes glitter. The torch flame catches the salt crystals that seem to be ingrained forever in his hair, on his eyelashes, even in the down of his face. 'It really is round like Grumpa said.'

Mara nods. She runs across the cave to dig out her backpack from the heap of mats that are her bed. She has had an idea. 'Tuck, listen . . .'

She hesitates. What would happen if they bumped into Fox? But would they? It's hard enough to find him when she wants to. She has been trying endlessly to find him in the Weave to explain about her odd exit from the World Wind. But she can no longer gauge, so deep in the mountain in this season of endless night, whether long days or even weeks have passed since then. It's long enough for her nails to have grown again though she keeps chewing them down to the quick. Surely they are unlikely to bump into Fox if she avoids the bridge.

Anyway, Tuck is just a friend, isn't he?

'I'll show you the Earth,' she decides.

Tuck looks blank, of course, and she tries to explain. 'It's a place I can go with the cyberwizz, a site that shows the Earth the way it used to be. People took pictures of it from the moon over a hundred years ago.'

Now Tuck looks at her as if she's crazy. Mara laughs.

'That's what I thought but it's true. People once went to the moon.'

'They had wings?' Now he's laughing with her.

Mara pulls the cyberwizz from her bag and begins to power it up.

'Oh no.'

The globe should charge up right away, at a touch, but it takes a long, dead moment to work up a pitiful glow. Mara's heart sinks. The power is running out. The solar

212

rods inside the globe need a blast of sun, but she is deep inside a mountain and the outside world is in the thick of the longest night of the Far North, a night that spans the whole winter, without a glimpse of sun. Blankets of icy fog make it hard to see the moon or the stars from the cave mouth. It's impossible to keep track of time. Finding midnight, that single point in the night, when the world around her is *all* night, has become a blind guess in the dark.

She owes Tuck something, she tells herself, because of his mother. And sometimes . . .

Mara clasps the globe in her hands, a snippet of temper heating her blood.

Sometimes a cyberfox is just not enough. It's his living, breathing self she wants, the one she can touch, and he's not here. The real Fox is as unreachable as the sun. He *could* have come with her. But he didn't. He chose to save his world instead. And she chose to save her friends instead of staying with him.

There's a disconnection between them that has nothing to do with missing midnight or fading solar rods.

Mara knows *his* reality, she can picture exactly where *he* is in his world; she knows the book rooms of the university tower, she's been there. But Fox has no idea, and she can't find the words to tell him, what it's like to be here, entombed in a freezing mountain at the bitter end of the Earth. Now they're no more than spirits in the ether and it's never enough.

Tuck's right here though. Mara can hear the fear on his breath as he sits beside her; the fear of a lone gypsea deep inside the Earth. The World Wind might, for a few moments at least, blow away that fear.

It'll only take a few minutes, only a tiny bit of power, to show Tuck . . .

And how long has it been since she had any *fun*?

Earth!

Not deadly and dark like the inside of the mountain but a blue-green pearl hanging in black space among the stars. All alive and aglow. Tuck blinks away tears as he watches clouds swirl across the tattered shapes of Land. And the oceans, what oceans of blue!

He could look at it forever but already Mara is digging him in the ribs. She warned him he could only have a glimpse.

Tuck takes an extra moment to fix the image in his mind. He shouldn't be scared of the dark innards of Earth, not now that he's seen this.

He crashes back into the dimness of the moon cave. The silver halo is taken from his eyes. He leans against the cave wall, dazed, and tucks the Earth-pearl into a keep-pocket of his mind wondering, as he watches Mara's soft mouth break into a smile as she slips on the halo, what other wonders exist in her magic machine.

The glow of the halo illuminates a patch of the story-carving on the cave wall behind Mara's head. It's the arm of a bridge exploding under a furious fist of ocean. A shock of grief hits Tuck, just when he doesn't expect it, as he remembers the *Arkiel* smashing the bridgeways of Pomperoy. He hurls the memory to the outermost corner of his mind. He can't think about that – not least because Mara, the one who made it happen, is right here beside him, so close that he can breathe in the warm, musky scent of her hair. Instead, he takes a peek into his mind's keep-pocket, where he has stashed the memory of the blue-green gem of the Earth. *This* Earth, the one that he cowers inside. Does it still hang so peacefully in space? Did all the drowning and destruction dim its glow? Those tattered shapes that were Land, full of cities like the one carved on the wall: are there any left? Or are they all sunk, like Ma and *The Grimby Gray*?

For the first time in his life Tuck wants to know. And there's something else. He wants to know why. *Why* did the seas rise up and drown the Earth?

Grumpa could have told him, but Tuck never asked.

Mara pulls off the cyberwizz with a sigh and stuffs it in her bag. She gives Tuck a wan smile and goes over to her sleeping mats where she makes her backpack her pillow, as she always does, lies down and closes her eyes.

But she's forgotten to seal up her bag. Tuck can see the gleam of the cyberwizz globe through a gap.

Mol said the cyberwizz holds the secrets of the past and she was right. He's just seen that with his own eyes. *Great Skua, it holds a whole secret Earth inside! Who knows what else?* Tuck waits until he's sure Mara is fast asleep then slips his hand into the gap in the backpack. He feels the curve of the globe, smooth as glass. If he could just ease it out without wakening her . . .

'Hands off, pirate,' says a voice at his back.

EARTH'S GREAT
WHITE WHALE

Mara is wakened by a spur of rock in her ribs and an idea spiking her dreams. Blurry with sleep, she rummages in her backpack, finds the cyberwizz halo and wand, but can't feel the globe. She takes her backpack over to the fire and peers inside, but it's not there. In cold-sweat panic she searches the craggy floor of the cave.

'This what you're missing?' There's a rustle close behind her. Rowan sits up. He unearths the globe from his sea-grass pillow and hands it to her. 'I caught pirate boy stealing it.'

'Tuck?' Mara frowns then laughs, relieved. 'Oh, it's OK. I took him on a trip into the Weave. He was probably trying to sneak another look at, um—'

She stops. Rowan doesn't know what she's talking about. She has always kept the secrets of the cyberwizz close to her chest. She is trying to work out how to explain when he shrugs and flops back down on his mat.

'Just keep your stuff safe,' he grunts.

And turns away. Mara stares at his back, stung. Why has he become so cold and strange? Maybe it's only now that they're stuck here in this dark hole in the Earth that he has been hit by the full misery of his twin's death and the loss of his parents. Mara remembers how she felt in the netherworld when the terrible loss of her family sank in. Now that Rowan has had time to think, is he blaming her?

Well, she blames herself. It was her idea to travel to the New World.

But if they hadn't, a voice inside pipes up, what would they have done? Stayed on Wing and let the ocean swallow them up? Everyone thought the North was in meltdown, that any land would be sunk; there was no way to survive there.

Whether they were right or wrong about survival, time will tell.

Mara picks up the cyberwizz, opens the globe and puts the halo over her eyes. She can't wait for Fox. She'll do this alone. With the wand, she scribbles a series of hiero-glyphs on the tiny screenpad inside the globe and . . .

. . . *dives into the ruined boulevards of the Weave. She whizzes through the crumbling network until she finds the site she needs and tumbles into the World Wind, zipping through crackling blue ether into black space where the vast, glowing gem of the planet looms up. A glinting, winged craft flies towards her. Mara boards the wind-shuttle and begins to zoom towards an immense blueness of ocean.*

A name glows beneath its surface.

The Pacific.

The names of lost lands and cities begin to flash at the faraway rim of the planet but the ocean is so large it covers this whole face of the Earth's sphere. Mara keeps a high altitude so that the images and echoes of the horrible history flags, planted all over the planet by old world wind-shuttlers, are weakened by distance.

There's a wide scatter of islands like pebbles upon the serene ocean. Solomon, Phoenix, Starbuck, whole shoals of names flash and fade as she zips past. A green and brown terrain looms up beyond a firework flash for Hong Kong. She follows the wriggling line of the River Ganges, skirts the purple peaks of Himalayan mountains, India and Sumatra behind her, the highlands of Pakistan and Afghanistan ahead, the River Volga shimmering far in the distance and cluttered plains of low-lying cities as far as she can see.

One name, flashing in the distance, catches her eye and a memory flares of sitting by the fireside with her mother in her lost home on Wing. Mara stares at the faraway nameflash. Ararat. Why does she know that? Mara dredges through her memories and she swallows hard when she remembers. Ararat was the mountain in the story of Noah and the Ark, an ancient legend of a flood. So that is where those long-ago people saved themselves from a drowned world.

*There **is** high land above the oceans, scattered across the Earth. How much is barren mountain rock? And how hot has the Earth grown? It's hard to believe the rest of the world is warm while they are stuck in cold caves. But Fox has trawled Weavesite ruins and what he found there has made him sure, he said, that the sunless winter at the top of the world is at odds with the searing heat further South, where no one can live, not even in a sky city. One thing has given Mara heart: Fox's certainty that once the long Arctic winter night is over and the sun returns, the mellow spring and summer of a warmed world awaits them.*

If only he's right.

If only they can survive until then.

218

For the first time in a while, as she scans the oceans and lost lands, Mara wonders about the other ships that escaped the sky city with the Arkiel. Did they survive and find land?

Mara stalls the wind-shuttle, lost amid her thoughts and the names that flash all around her. Where in the world is she? She could zip back into realworld and ask Rowan, who spent entire winters engrossed in old atlases and books, but she can't face another of his rebuffs. No, she'll do this herself. She can't make up for the deaths that have already happened but she will do everything in her power to save the people she's brought to the top of the world.

Mara wings a prayer of hope across the Earth to wherever the other ships might be and focuses on the task in hand. She casts her mind back to the tattered atlas that used to lie on Tain's cottage table. If only she'd paid more attention when he'd tried to teach her about the world beyond the island, instead of twitching to be out playing in the wind with Rowan and Gail.

Wing was in the North Atlantic, a pinprick in the seas beyond the land mass of Europe. That she knows for sure. She closes her eyes to block out an insistent red SOS from Bangladesh, as the wind-shuttle flies over it, and tries to remember more. Europe leaned on the shoulder of Africa. That was the dead continent with the **HELP** flags she saw on her trip with Fox; she's almost sure of that. Far West, across the Atlantic Ocean, was the huge mass of North America, trailing its southern lands on a string.

Mara takes a guess and zooms East, back across the Pacific Ocean until she sees a gigantic golden archway with a banner flashing **USA** in red, white and blue. It bridges the entire land mass that lies to the north-east. And, yes, there are the southern Americas attached to the North land mass by a thin string of land.

Peru, Ecuador and Colombia flash past. She zooms over the string of land – and jumps with fright as a crowd of orange ghosts rise like distress flares from a bay on a long island that is the shape of a wrenched arm. The name of the island, Cuba, flashes but there is no message flag or blog from the bay of the orange ghosts.

Unnnerved, she speeds on to the ridges of the Rocky Mountains where a roll of beautiful names echo the undulations of the land. California, Arizona, Colorado, Oklahoma. Dizzied by flashing towns and cities, she heads for the calm blue of the ocean that lies beyond the lowlands of Mississippi and Florida, now surely drowned.

The Atlantic! The name shimmers on the surface of the ocean and Mara's excitement grows as she veers sharp North, following the eastern seaboard towards the part of the world that is home.

A rumble vibrates the wind-shuttle. Far below, two towers, as tall as any sky city, implode into dust.

Mara rushes onward, following the flashes of Toronto, Montreal and Quebec along a trail of waterways that lead her North, tracking the line of the coast. As the wind-shuttle takes her over the huge water bowl of Hudson Bay, she remembers something and glances back West. But there are too many lakes, scattered like shattered glass across the rugged terrain of the North. Somewhere among those lakes and forested highlands lived the Athapaskans whose story first inspired her to find a homeland in the Far North. She hopes the Athapaskans survived.

Now all her hopes and wishes fly North, like a spur of boreal wind because there it is at last, like a great white whale at the top of the world.

Greenland, the biggest island on Earth.

A patch of island, a cuttlefish beside Greenland's giant

whale, comes as a shock because it's due North, surely, of where Wing, her home island, must lie. Mara peers out of the wind-shuttle window.

The name flashes up.

Iceland.

She remembers tales of an ice land full of molten fire. The oldest island folk swore the tales were true. Mara digs into her memory. Wasn't there a mention in her Greenland book of a volcanic island in the northern Atlantic? The old people's stories were of a violent land, so hot it melted the soles of your feet and guarded by a people so fiery they could burn a stranger's eyes to blackened sockets with a glance. Not a soul on Wing suggested they go there, not even when the sea reached their doorsteps.

Mara pauses the wind-shuttle. Now that she's here, she knows it's been in the back of her mind to do this all along.

Just to see.

She descends to a speckle of islands that lie south of Iceland and North of the British Isles. She's using up too much of her precious power but she doesn't care. She circles the speckle of islands. It's the largest, most southerly one.

Mara stares at the island. Her vision blurs and her throat tightens.

In realworld she scrubs tears from her eyes. In the cyber-world she swoops low over the old satellite image of Wing, her island, her lost home.

How long ago did some satellite orbiting the Earth capture this image of what no longer exists? Was it when Mum and Dad were young? Before they were born? A century ago, before the seas rose, when Granny Mary and Tain were young? Mara zooms deeper into the satellite image, as close as the World Wind allows, until she is no higher from the ground than a sky city tower. That grey clutter near the sea must be the rooftops of the old village – before the sea forced the villagers further inshore. There's a scattering of farms on the hillside that didn't exist in her lifetime. It was the field of windmills. Mara's heart beats painfully as she follows the coastline of her island until she finds the horse-shoe shape of Longhope Bay.

There it is. She can hardly believe her eyes. Far below is the grey rooftop of a farm cottage. Her own home. And there, further up the hillside, is Tain's cottage roof.

Mara can hardly breathe as she gazes down at this lost world, her world, from a time long before she was born, before the Earth drowned.

Two specks are outside Tain's cottage. They could be rocks. Or they could be people.

They might be Granny Mary and Tain.

She can't take any more.

Mara revs the wind-shuttle and zooms away as fast as she can from the ghosts of the past.

HERE, NOW

Mara takes the wind-shuttle up the eastern side of Greenland, across endless fjords. In realworld, their mountain could be in any one of the fjords that fritter the edges of the great white island like frosted ferns.

She zooms over the ridge of the mountains that enclose the mass of ice and snow in the interior. The snow is melted now so the mountains must surely cup a lake so vast it would seem like a sea.

Mara thinks of the dead tree root in the cave roof and wonders. She remembers the Athapaskans who lived among the boreal high lands and lakes. Anything is possible, she reminds herself. It's a thought she hasn't had in a while.

She is about to pull the wind-shuttle back from the Earth to find its parking bay in electronic space when she pauses. Thinks hard. Then scribbles on her screenpad and hits the message flag button on the control panel. Maybe no one will ever see it but Wing, her island, deserves a flag of its own.

Now she revs up the wind-shuttle, ready to exit Earth.

She's seen what she needs to know, and far more. Of one thing she is sure.

They need to go through the mountains. They need to find a way through to the interior sea.

SNAKE IN THE BOOK

Tonight, at long last, he found Mara on the Bridge to Nowhere. Fox replays the precious moments in his head. She seemed so lost and upset. When he asked her what was wrong, she hardly made sense. Before she left, she asked him such an odd thing.

Have you ever seen the sign of a snake coiled around a stick?

She described a symbol she'd found among the carvings on a cave wall. The same sign, she murmured, was burned on to her arm.

Burned? By who? Fox demanded, appalled. Not now, she muttered, she'd tell him another time.

He has only seen her for a few snatched moments since her sudden, strange exit from the World Wind. Now he's too worried to focus on his own task. Who could have done such a thing to her? The gypsea? Yet Fox remembers, all too clearly, how fondly she speaks of him.

Finding out about the snake sign is the only thing he can think of to do, so Fox searches the tower bookstacks, trying to calm his spiralling fear. The image is niggling at the back of his head. It's only when he turns over a book on serpents and spots a tiny snake coiled on a stick on the corner of the back cover, that he realizes what it is.

Of course! It's all over New Mungo and the Noos.

It's a dollar sign. The trading symbol of the New World.

Fox grips the book. The sign of a *dollar* is branded on her arm?

'What's branded on whose arm?'

Candleriggs is frowning at him.

Fox could kick himself. He must have spoken the words out loud.

The gnarled hand on his arm is like a claw.

'What's happening?' demands Candleriggs. 'You told me they'd found land, that they're safe and settled for the winter in caves by the sea.'

He said exactly that. Fox has been very careful about what he has and has not said. Mara was adamant about that.

'What's happening?' Candleriggs repeats. 'Is someone sick? Broomielaw and the baby, are they—'

'They're fine,' he says, too quickly.

'What's *happened*, boy?'

Fox shakes his head. With Candleriggs's owl eyes fixed on him so fiercely, he can't lie any more.

When he tells all he knows she doesn't break down. She hunches deeper into her earthen cloak, says nothing at all, just walks away.

Night has fallen when he hears her wail somewhere deep in the book rooms. Her cry mingles with the moans of misery Fox is sure he hears, carried on the wind, from the boat camp on the other side of the city walls.

He couldn't tell Candleriggs what else Mara said.

If my power dies, don't give up on me. If something hap-
pens, if we lose contact, don't ever give up.

What's wrong? he kept asking. What happened that
night you disappeared?

I'm running low on power, she said. I'm – I – I don't know
what's wrong. Everything's wrong. Just don't give up on me,
promise?

He promised, of course he did. There was nothing else
he could do.

Now he has found the snake sign but when will he find
Mara again? Fox is filled with a terrible foreboding. All he
can do is wait on the Bridge to Nowhere and hope that
she comes.

ANGEL ON THE RISE

There are skeletons in the nooks and crannies of the deep caves, and the scattered belongings of the people they once were. Broken watches, jewellery, unfathomable gadgets from the past, all kinds of useless stuff. Useful things too. Clothes and shoes and blankets, pots and plates, empty cans, knives and spoons, plastic bottles and bags.

The urchins have found a collection of small metal and coloured plastic boxes, some of which still magic up a flame when a switch is flicked. Ibrox sniffs the unfamiliar oil that fuels them, impressed at these ingenious fireboxes of the old world.

Mara shudders at the thought that the skeletons were once the same people who carved the story of the world's drowning on to the cave wall, though she overcomes her qualms and gratefully pulls on their warm clothes. Did they die here waiting for winter to pass? Their remains can't be buried. The ground is solid rock. So the urchins play with the skulls and bones, turning them into bats and balls, guns and swords, and sticks to batter out a drum bash on the rocks.

The urchins make treasure hoards of the bright litter

they find scrunched on the ground. They dress up in motley assortments of clothes, drape themselves in jewellery and broken watches and take apart the gadgets to see what's inside.

Scarwell has moved into a cave of her own, a low cavern along one of the tunnels that branch off from the moon cave. She has filled it with precarious bone-heaps, gruesome things that scare the other urchins off her treasure hoard, each one topped by a skull with a gleaming pair of firestone eyes. In the middle of them sits her constant companion, the plastic apeman from the drowned museum, who is almost as big as herself. He looks strangely at home in his cavern, hunched over Scarwell's treasure, surrounded by human bones.

It was Scarwell who made the skull lanterns, by turning skulls upside down and burning small chunks of driftwood soaked in fish oil inside. Everyone was horrified, but the darkness of the mountain and the outside world had crept into the moon cave. It seemed to sap the thunder of the waterfalls and the soft moon glow that lives in the cavern rock. Now Scarwell's skull lanterns are a welcome, if grotesque, source of light.

Ibrox, whose fire-making tricks have been dwindling fast, hoards all the fireboxes that still have dregs of fuel. Every so often, he uses one of the fireboxes to spark the embers of the fire. It's the signal for everyone to gather in semblance of the Treenesters' old sunup and sundown ritual. No one can be bothered to shout out their names any more but they gather together and Gorbal reads from *A Tale of Two Cities* or a snippet from Tuck's book, or he unwraps a poem or story from his own head and warms it by the fire. The ache of their empty stomachs fades a little as they fly on the wings of the words, escaping their entombment in the caves. They fall asleep with the story infused in their dreams.

Human sounds, a sneeze or shout, begin to jangle nerves and graze the ear like grit. There's no longer any sense of day or night, hours or minutes. Time hibernates in the long night of winter, nestled in the beat of a heart.

And then . . .

A wind enters the cavern with a clean, sharp scent that cuts through sleep. Everyone wakens.

'That's not a sea wind,' says Pollock. He jumps up from his sea-grass mattress, alert. 'No scent of salt.'

'A tree wind,' whispers Mol, more hopeful than sure.

'Smells green,' Ibrox agrees.

'We'll track it,' says Pollock. Possil has already disappeared into the cave tunnels, quick on its trail.

Tuck sniffs the air. He's never breathed any that isn't salty with sea.

Mara knows the green scent of grass in the wind. This wind is fresh yet it comes from deep inside the tunnels, not from the cave mouth. It can only come from somewhere beyond the mountain.

From the interior?

If that's where the green wind comes from, Mara is sure there must be a way through. And they need to find it soon or they might end up as a litter of skulls and bones too.

She should go with Pollock and Possil and follow the wind, right now, to wherever it comes from but she's so tired. Her mind keeps slithering into sleep. Later, once she's slept, then she'll track the wind.

But something keeps nudging Mara out of sleep. She tries to ignore it but every time she is about to drop off it nudges her once more. She lies in the dark, wondering what it is. Not a noise, but a movement in the pit of her stomach. The strangest sensation. Not pain. Mara rolls on to her back, places a hand on the spot, feels it again. *It's like . . . like a key turning in a lock.* Mara's heart beats like a clock. There's a strong taste in her mouth again. Something to do with the sulphurous tang in the air from the hot spring? It makes fish and seaweed taste of metal and she can hardly eat them, though that's all there is and she's hungry all the time. Her eyelids, the soles of her feet, the insides of her wrists, every part of her tingles, as if her skin has grown too thin and her nerve endings are raw. Sore and tender, she sits up. The ghostly glow of the cavern seems to seep inside her fuzzy head.

'M-Mol?'

She almost called for her mum. Her voice echoes around the caves. Mol doesn't answer. Maybe she's gone tree-wind-tracking with Pollock and Possil.

There's a grunt from across the cave.

'Mara?' Mol's voice croaks with sleepiness.

'Something's wrong,' Mara whispers. 'I don't feel right. I saw stuff in the cyberwizz – things I shouldn't have looked at . . .'

The darkness hisses with her whispers. She hears Gorbals mutter in his sleep. Beside her, Rowan is snoring lightly. Suddenly Mol is beside her. She puts a cool hand on Mara's forehead.

'What things did you see?'

'Things from the past. My home. My Granny Mary and Tain.'

'Dreams, Mara. You've just had a bad dream. There's no fever. I don't think you're ill.'

'I feel so strange. Not sick, just *strange.*'

231

Mol takes a breath, lets it out, long and slow. She puts her mouth to Mara's ear.

'Are you still bleeding every moon?'

Mara lets the words sink in. Her heart hammers.

'We can't see the moon,' she mutters. Then, in a whisper, 'No, but so much has happened and we're half starved . . .'

Mol takes her hand and pulls her over to the low ember fire. 'It *is* the strangest feeling,' she whispers. 'Like moth wings or tiny fish.'

'Like a key turning,' breathes Mara, 'deep inside.'

Mol nods. 'And you dream a lot too. Strange dreams.' She squeezes Mara's hand. 'You're not sick, you're full of life.'

Mara feels a cold hand grip the key that's still turning, slowly, slowly, deep inside.

No.

'I *can't* be . . .'

And yet she knows she is.

'It's only a baby,' whispers Mol. 'Don't be scared of that.'

A baby.

'I can't, Mol. It's too scary. What'll I do?'

'Nothing,' says Mol. 'Stop panicking. The baby grows itself. How can you be scared of a baby after all you've been through?'

'What if something goes wrong?' Mara has a sharp memory of the cold waiting and wandering in the field of windmills as a trail of grim faces rushed into the cottage during her little brother Corey's difficult birth. Most of all, she remembers the sound of her mother's agony mixed with the moan of the wind. 'No one here knows anything about babies.'

Molendinar's eyes drop. '*I* know.'

'I wish Broomielaw was here.'

'Me too,' admits Mol. 'But listen, Mara, I helped with her birth and it was a tough one. We got there, though. Broomie and Clay were . . .' She falters, bites her lip. 'They were *fine* in the end,' she says firmly. 'You will be too.'

'I want my mum.'

Mol squeezes her hand tighter still. 'I know. But I'm here. Mara, this is not a bad thing, it's good. We need new, strong blood. We need to grow new people.'

Mara hears the ring of relief, as well as friendship, in the other girl's voice and she knows why. It's to do with Tuck. Mol's heart is in her eyes whenever she looks at Tuck. Everyone can see that; everyone but Tuck. And Mara knows who's to blame for that. She is, because Tuck only has eyes for her. But once Tuck finds out she's going to have a baby . . . Mara sighs. Well, he's bound to feel differently then.

'It's new life,' Mol whispers, 'something warm and good, like finding the hot spring in the middle of the killing cold. My mother used to say that wherever a devil is roused, you'll always find an angel on the rise. You'll always have a bit of your Fox now. Think of that.'

Think of Fox, not Tuck, is what she means.

Back in her bed, Mara's thoughts whirl. She's having a baby. Fox's baby. The idea is so enormous and strange, but when the slow, fluttery key-turning comes again, a feeling as clear and sharp as the green wind rushes through her and the dread seeps away.

Like the green wind, the baby is the key to the future. The baby is the way through.

Mol is right. She will always have a bit of Fox now.

233

Part of him is alive inside her, closer than ever, growing into a baby that they have made.

The women on her island used to call every newborn baby a tiny miracle and Mara never gave it any thought, never understood. Now she does.

Amid the bones and primeval dark of the Earth, her own tiny miracle has bloomed. A miracle that links her across the waves of time to Granny Mary and Tain on the island. And to Fox in his netherworld tower, an ocean away.

THE SILENCE OF
THE FALLS

Pollock stops dead. The torch flame flickers on the rugged
rock of the cave tunnel.

'Listen.'

The others strain to hear.

Mara shrugs. 'Can't hear anything.'

'That's it,' says Pollock. 'There's nothing. There *should*
be a waterfall here, louder than the biggest roar of thunder I've ever heard. It made a wind that nearly blew me off
my feet.'

They listen again but there's only the jangling of the
urchins' jewellery. Their arms and legs are adorned with
dead watches and flip-top wrist phones, old world junk
that Granny Mary and Tain used to hoard under their
beds.

Wing is a ridiculous sight, zipped in a big blue snow
suit he found in one of the tunnels, rattling with neck
chains hung with the ring tops from empty cans, his ears
plugged into a gadget that's long dead. He is almost up to
her shoulder now, Mara sees, and wonders how he has

grown having had so little food for so long in these dark caves.

'Shh!' Pollock hisses fiercely and everyone stands stock still.

'Maybe this is the wrong tunnel,' Rowan suggests.

Pollock lowers the torch to show two human leg bones, one crossed over the other. 'I left crosses to mark the way. I've been tracking these tunnels ever since we got here.'

'A waterfall can't disappear,' says Mara.

'No,' says Pollock. 'But it can freeze. Haven't you noticed they've all grown quiet? The streams of water that run along the floor of the tunnels are only trickles now because the waterfalls have turned to ice. It's only the hot spring that keeps our floor from icing up.'

'We must be right in the heart of the winter,' says Mara, shocked at what she has missed. She has been so eaten up with worry about the baby that she was glad when the din of the waterfalls dimmed, and didn't even ask why. She never even noticed the streams had shrunk or wondered why the others were melting slabs of ice to drink. She has been too caught up in herself.

'We could all die here,' she says quietly.

'Not if we find a way through,' Pollock responds.

'You think this is the way?'

Pollock nods. 'It's the way through to somewhere. Don't know where though. The scent of fresh wind used to be strong in this tunnel and I used to see a star here. Sometimes it peeked at me through a waterfall chute.' He shows them the skeleton hand he's placed on a rock, its ringed forefinger pointing to the ceiling of the cave. 'But it's gone and the water's gone too. The chute must be iced up, high in the mountain.'

'The wind came from beyond the waterfall,' adds

Possil, 'from a place where the air is full of the smell of plants and earth, not salty sea.'

Mara feels a sharp surge of hope. If only Possil and Pollock are right.

They follow the bone trail further until the cave tunnel ends in a solid wall. Possil bends and lights the skull lantern left from a previous visit. Pollock lifts the torch and the wall gleams with ice.

'This is it!'

The wall is not rock. Mara can see from the gleam cast by the skull light that it is solid ice. The huge waterfall has frozen into a thick wall that blocks the way through to the place of the green wind.

'What do we do now?' Disappointment is as sharp as the burst of hope. But she will not cry. The situation is too desperate for tears.

Pollock sighs. 'Wait for spring.'

'*Spring?*'

The baby will be born in the spring. She can't give birth in these deathly caves.

Rowan picks up a sharp-edged rock from the ground and one of the long bones Pollock used to mark the way through the cave tunnels. He places the rock at the end of the bone and frowns.

He steps forward and stabs the ice wall with the rock. A splinter of ice shears off. He holds the bone in one hand, the sharp rock in the other.

'We'll make axes,' he says. 'We'll hack our way through.'

Mara has spent what feels like weeks collecting flat rocks from the floor of the caves and tunnels, chipping them into axe heads then binding them on to bones with tough seaweed rope. Sorting out long, strong bones from the piles in the caves then filing and sharpening the axe heads with other rocks has become an intense craft that takes her mind off her worries. Her first axes were wobbly, useless things but this last one looks good and strong.

But not as good as Tuck's. Mara watches his nimble fingers weave intricate braids of seaweed up the bone handle and around the axe head. He knots the braid and cuts it with a flash of his cutlass. His finished axe is a beautiful thing, thinks Mara, unlike her clumsy, functional tools.

'Come with me?' she urges. Tuck shakes his head. His trip in the World Wind has not shifted his fear of the mountain. He will endure long treks through the tunnels to the cave mouth to fish and collect seaweed and driftwood, but he refuses to go any deeper into the Earth.

So Mara follows Pollock's trail of fire stones and crossed bones to deliver the axes to the frozen waterfall where the others are trying to hack a tunnel through the solid wall of ice.

Rowan tries out a few axes. Mara wants to tell him that she made the axe he settles on but he is in a brittle, sullen mood and she can't help thinking he deliberately did not choose Tuck's, even though his axes are clearly the best.

It's only when Mara picks up an axe that he looks at her then grabs it off her, chucking it on the ground with a gruff *no*. Mol pulls her away from the ice wall.

'You can't, silly. You have to take care of yourself.'

Mara looks from Mol to Rowan. Has she told him? Does he know?

The axes smash the ice into chips and daggers. Mara yelps as a splinter hits her in the face. She backs off, a trickle of blood on her cheek, leaving Rowan and the others to attack the ice wall. As she thinks of what she needs to tell Fox, before the cyberwizz finally dies for the rest of the winter, she feels as if the ice splinter has slipped into her bloodstream and lodged in her heart.

THE OTHER SIDE
OF WINTER

'Fox . . . power's dying . . . you there . . . ?'

Fox zips along the Bridge to Nowhere. Mara is here again, at last. He's been worried sick. Every night he waits on the broken bridge and the one time he almost sleeps through midnight, she's here, waiting for him. Her eyes and her voice are scared. Her electronic image flickers. Her lips are moving but now he can't hear her speak. Fox moves closer and tries to lip-read.

What is it? I don't know what you're saying.

She reaches out an arm to him. Fades. And then she's gone.

Fox waits, heart thumping, but she doesn't come back. There's nothing to do except wait. A moment seems to stretch for hours. He can't bear it. She's gone.

Fox commands his godgem to save and re-run Mara's image, but his lip-reading skills are no better this time around. Yet there's a way to decode anything. Fox digs up a program that will make an electronic cipher translate her silent words. He runs the program and now Mara speaks to him in an alien voice.

'Someving I need to tell you bevore my bower diezzz,' the bland voice of the cipher says through Mara's lips.

It's not perfect. Some of the sounds are wonky, but he can make sense of it, just about.

'A – a bavey,' Mara stutters, *'in the zpring. I'm zorry – zzzzz – power'z going. Can't recharge till the zun comez dack in the zpring and by ven . . . well, by ven . . . zzzzzzZZZ . . . the bavey . . . sssssssss.'*

The cipher voice breaks up, buzzing and hissing. Mara's face flickers. He holds the look in her eyes until she fades out.

'Above you.'

The cipher voice cuts through the ether. Fox looks up above him, but there's nothing except empty static there. There's no voice, no Mara. He is alone again on the broken bridge.

She's lost him. Her power's all gone. Mara unplugs from the cyberwizz and shakes the globe, in case there's a trickle of power left. She tries again but it's dead. Did she get through? Did he hear her at all?

Mara puts her head in her hands. Her heart thumps a painful, hard beat.

Darkest winter grips the top of the world. How will she ever make it through to spring?

Fox replays Mara's message on the bridge. She was trying to tell him something important; he could see by the look on her face. Something about a *bavey*. Didn't she say the word twice? Fox tries out endless permutations of the word but there's only one that makes any sense.

Baby.

A baby in the spring?

She will come back. She must. He needs to speak to her and be sure that's what she said. He can't believe he might not see her until the spring. That seems a lifetime away. And in the spring . . .

. . . she'll have a *baby*?

His heart pounds. It's the last thing he expected. They were so caught up in each other and their desperate, dangerous plans – but they never planned for this. They were together so briefly, everything happened so fast. Fox's emotions are in turmoil. He is hit by sudden doubt. Is the baby his? Who else is she close to? There's Rowan, her old friend from her island. Gorbals and the Treenesters. And Tuck, the gypsea. His voice sounds like the sea, she once said, and something in the way she said it made the back of his neck prickle. It could be Rowan's baby or the gypsea's. Couldn't it?

But she told *him*. Fox pulls himself together. Of course it's his. He remembers how it was with him and Mara and he feels sure.

All of a sudden he doesn't want it to be true because he will never see their baby, never know the child they've made. The thought chills his soul. Mara is so far away she may as well be on another planet. She may as well be dead.

Fox replays her message again on his godgem. It ends with those strange, stark words.

Above you.

Bewildered, Fox wonders.

What did she mean by that?

The baby makes a sudden wild leap that makes Mara gasp.

Mol catches her eye.

'It's leaping like a dolphin,' Mara whispers. 'Head over heels. Like it's having fun.'

The moon glow of the cave can't soften the envy on Mol's face. She looks away. 'I lost a baby once,' she murmurs. 'Bad blood, that's what everyone said.' She glances back at Mara's shocked face. 'One of the New Mungo sea police.'

Mara can't quite meet her friend's eye. The sea police are ruthless agents of the New World.

'What happened?'

'Oh, nothing bad.' Mol gives a weak smile. 'I met him in the ruined cathedral.' She gives a tiny sigh. 'He wasn't like you'd expect. Not like the others, not a brute. He was . . . nice. Just a person, same age as me. He had sunlight hair, just like Tuck.'

Is that why she is so drawn to him? Mara wonders. She remembers the young policewoman she found dead in the cathedral in the netherworld. *She looked such an ordinary girl, not much different from me.*

'Did he know about the baby?' Mara asks gently.

'I was going to tell him, but then I lost her. She wasn't even as big as my hand but she was perfect. A baby girl.' Mol tugs at a knot in her long braid of hair, a quiet but frantic gesture, as if trying to tug the memory out her head. 'Once the others found out what had happened, they wouldn't let me see him again. I was putting all our lives at risk. But he would never have told. Never. I – I don't think so. Well, we never had a sea-police raid so he couldn't have. I never told him we lived in the trees, though. He was from the sky city. I would have seemed like an animal. Anyway, I never saw him again.'

'I'm sorry,' says Mara. She knows that kind of pain, can't think what else to say.

Mol swallows a sob. 'But *you* have your baby. Think of that.'

Think of that, and don't think of Tuck, she means. You have your baby, you don't need him. Tuck, who spends most days hunting seaweed and driftwood and fishing at the mouth of the cave, not bothering much about Mol.

The baby gives another dolphin leap. Mara lies on her back and tunes into the feeling. For the first time she imagines a baby, a real live baby inside her, jumping head over heels. It must be sending out waves of joy because she feels them vibrate through her, feels something close to pure happiness for the first time since she was in the sky city with Fox.

She's the lucky one, she suddenly sees, because Fox is on his own without her. But she has a part of him now, to keep.

The thought shakes up a surge of energy. She sits up, eager to find a scrap of food. Now there's a reason to eat, a need to make it through to spring. On the other side of winter is a little piece of Fox.

WATER TO A WAVE

'Nice of the pirate to give us a hand.'

Rowan jerks his head towards Tuck who is dozing in a nook of rock. He plunges into the hot spring with a groan, ice-bitten after a day spent hacking the frozen waterfall.

Tuck has fallen asleep after a long trek to the cave mouth with Scarwell and Wing. Everyone is sick of seaweed and fish, but there were no eggs or birds on the shore, only face-sniping wind and a darkness that never lightened, not a pinch, said Tuck, though they hunted as long as they could bear the cold. Still, they didn't return empty-handed. As they gathered seaweed for soup and driftwood for the fire they came across a lone seal on the shore. Tuck killed it with his cutlass and somehow the three of them managed to haul the dead seal all the way back through the tunnels to the moon cave.

'He's been busy enough!' Mara retorts. 'This will feed us for weeks.' Sweat drips from her forehead as she works on the large carcass she and Scarwell are struggling to cut up with sharp stones.

Rowan climbs out of the pool and comes over. 'A seal!' he exclaims.

'The *pirate* found it,' says Mara sarkily.

'Use every bit of it,' is all Rowan says, though his eyes gleam with hunger as he watches Mara cut through tough skin and thick blubber to reach the meat. 'Keep the fat for soup and lamp fuel. We can use the skin for all kinds of things and the liver is full of iron—'

'I know, I know,' Mara interrupts. Has he forgotten she lived on the same island as him? She knows what to do with a seal – though she has only ever watched before.

But why is Rowan so moody? Now he's growling at Scarwell for licking lumps of seal fat from her fingers. And he's always ready to give Tuck a tongue-lashing when, right now, he should be praising him to the skies.

'What's your problem with Tuck?' Mara demands.

'Don't trust him.'

'You've said. But you don't like him either. Why?'

'I caught him trying to steal your cyberwizz, *remember?*'

'Caught him *looking* at it. He thinks it's a toy.'

'Mara, I know you feel guilty about his mother and everything but—'

'But what? He needs us. He's lost his own people, *remember.*'

'We all have,' snaps Rowan. 'Anyway, he hasn't lost his people, he abandoned them. You can't trust someone who does that.'

'He abandoned a lot of murdering pirates because he doesn't want to be one.'

'Still think he's dangerous,' Rowan growls.

'*Dangerous?* Don't be stupid, Tuck's the least of my worries.' This is her chance, thinks Mara, to tell Rowan

246

about the baby, though she suspects Mol already has. He is her oldest friend in the world but somehow she hasn't been able to find the right moment or the words. And somehow she knows that her not telling him might be at the root of his filthy moods.

'What about your Fox?'

Mara starts at the unexpected question.

'I – I can't reach him any more. My power's dead.'

Her voice breaks and she bites her lip.

'Is he so important?' asks Rowan, in a strange, curt voice.

But he reaches down and draws a strand of hair back from her hot face with a gentle hand that is at odds with his tone.

'He's important.' Mara's face crumples and she lowers her head to hide her tears and digs at the seal with her cutting stone. 'I tried to tell myself he wasn't. He's so far away that he didn't seem real any more. But I need him now.' She swallows and scrubs tears from her face with a greasy hand. 'It's not just that. Rowan, the cyberwizz took me into the past. I went to Wing and I saw—'

'Mara! Forget those silly games. We're beyond all that.' He hesitates then blurts out. 'Just when are you planning to tell me?'

Mara tries to speak but no words come.

'All that sickness and fainting.' Rowan crouches beside her. 'We're all starving yet you're getting big. And weepy and strange. Anyway, Mol doesn't keep a secret well.'

The look in his blue eyes makes her hot inside.

'I – I *was* going to tell you.'

'Yeah?' The word feels like a slap. He stands up and turns his back on her. 'So who's the father?' he mutters. 'The pirate or the Fox?'

Mara could hit him. She glares at the back of his head, hardly able to breathe. But she knows how to rouse Rowan's temper, just as he knows how to rile her.

'Urth!'

She spits Tuck's favourite gypsea curse at him and flings her cutting stone at his back, splattering him with blubber and blood.

That does it. Rowan turns on her.

'How many chances does one person get? How many stupid mistakes . . .'

He tails off.

Mara gulps. 'You mean me?'

He begins to speak, sighs, stops.

Mara stands up. 'I get it. This is about Gail. She's dead because of me. How do you think I feel about that? She's not just *your* sister. She was my best friend. My own little brother, my parents – they're dead too because of me and I've got to live with that. Now I'm pregnant and we're stuck in a hole at the ends of the Earth and we're probably all going to die. That's my fault too because coming to Greenland was another one of my brilliant ideas. Except,' anger blazes through her, 'you all do what I say, don't you? You don't have any brilliant ideas of your own but you'll follow me and blame me when it all goes wrong. I'll tell you something else though – you haven't a clue just how bad I am.'

She takes a seething breath. She should swallow back the next words but she's surfing a wave of temper and can't stop. 'I killed a man. I mean it, I did. In the sky city. I thought he was going to kill me, so I – I killed him first. If I hadn't killed him we wouldn't be here now. You would still be a slave, building bridges for the New World till you dropped dead. You might even be dead already . . .'

248

'Mara—'

Rowan is on his feet, trying to hold her, to calm her down, but she flaps him away.

'So just *how* many people have I killed? How many have I saved? Let's count them up . . .'

'*Mara.*'

Rowan grabs her by the shoulders and shakes her. Raging, she shoves him in the chest.

They look at each other and stop.

They were like this as little kids, when their bad moods clashed. They'd end up blazing at each other and someone would have to drag them apart before fists flew – usually Mara's, first.

Wonder where she gets her temper from? Tain's eyes would twinkle and Granny Mary would give him one of her looks.

In time, they learned to keep their tempers in check but it was easy back then, in their ordinary life. Now, nothing is ordinary. Everything familiar is gone. All they can depend upon is each other, yet here they are, brawling with each other, ready to fight like a couple of farm cats.

Rowan gives her another shake, gentler, a rough kind of hug, almost.

'Mara, I'm sorry. I just needed to blast off at someone,' he confesses, 'and you're – well, I *know* you, so you got it. What happened in the sky city,' he looks bewildered, upset, shakes his head, 'we'll talk about that sometime. But Gail and our families – you're not to blame. You're right, we backed you all the way, all of us. I never should have said what I did, I just – I *miss* Gail so bad. It's like I lost a bit of myself. It's like—' he screws up his face, 'like chopping the leg off a stool. I feel . . . toppled.'

'I know.'

Gail was his twin. Twinned in looks though not in nature, they were as necessary to each other as water to a wave.

'I want them all back.' Mara feels a terrible grief rising; her nails are puncturing her palms. 'I want our old life back. Everything's gone.'

She thinks of the specks of people on their island, the ones that might have been Granny Mary and Tain. There were other specks near the village that might have been Rowan's ancestors. When the sun returns and she can power up the cyberwizz, she'll show him then.

Rowan looks her in the eye. Like her, his temper is all burned out.

'We're all ripped up by what we've seen, what we've lost – and what we've had to do to get here. We've all got blood on our hands. Me too. There are things I did—' Rowan stops and stares at the carving of the Wreck of the World on the cave wall. 'We've survived a catastrophe like nothing else that's ever happened. The seabed's crowded with people who didn't. How are we supposed to live with that?'

He rubs a hand over his eyes and turns away from the carving on the wall.

'Maybe there's still something out there in the world for us,' Mara whispers. 'Some kind of future.' She's not sure if she believes that any more but she can't give up hope.

'You've got your baby now,' says Rowan. 'You've got that.'

He says it softly but she knows him so well she can hear an edge in his voice. A strange, snaky feeling is uncurling deep inside.

It's only the baby moving, she tells herself.

Too much has happened, too much has been lost. Too much hard life has junked up the innocent bonds they once had. He is not Rowan from the island any more than she is the same girl she was back then. Everything has changed. They are not the uncomplicated friends they once were. How could they be?

Their eyes meet in a confused glance.

But what are they now?

BROKEN HEARTS

Possil bursts into the moon cave with a yell, his axe still grasped in his fist. At last, they have broken through to the other side of the waterfall! It was his axe, Possil boasts, that made the final chop.

Excited voices echo in the tunnels and soon the others pour into the cave. Tuck is woken by grateful slaps on the back when the ravenous ice-diggers see the seal carcass and the strips of meat sizzling on hot stones around the fire.

What a day this has been, they say, licking their fingers, although whether it's night or day no one can tell.

Once they have slept, they will pack up and try to make it through the ice tunnel and the mountains into the interior of the land.

'We can't leave without Broomielaw and Clayslaps.' Gorbals is hit by panic now it's almost time to go. 'They could be out there somewhere. We don't know. We have to wait until the sun comes back and search the bay again.'

'We *have* searched, Gorbals,' says Ibrox firmly. 'Many, many times.'

Gorbals stares at the ground and shakes his head.

'I'll stay and look for them,' Tuck offers.

Everyone stares at him in surprise.

'You? How would you know who they are?' scoffs Pollock. 'Even if you found them, you'd never bring them through the mountain. You only want to stay because you're afraid, gypsea,' he taunts.

Tuck clenches his fists and shifts from foot to foot.

Pollock raises his chin. His dark eyes are fierce. 'Anyway, *I'm* staying.'

Gorbals's face stiffens. 'Why would *you* stay?'

'Clayslaps is my baby. Remember? I searched the bay even when the firebombs were falling.' Pollock turns on Gorbals. 'Didn't see *you* out searching at all, wordslug. Too busy digging in your thick head for poems? Too scared you'd get another finger burned? You go. I'll search again for Broomielaw and my baby when the sun returns. Possil can mark a trail through the mountains and I'll track you all down in the spring.'

Mol pushes between Pollock and Gorbals. Her mouth trembles and she twists her hands.

'Broomie and I were like sisters. If I thought she was alive out there with Clay, would I have stayed in these caves all this time? We only survived because we found the hot spring. How long would we have lasted out there in the dark, any of us, alone? I've thought and thought about it and I know they must have drowned when the ship sank. The wreckers would have rounded them up with the rest of us if they'd survived.' Mol covers her mouth with her hands to catch a sob.

After long moments, Gorbals steps towards Pollock.

'No more fighting,' Mol pleads.

But Gorbals only puts out his hand.

Shocked, Pollock looks as if he'll refuse the out-
stretched hand.

'She's right, Pollock,' says Gorbals. 'They're gone and
we're still fighting over them.'

Pollock looks at the hand, gives a tiny shake of his
head, as if he doesn't know what to do.

'We'll come back in the spring,' Mara urges, 'and we'll
make sure. We won't give up on them. But we need to survive. We can't look for them if we're dead. Come with us
for now, Pollock.'

She sees the pain in Pollock's eyes. He's so practical
and fierce in nature that everyone thought he felt little for
the baby and Broomielaw. He's been hurting all this time.

Gorbals has taken back his hand and stuffed it in the
pocket of his sealskin coat. Mol grabs his arm before he
turns away. She grabs Pollock's arm too and forces them
into a handshake.

'Enough, you two,' she says wearily. 'Time to move on.'

BROKEN MIRRORS

Once everyone has had their fill of rich seal meat and is yawning, Tuck slides up close to Mara.

She turns to him with a tired smile. 'There's no power left, Tuck.'

'It's dead?'

'Till spring. It needs sunlight.'

'Me too,' sighs Tuck.

He digs in his pocket and holds out a closed fist to Mara.

She looks at it, puzzled.

Tuck turns his hand over and opens the palm. Mara leans forward to see. A small, three-cornered mirror, the shape of a boat sail, lies in the palm of his hand.

'The box,' says Tuck. 'Your little box with the mirror inside. Let me see.'

'Why?'

Tuck only smiles, so she rummages in her backpack and finds the wooden box Tain made for Granny Mary so many years ago. He gave it to Mara for her fifteenth birthday, her last birthday on the island, the last of her birthdays he'd ever see. She runs her fingers over the beautiful carvings on the lid, glad she didn't know that then.

'Open it,' Tuck urges.

In the instant she opens the lid, Mara understands.

On the inside of the box lid is a broken mirror. Mara remembers the moment she kicked it by accident across her bedroom, in a fit of temper, soon after Tain gave it to her. The mirror was left with a jagged crack across one corner but all the crashes and bumps the little box has taken in her backpack since then have crumbled the broken corner into fragments.

Tuck takes the box and blows away the fragments of mirror. He presses his three-cornered mirror into the lid. It's not perfect; he has to force it and there are gaps where the edges don't quite meet and the dark grain of wood shows.

'That's amazing.' Mara stares. 'It almost fits. Where did you find it?'

'My Grumpa gave it to me.'

Tuck pauses. 'You keep it,' he says. 'It belongs there. It bridges the break just fine.'

Mara looks into his eyes. 'Thanks, Tuck.'

'The wizz machine,' he hesitates. 'Mol said it holds the secrets of the past.'

Mara nods, looking at her reflection in the broken mirror for the first time in months. Eyes like midnight, Dad used to say, but there's an indefinable darkness that was never there before. The patched-up mirror makes a jagged tear across her face.

'What are the secrets of the past?'

Mara looks up and catches the hungry look on Tuck's face. She shrugs.

'Things people used to know before the world drowned. I'll show you when my power comes back.'

'Tell me now.' Tuck persists. 'What kinds of things? I want to know what else is inside the globe. What do *you* know about the past?'

Mara's heart jumps. The words are an uncanny echo of what Fox said to her the very first time they met in the Weave. She puts the thought from her mind and tries to answer Tuck, but that only takes her back to that disastrous trip with Fox on the World Wind and the chilling warning of the lone voice from the NASA satellite.

'People knew the world was growing hot,' she remembers. 'They knew the ice caps were melting and the oceans would rise but they ignored it. They made it all happen, I think.'

'The world's not hot.' Tuck touches her face with cold fingers and she laughs.

'Not here, right now. But the top of the world used to be a land packed with snow all year round.'

'This is the top of the world?' Tuck looks amazed.

Mara nods, remembering what Granny Mary told her and what she has worked out. 'Once upon a time the sea out there was solid ice. You could stand at the North Pole. It's still freezing cold in winter because there's no sun but it'll warm up in summer. It must do or the ice caps wouldn't ever have melted. In summer, there's no night. Imagine it, Tuck. We can lie in the sun all night long.'

In the summer, she will be able to meet Fox on the bridge all day and all night if she wants and never run out of power.

'Why did the world grow hot?' Tuck persists.

Mara shakes her head. She cannot explain something she barely understands herself. Then she has an idea.

257

She picks up a skull lantern and takes it over to the carvings on the cave wall. Gorbals is snuggling down to sleep but Mara calls him over and lifts the lantern to light up the story preserved in the rock.

'We should learn this story, Gorbals. The people who left this wanted us to know.'

Gorbals studies the carving with large, tired, owlish eyes. He scratches his head till his hair stands on end.

'Can you make it into a story? Tonight? Before we go?'

Slowly, Gorbals nods. 'Gather everyone around. I think I know this story. My mother told it to me.'

Once everyone is gathered, grumping and yawning, the urchins squabbling with tiredness, Gorbals begins.

'Once upon a time, before the world's drowning, people lived in cities that covered the lands of the Earth.' Gorbals points to the picture of the city. 'At night, the lights of the buildings and cars and buses and trains and planes sparkled like stars. But the sky grew dull with the dust and dirt from the city. Soon, it grew jealous of the city's sparkling lights. So the sky cried out to its mother sun and brother wind and sister ocean and asked them to brew up a storm of weather to punish the people of the world who had stolen its glory. And so they did.

'The sun beat hard upon the Earth. The wind and the ocean brewed up terrible storms. The people of the world cried for mercy and the weather answered that all would be well if they gave up their sparkling lights to the sky. But the people would not.

'So the sun burned ever hotter and the wind blew harder and the ocean rose up and snatched the lights of the world in its arms. Then the wind flung the world's lights up into the sky!

'And they're still hanging there, above us, like stars – all the lights that once lit up the world.'

There's an awed silence when Gorbals's story ends. The skull lights shiver on the moon-cave wall.

'Maybe one day they'll fall back to Earth,' says Fir.

It might not be exactly right, thinks Mara, but it's a strong and beautiful story that everyone will remember. It'll have to do for now.

'This story – is it a message from our landcestors?' Tuck asks, as the others settle back down to sleep.

Mara's eyes crinkle, puzzled. 'Our *what* . . . ?' Then she understands and smiles. 'Yes, it's a message from the past.'

Tuck leans close and lands a kiss on her mouth.

His lips are cold and unexpected. Mara jerks back, crashing her head on the cave wall.

'Don't.'

Now Tuck looks as if he's the one who cracked his head.

Mara steals a glance at him. All the salt crystals in his hair and his eyelashes are gone, though she still hears the wind and the ocean in his voice.

'I'm having a baby,' she falters. 'I love someone else.'

Tuck's hand strays to the cutlass handle. Mara sees and stares.

'Who?' he demands. 'Rowan?'

Mara shakes her head. 'He's an ocean away.'

Tuck relaxes. His hand slips from the cutlass. 'Well, that's no good. I'm right here.'

But when he tries to pull her close Mara pushes him away. Tuck shifts from foot to foot, unsure of his ground.

In the glow of the moon cave her hair gleams like an ocean slicked with oil. The skull light flickers in her dark eyes. She's feisty like his Ma but soft-faced like his little

259

sister Beth. And she knows things about the Earth and the past like his Grumpa did. She's a Lander with the ocean in her island blood. Her kiss tasted of the sea. Tuck knows she's the one for him, baby or not.

Yet she pushed him away.

He is not Fox.

But he's here and Fox is not. And more than that, there's something about Tuck she understands – a wayward spirit, a restless curiosity that has brought them both to this cave at the ends of the Earth. And yet . . .

He's not Fox.

His kiss wasn't cold and strange like Tuck's. Fox's kiss was a golden beam of energy that shot right through her and still tingles deep inside whenever she thinks about him. It's the difference between the moon and the sun.

And yet she is drawn to Tuck, this stranger she has found in a strange land who has something of the same fire in him as Fox, as herself, and who comes from her ocean world.

Mara lies down, exhausted by clashing thoughts and feelings and by the urgent, kicking life force of the baby. A thought nudges her. But she is sliding into sleep and it slips away.

Tuck waits until the fire is at its lowest ebb and every skull lantern has died. He slips as quietly as he can from the heap of rustling seaweed mats that are his bed and glances around the wide cavern. *All asleep.* He double-checks Rowan. He's snoring lightly. Ibrox is snoring hard. Before he turns to his task, Tuck creeps over and lifts the lid of a pot beside the fire. He delves into the hoard of light-makers that Ibrox stores inside the pot and takes the silver one he's had his eye on. It's a match for his silver eyebox. Tuck does a quick count. Eleven left. Ibrox won't miss one.

Now Tuck creeps over to Mara. He slides a hand between her body and the cave wall until he feels the bag that's wedged there. *Gently now.* He unzips the bag and slips his hand inside, feels the intricate carvings on the lid of the wooden box, the one with his broken mirror inside. But that's not what he wants. *Ah, here it is.* Tuck rolls out the globe and slips it into a deep pocket of his windwrap.

He's not looting, he's just taking a loan.

Man is a rope over an abyss.

Nietzsche

A MOMENT LEANING OUT OF TIME

Young Clyde, thin as a stick, crawls through the tunnel in the frozen waterfall. Everyone holds their breath, willing him to reach the other side. When he returns he is vague and nervy about what lies there. It's hard to see in the dark, he says. Mara's heart sinks. She'd been hoping there would be the miracle of light at the other side. How deep into winter or close to spring they are, she can't guess. Time has lost itself in the unending dark maze of the caves.

There might be light in the morning, she tells herself. This might be the middle of the night.

'Ready?' Rowan looks from face to face. 'Take it slowly. It'll be a tight squeeze.'

Mara is sure he is speaking to her most of all. She feels heavy and huge. Her sealskin coat has grown too tight and she had to swap it for a roomier parka they found in the tunnels. She has a horror of getting stuck.

But she will get through. She must.

A tense silence falls as they line up to crawl through the

tunnel in the wall of ice. Then Mol bends down with a cry and reaches into a nook of the cave. 'What's this?'

She pulls out a box covered with frozen moss and slime. Grabbing an axe, she kneels down to prise the lid open.

'What does this say?'

Mara tries to see but it's hard to bend with the bulk of the baby inside. Mol jumps up and shows her the name on the box.

'Tupperware,' Mara reads. 'Rowan, didn't your mum have one of these? She used to keep oatcakes in it.'

Rowan looks over her shoulder and his face softens as he looks at the box. 'She wouldn't throw it out. It belonged to my great-grandmother. It kept things fresh.'

Something inside the box shifts and rattles. There's a tight band around it that stretches and pings when Mol pulls it off.

'Keep that,' says Pollock, grabbing the stretchy band with interest.

It's not easy to prise off a lid that has been stuck fast for an age with winter ice and summer slime, but Mol shrugs off help. At last she breaks open the lid and stares into the box.

'What is it?' Mara demands, as Mol begins to cry in great, heaving sobs.

'I'm sorry,' she gulps. 'I lost all my cuttings from our Hill of Doves when the ship sank and I never thought I'd find anything to grow again.'

Mol holds out the Tupperware box for the others to see. It's full of seeds. The cold and the Tupperware seal have preserved them. Most still look good enough to plant.

Mara crouches beside Mol, ignoring her aching back.

She hugs her friend tight. It's not just the lost cuttings or this unexpected gift Mol is crying for. All the grief pent up inside for her lost life and for the loss of Candleriggs and Broomielaw and Clay and Partick has come pouring out over the box of seeds.

'They must have been left here for you.' Ibrox puts a fire-grizzled hand on Mol's head then pulls her to her feet. She seals the lid of the seedbox and tucks it securely inside her skin coat.

The skull light catches on words that have been gouged into the cave wall, right above the nook where Mol found the box. Mara peers at the message left in the stone:

THIS IS NOT HERE

But the seedbox is.

'A sign set in stone,' Mol exclaims. 'What does it say?'

Mara reads it out and they puzzle over the odd words.

'Was it written by the people who died here?' Mara wonders. 'Or by those who made it through?'

A jittery silence falls once again and Mara wishes she hadn't voiced her thought.

Pollock goes first. A hundred heartbeats pass before they hear him yell.

'OK?' Possil shouts into the ice tunnel.

'Ooooo,' Pollock's voice echoes back.

Possil sits back on his heels. 'He's through. Who's next? Hey, one at a time. No shoving, you lot!' he barks at the urchins. 'Scarwell, you can't take *him*!'

But Scarwell is already shoving her apeman into the hole in the ice. Where she goes, he goes too.

The urchins scrabble through the tunnel after her,

rattling with all the old world junk they have stuffed into the pockets of their clothes. One by one the others crawl through, with the caves' hoard of pots and utensils strapped to their backs. Tuck counts them as they go. *Twelve Treenesters, seven urchins.* Now only Mara, Rowan and Tuck himself are left.

He shifts anxiously from foot to foot.

'Mara, you go now.' Rowan gives her a quick hug. 'Take it easy. You'll be fine.'

She crawls into the tight space. The frozen air nips her face. Her back aches with the baby's weight. The tunnel presses in on all sides and she can only move slowly, her hands and knees slipping on the ice. Behind her, the light from the skull lanterns grows dim. She comes to a dark bend in the tunnel, can't seem to get around it. Can't move forward or back. Can't see a thing. She panics.

'I'm stuck!'

Rowan calls to her and though she can't hear what he says the sound of his voice calms her. She begins to slide her body around the curve of the bend, to push herself forward limb by limb. Before she knows it, Gorbals and Pollock are pulling her out at the other end.

Gasping and sweating, she leans against cold rock.

Starlight stings her eyes. The moon is in full sail above dark peaks. Mara stares at the enormous sky. They are at the other side of the mountain. They have made it through!

'All right?' Pollock is gripping her arm. 'But don't move. We're on a little shelf. Five steps from here the Earth falls away. I threw down a stone and it took ten fast heartbeats to land. If those ratkins don't stop squabbling, they're going to fall over the edge.'

Down beyond the ledge is a darkness so dense it might

be made of rock. Mara speaks sharply to the urchins to make them sit still. Rowan emerges from the ice and now there's only Tuck to come.

As they wait, the niggling thought that sleep nudged out of Mara's mind pops up again – the thought that Tuck must have been rummaging in her bag and looking at all her things. How else had he known she had a box with a broken mirror inside?

He can't go into the tunnel. He just can't.

The skull light glints on whorls of water stunned into ice. It looks like a frozen wave. Waves don't stay still, every gypsea knows that; they come crashing down. Every time Tuck tries to push his head into the tunnel fear sends him ricocheting back into the cave like the band that pinged off Mol's box of seeds. There is not a sniff of salt or sea in the air.

He can't go through. He's too much of a gypsea to live deep in the Earth, so far from the sea. But not much of a pirate or he'd be able to kill his fear. Yet he *must* force himself through the tunnel or he'll be left behind on his own.

To stir up his courage, Tuck rips his cutlass from its scabbard and clangs it once, twice, three hard times on the ice then lets out his best pirate yell.

The frozen waterfall answers with a deep, rumbling growl.

'Where's he got to?' Rowan is down on his hands and knees at the tunnel. A clang echoes through the ice. 'Tuck, what's up? Come on!'

'Listen,' cries Mol. 'What's he saying?'

Tuck is yelling something from the other end, but they can't hear what.

The Earth gives a roar so fierce Tuck's knees give way.

THIS IS NOT HERE, say the words above the nook of rock in front of him. It's the last thing he sees before the skull lantern is smashed by the fist of the Earth.

'He's scared,' Mol cries, 'You've seen how he is. The tunnels and caves terrify him, just like the ocean terrified us because we were Treenesters, used to our netherworld. It's the other way round for him. He must have taken fright. We need to go back and get him.'

From deep inside the mountain comes a rumble. In moments it has grown into a ferocious roar.

'*Urth!*' Pollock steals Tuck's favourite curse. 'Everybody move! Keep close to the rock wall but get away from here!'

'What's happening? *Tuck!*'

Possil grabs Mol and forces her to follow the others round a sharp bend. Mara is crushed between Rowan and the mountain as rock and ice hurtles down on to the shelf of rock they all stood on just moments before. Beyond the roar of the landslide, they hear the rocks and ice falling into the black abyss. They land so very far below they sound as harmless as a handful of pebbles chucked on a shore.

ONLY ALIVE

It feels like an age until the Earth roar ends. Once the last broken echoes die in the abyss, Ibrox begins calling out the names of the Treenesters, Mara and Rowan and the urchins.

'Are we all here? Is it only Tuck that's missing?'

Mol erupts.

'*Only* Tuck?'

'I didn't mean – Mol, I just meant that *we're* all here.'

'We're *not* all here. *He* isn't.' Mol pushes past Ibrox and runs back around the bend.

Mara follows her, ignoring the others' warning shouts.

Round the bend, she stops dead. The ice tunnel and the frozen waterfall are gone. Starlight pours down upon a fallen slice of mountain, a great clutter of rock.

Mol is on her knees at the place the tunnel mouth should be. *Tuck*, she sobs, again and again. Echoes of his name spill into the abyss.

With axes and bare hands, they all try to shift the huge rockfall. They pull away what rubble they can until there's another rumble and the land begins to slide once more.

Ibrox calls an urgent halt. 'We're going to bring it all down on our heads.'

They stand in stricken silence and wait for the Earth to settle. Then Ibrox kneels down beside the rockfall and calls Tuck's name one last time.

There's no answer, only a trickle of rock.

'He rescued me from the sea.' Gorbals's voice shakes. 'I should rescue him from the Earth.'

Mol turns to the mountain and batters her fist on it with a wail.

Mara feels numb. She knew Tuck was scared but was sure his curiosity, like hers, would overcome his fear. She can't believe that the very thing he dreaded has come true. She should have spoken to him before she went into the tunnel, but she was keeping her distance. What happened between them last night replays in her head. She begins to tremble as she feels the ghost of Tuck's cold kiss on her lips.

The baby kicks and turns inside her, oblivious to the world outside.

'Look,' says Rowan.

His eyes glitter with starlight or tears. Mara turns to see. Far away, a thin red fire burns in the black night.

'What is it?' Mara whispers. She imagines a phantom fleet of fiery pirates, all coming for Tuck.

'The sun,' says Rowan. He sounds choked. 'Tuck just missed the sun.'

The sun never rises above the mountains but its ember fire kindles in a twilight sky. The wind is flint-sharp after the vaporous fug of the moon cave. Starlight shocks eyes used to the darkness of the mountain caves. More shocking still is what the stars reveal.

The path they edge along is a wrinkle on the rim of a vast abyss. Far below, what remains of a glacier glimmers with a cold blue light. Mara can't begin to imagine the aeons of ice that gouged out such a deep, wide gorge.

When they stop to rest, she wonders how much longer she can go on. The pain in her back is grinding but every time she wants to cry or complain, she remembers poor Tuck. She can hardly bear to think of him crushed under so much rock. She must fix her mind on something else. Is there anything to give her hope? Mara scans the sky for the Star of the North. At first, she can't find it. Then she sees her sky markers: Queen Cass's zigzag crown and the Long-Handled Ladle. And there it is. The jewel that is dropping off Queen Cass's crown into the Ladle. The North Star, the sailor's steering star, the wanderer's lodestar.

Her anchor in the world. And for the first time she sees that the star is not pointing North. Now it's right over-head.

We're here at last.

NOT HERE

THIS IS NOT HERE, say the words that are gouged into the rock above his head.

Tuck wondered what they meant when Mara read them out. Now he knows.

The Earth has roared and smashed its fist. Now Tuck is trapped in that clenched fist. He thinks of the box of seeds that Mol found here in this very nook of cave. Maybe he, like the seeds, can survive until they dig him out. Surely they will.

Tuck makes his windwrap into a tent and huddles inside, trying to ease a trapped foot from the rubble.

This is not here, he decides, *and neither am I.*

He reaches into a pocket of his windwrap and feels the cold curve of the one thing that might have the power to keep him safe. He hugs it close, hoping any trickle of power that remains will save him from this savage Earth.

FROM THIS ABYSS

The moon is like a breath-misted mirror among the clouds that cling to the western peaks.

Mara slips a freezing hand into her backpack and finds the little wooden box. She pulls it out and opens the lid that Tuck tried to mend with his Grumpa's triangle of mirrored glass. Stars glitter in the cracked mirror until her breath clouds it. Mara closes the lid, wishing she could capture a boxful of starfire to keep herself warm.

She puts the box back in her bag then, as always, checks that her cyberwizz is safe. She feels the crescent of the halo but the globe must have rolled out of its inner pocket into the main part of the bag. The tiny wand is slotted inside the globe.

Mara's heart beats faster though she knows the globe must be there. She checked it twice last night before she went to sleep and she hasn't opened her bag since.

'What's up?'

Her frantic rummaging makes Rowan raise his head from his pillow of freezing rock.

'I can't find my globe.'

Mara begins to take out her only possessions, lays each

one on the ground. The cyberwizz halo, Tain's carved box, Charles Dickens's *A Tale of Two Cities*, the small black lump of meteorite she found in the netherworld museum. The clutch of herbs from her mother's garden are only crumbs now, their scent almost gone. The red shoes Candleriggs gave her are in Ilia, and her book on Greenland is at the bottom of the sea. She can account for each and every one of the precious things she brought from her island or found along the way, but the cyberwizz globe is not there.

She rummages again in the empty backpack, every corner. Searches the pockets of her clothes. But it's not there.

The globe is gone.

Mara slumps down against the rock wall of the mountain. Everything feels distant and unreal.

A voice with the roll of the ocean and the whinny of sea winds echoes in her head.

Mara closes her eyes.

I am not here.

'I see a beautiful city and a brilliant people rising from this abyss.'

Gorbals reads the words in a low, trembling voice by the light of the meagre fire Ibrox has kindled almost out of thin, cold air.

Mara hauls herself to her feet and staggers towards him. She rips *A Tale of Two Cities* out of his hands.

'*No*,' breathes Gorbals, thinking she's about to feed it to the fire. 'It's our only book.'

Mara flicks through the pages so harshly that she rips some, until she finds the page she wants.

'Far and wide lay a ruined country, yielding nothing but desolation,' she reads in a voice so bitter and harsh it

doesn't sound as if it's her own. She flicks the pages again. '*I see the evil of this time and of the previous time of which this is the natural birth.*'

She glares at the others but no one looks at her. They don't know what to say. Mol's head is on her knees and her arms are wrapped round her head.

Gorbals gets to his feet. There are tears in his eyes.

'*I see a beautiful city and a brilliant people rising from this abyss!*'

He chants the line over and over again, his voice growing stronger each time, until the glacier gorge is filled with the echoes of the words.

SNAKE IN THE STONE

Midnight is an empty place now that Mara never comes. Fox's only company are the hosts of owls that nest in the tower by day and flit like ghosts in the dead of night all across the netherworld.

Who you, they hoot in ghoulish voices, *who you, who?*

Once upon a time, after a day's work in the Noos, night was when Fox went prowling into hidden corners of cyberspace. That was how he first found Mara in the Weave. Now his days are spent finding food and fuel and water. In the evenings, between dozes and yawns, Fox crafts his plan with the utmost care. The rooks are now on constant security alert. Searching for cracks in the system is achingly slow, tentative work. It's all he can do to stay awake until midnight in the forlorn hope that Mara might come to the bridge. When she doesn't, he wanders the Weave's lonely boulevards or creeps out to forlorn nooks and crannies at the edges of the cybernight; but the thrill is gone and nothing feels the same.

Asleep, he dreams that he left on the ship with Mara. Awake, he wonders if part of him really did – if the wrench of her leaving split his cyberfox self from his realworld self, the one who is called David Stone. Maybe David is living at the top of the world with Mara. Maybe that's why he feels so lost and dead here.

Who you? hoot the owls and he wonders. Is he now a phantom Fox? He looks down at the drowned city that glimmers with eerie phosphorescence under the water. Has he, like it, become a netherworld ghost?

A wind full of stars gnaws his face as he stands at the tower window. A wind that feels as if it has travelled the oceans of the Far North. *My heart is with you*, he reads in an old, gold-edged book by someone called Ovid. *Only my husk is here.*

His husk has entered a state of winter, a cold and barren zone.

Candleriggs is weak. She misses her people badly and Fox knows he can't fill the gap so he doesn't even try. There's a scraping sound to her breathing and a waxy look to her face. Her large owl-eyes are dull and yellow and she sleeps a lot.

'I'll go and look for some dinner,' he tells her. If he doesn't, there's only the dandelion and rainwater soup that he hates, boiled up and thickened with the gluey bindings of books.

Candleriggs tells him that Molendinar's winter crop of root vegetables should be ready over on the Hill of Doves.

Fox makes the long trek down the stairs and through the many halls of the museum until he reaches the stone arches of the watery undercroft at the foot of the tower where the raft is tied to a pillar. Fox rows out across the stagnant sea of the netherworld towards the Hill of Doves.

He has tracked Mara's trails in the netherworld. He

279

has rowed over to the ancient cathedral and felt the peace of centuries preserved in its stone – and found the recent remains of bodies entombed there. He has explored the Treenesters' old home, the tiny island of the Hill of Doves, where Mara lived for a while.

A sudden wail of sirens catches him on the open water. Heart pounding, he drags on the oars to steer the raft in the opposite direction, away from the sirens towards the nearest shelter, the one place he has avoided all this time: a building with archways full of statues, topped with turrets and towers. It's here in one of the archways, so Candleriggs says, that Mara's face is carved in stone.

As the sirens reach a head-splitting pitch and the netherworld fills with the flashing lights of a fleet of sea police, Fox rams the raft into a nook in the turreted building and loops the rope around a jutting piece of stone. Knotting the rope, he sees that the stone is a hand, reaching out into thin air. His heart thuds harder. He draws back. The statue is up to its waist in water so he is on a level with the face. Time has weathered away the features but even so, Fox is sure it's not Mara.

Light flashes in his eyes and Fox drops flat on to the raft. Lasers and gunfire ricochet across the netherworld. Fox clenches every muscle. Is this how he is to die? Not in some glorious fight for a better world but here, for no good reason, on this rickety raft?

But the fleet of police on waterbikes is passing, with a huge white cargo ship in its wake. There's no way of knowing when the ships arrive. Their timings are kept random, Fox is sure, to thwart attacks by the boat-camp refugees. He clings to the raft as it crashes against the building, willing the stone hand that anchors him not to break. When the netherworld dims back into calm, he raises his head, sits up cautiously – and grabs the stone hand in fright.

A small body has washed up against the raft. Fox stares into the pale, unblinking eyes of a young child. He is so shocked he doesn't know what to do and in the moment he hesitates a wave hurls the child out of reach. He should untie the raft and – and what? Fox saw the black hole burned deep into the child's forehead: the wound of a laser gun. The child was dead.

He is still grasping the statue's cold hand as he watches the small body float away into the gloom.

Beyond the old stone tower, at the foot of one of New Mungo's vast trunks, the white cargo ship is unloading its goods under the protection of the sea police who killed the child. A new, hot, dark anger burns inside Fox. *This* is what his world does. Kills children like vermin when they get in the way. Mara's plight made him understand the kind of world he wants to fight for. Now he has seen for himself the callous inhumanity he is fighting against.

Already, the short day wanes. A fat full moon is rising above the city wall. Soon night lights will glow in the sky-city tunnels high above him – the very tunnels he used to skate through in his old life.

Above you.

Those strange, last words Mara spoke to him on the bridge. He still can't fathom what she meant. Was she trying to tell him to go back up there? Or telling him to remember why he's down here? Fox stares up at the sky city, feeling desperate. It's not Mara who may as well be dead; she's growing a whole new life. *He* may as well not be here.

Above him is his destiny. Could that be what she

meant? He has lost his way these last few months, grieving for the life he left and for the one he could have had if he'd gone with Mara on the ship. Well, he's done enough grieving. He can't bear to live this ghost life any longer, yearning for Mara and the baby he will never know.

The moon slides out from behind a tower. Its light falls on the faces of the statues in the archways. The oars *sloop* through the murky water as Fox moves around the building, studying each stone face. At last he stops. Draws in a breath.

There.

It's her. Mara. The statue is cracked and furred with moss but the likeness of the stone face is astonishing and true.

Fox wants to reach out and touch her face but he can't see a way to secure the raft. All of a sudden he knows what it is he must do now he is here. He must say a goodbye of sorts. He won't give up on her, he couldn't; he will leave a cyberfox to wait for her on the bridge in the Weave. But he must stop dwelling on the path he did not take. He needs to move on, grow his own new life.

What he must do, he sees, is turn all his pain into energy. He needs energy to do what Mara must have been urging him to do – not to dwell on her and the baby but push on hard to change the world right above his head.

Dreams can slip through your fingers like water. Crafting dreams into something solid and real, Fox now knows, is one of the hardest tasks in the world.

He studies Mara's statue; the dream that some long-ago craftsman, who never knew her, carved into stone. And he looks up at his grandfather's dream in the sky – a wonder of the world that is rotten at the core.

Something slithers and hisses at the mud-caked base of

282

the statue. Fox draws back. He raises his oar, ready to strike. Some slimy netherworld creature is coiled in a heap at Mara's stone feet.

In the dim light, Fox thinks it's a snake. The creature begins to uncoil, hissing louder. Fox stares at it through the gloom. It's huge. Better just row off, fast as he can.

The snake unfurls arms and legs from within the heap of itself.

Fox peers at what he thinks is a round, entirely human head with two large, bright eyes. The thing hisses, stands up, and chucks a handful of clay that hits him *splat!* on the head.

'*Hey*. Stop that!'

A child's giggle bursts out. The giggle is so full of sheer naughtiness it makes Fox smile, despite his dripping hairful of muck. He takes a clump of dirt out of his hair and flings it back. The child giggles again.

A child so caked in mud and dirt she looks as if she's made of clay.

THE CLAY CHILD

'I found her by Mara's statue.'

Candleriggs raises her head from her book. Her eyes
moisten when she sees the urchin beside Fox.

'Were you left behind, little one?'

The child hisses back.

'She doesn't talk, just does that hissy snake noise.'

Fox flops down on a lumpy heap of books in the
corner of the tower room that he has made his bed. The
journey across the netherworld and back has made him
dizzy and weak. His neck and arms ache from rowing.

'I didn't know what to do with her. She crawled out of
the water and sat at Mara's – I mean, the statue's – feet. I
think she's all on her own.'

He finds he can't speak about the other child, the dead
one.

'You found her at the Face in the Stone?' Candleriggs
looks startled then rummages on the floor among a scatter
of books. 'Now, where is it? I was reading a Greek legend . . .
it's such an old story it surely can't do me much harm.'
Candleriggs mutters, fumbling in a book.

Fox has to smile. She's surrounded by hillocks of

books, sleeps upon them, the floor is carpeted with pages and they burn them to keep warm, yet Candleriggs can't shake off her belief that books are dangerous things.

'Ah, here it is.' Candleriggs smoothes the page, so intent on the words of the story that she momentarily forgets her fears. 'The legend of Pandora, a child made of water and earth. Made of clay, really . . . and you found this clay child at *that* statue. That's important. Must be.'

Fox yawns. The old woman is fixated with signs in stones, with coincidence and what's meant to be – as if the future is all laid out, already set. Fox is clinging to the hope that the future is still up for grabs. He has to believe that, or why else would he be cooped up here in a cold stone tower in a netherworld with an ancient, owl-eyed Treenester and a child made of clay?

The urchin is staring at the fire, hissing. Before either of them can stop her she reaches out and picks up a glowing ember. And drops it, screaming, her hand singed.

'Hey, hey, come here.' Fox grabs a can full of rainwater and plunges the burned hand into it. The child wails at the top of her voice, a sound that mimics the sea-police sirens. Fox points to the fire and copies the siren noise. 'Don't touch.'

'You're a Pandora all right.' Candleriggs dips a corner of her mossy cloak in the rainwater and begins to clean the urchin's mucky face. 'Too curious for your own good.'

Candleriggs scrubs the urchin's clay-caked face and body. A green-eyed, wild-ringleted cherub emerges from layers of netherworld muck. In the firelight, when Candleriggs shows how to warm hands and feet by the fire without getting burned, Fox stares at the urchin's leathery, thick-downed skin and the faintest of webbing between her fingers and toes.

Once she's eaten some scrambled egg and spat it out in disgust, Pandora prowls the tower room, curious and wary. Fox eats her leftover egg and watches her grab an uncooked one and munch it, shell and all. When Fox laughs she snatches his green headgem from the bookshelf behind him, hissing like a snake. Fox smacks her fingers but Pandora won't let go of the gem. He has to force her fingers open. She bites his hand.

'No!'

Pandora just looks at him with beautiful green eyes and laughs. She points to the headgem that's the same colour as her eyes, with another hiss.

'What's the hissing for?'

'I don't know. She's copying something, as children do. The waste air that's pumped out of New Mungo, maybe? There's a waste pipe near the Face in the Stone. No, listen – she's speaking,' says Candleriggs.

Fox can only hear a serpent hiss.

'Whississss,' Pandora hisses, still pointing at the green gem.

'What's this?' Candleriggs's face creases into a thousand wrinkles as she smiles at the child.

'Thisss,' says Fox, imitating the hiss, 'iss mine. Iss not a toy.'

'Ah, but I've got a toy,' declares Candleriggs.

She digs into a pocket in her mossy cloak and brings out a little wooden snake, hardly bigger than her hand. The snake is made of a train of short stubs of wood, linked on a string, so that it wriggles whenever it's moved. The greenish tinge the wood has been stained with has almost all rubbed off.

'Whississss.'

'It's a toy snake. See? Sssss.' Candleriggs runs the

286

wooden snake up Pandora's arm. The little girl squeals with delight and grabs it. 'It was my son's,' says Candleriggs, laughing. 'I made it for him when he was a baby. You can play with it now,' she tells the child.

Candleriggs has a son? One of the Treenesters who have gone with Mara?

Candleriggs reads the surprise on Fox's face.

'He died when he was a baby.'

Fox takes this in. 'You had a baby with my grandfather? Is that what you mean? And he still threw you out of the city? With his own baby? What kind of a man could do that?'

Anger flashes through him. The thought of Mara with his baby, an ocean away, haunts Fox night and day.

'Caledon never knew,' says Candleriggs. 'It was my revenge. But revenge didn't do me any good when my baby died,' she pauses, her eyes bitter and dry, 'of an infected mosquito bite.' Candleriggs gives Fox a look that makes him shiver. 'Maybe he'd have looked something like you, if he'd lived.'

Everything might have been so different. What if Candleriggs hadn't rebelled against the New World, where people are safe in their sky-city havens and everyone else, like Mara, is abandoned in the drowned world? If Candleriggs had stayed with Caledon and her baby had lived, his grandfather would never have married his grandma. He, Fox, wouldn't have been born at all.

Fox has a glimmering of all the great and small flukes of fate, all the twists and turns in the lives of his ancestors, that must have happened to cause him to be born, to be alive, here, at this point in the world.

He's hungry, miserable, his life is a wreck, and the idea that he could change things seems like a mad fantasy. The temptation to go back home is huge, to plead for forgiveness from his family and claim his disappearance was just a teenage prank that got out of hand. Night after night, too cold to sleep on his lumpy mattress of books, he's on the verge of giving in. But he always comes back to Mara. Mara and a ship of refugees at the top of the world. Wasn't it a mad fantasy to think she could do that? Wasn't it a mad fantasy of his grandfather's to imagine up a whole New World of skyscraping cities studded across the globe of a flooding world? Yet he made it real and became the Grand Father of All the New World. His grandfather and Mara both chased their dreams and made them real.

'Your parents,' Candleriggs interrupts his thoughts. 'They must be missing you, worried sick.'

It's not the first time she's said it. She keeps urging him to post them a note in the Noos, at least.

'I hardly knew them,' says Fox, aware as he says it that he's put his parents behind him, in the past. 'They were never there. Their work came first.'

The idea he's been crafting all this time feels like mad fantasy too. But maybe, just maybe, it'll work. The Noos is more ruthlessly guarded than ever before, but Fox knows that trying to police cyberspace is like trying to police the universe. You can't. And now he has created a new wonder for the stunning cyber-universe of the Noos.

A galaxy of peekaboo moons.

He found the idea in old Weavesites: pesky adverts that pop-up in your face. Yet the occasional one would catch his eye and he'd be curious to see what it was about. So Fox has created another kind of pop-up: a peekaboo at a buried past and an unknown world of the present that exists just beyond the city walls. It's a pesky pop-up of brutal truth the people of the New World need.

Someone, surely, will take a look to see what his peek-aboo moons are about. The bored and the too-curious, the brilliant and the lonely. Some daredevil Noosrunner like he once was, who still has a glimmer of wonder and might stop for an instant amid the frenzy of invention and cyber-trading that engrosses the New World.

That's who Fox is seeking. People of a mind like him. In the unguarded moment they stop to take a look, their godgem is open to him. That's his chance to sneak a secret connection with the godgems of all the curious minds. All he can do is hope there are such people left in the cosseted cities of the New World.

If there are, he'll pop them a shock of truth.

I chased the clouds of my Thrawn Glory
Looking for my Kingdom Come
Slip the chains of Fate
Don't tell me it's too late

'My Thrawn Glory' by James Grant

A man's reach should exceed his grasp or what's heaven for?

Robert Browning

THE TECHNOLOGY
OF A WORM

The globe is a dead and useless thing. It has no power to get him out of here.

Tuck wriggles inside the tent he's made of his windwrap as something trickles down his neck. A fragment of the rockfall that traps him, or an insect, he can't tell.

An insect.

Tuck has been trapped long enough to latch on to the slightest slither of thought. He gave up counting heartbeats once he reached twelve thousand and after that there was nothing else to count. He doesn't know much about insects. There were few in Pomperoy. Lots of woodworm though.

Worms. They live in the Earth as well as in wood. Maybe it's a worm that's gone down his neck.

He waits, feels nothing except the pain in his trapped foot, but a thought slides out of a corner of his mind.

Worms and insects. Dead insects. Dead, black insect words.

The book.

Tuck rummages in the pockets of his windwrap, willing the book not to be lost. In one of his pockets he finds a trickle of small, smooth stones. They run through his fingers and Tuck remembers with a shock what they are: the seven pearls that Pendicle gave him on the day Ma died. He'd forgotten all about them. Tuck's heart beats faster. It feels like a sign. But a sign of what?

Great Skua, this is not the day *he's* going to die.

What about Pendicle? Is he loose on the ocean or safe back at the rig? Or is he lost at sea just as Tuck is lost at Land? And the bridgers? What about the rusted barges and ferries and the leaky old *Waverley*? Did they all survive the harsh oceans of the Far North?

What folly to rush headlong after the *Arkiel* like that. Pomperoy acted on pirate impulse with no thought to what might happen or how to get back if it all went wrong. Just as he rushed headlong to Land.

Don't build a bridge into thin air, Tuck.

An old bridger saying that Da used to quote. Before, it was just words but now Tuck understands.

He's found the book in a pocket and grips on to it, visualizing the tatty cover in his hands, its words like thick black oil. He fixed those words in his head.

NATURAL ENGINEERING by C. D. STONE

There were worms and insects in the words and pictures of the book.

Tuck *is* trying to build a bridge out of thin air – to every dead insect word and every picture from the dark days and nights when Gorbals read to him by skull light. He knows there are three hundred and thirty-seven pages and forty-two pictures, but remembering what's in them is hard. Tuck tries to turn each page in his mind, pages upon pages on the dam-building of beavers, the web-weaving of spiders, tower-building of termites, nest-knitting of birds, the industry of ants – and the tunnelling of worms.

The tunnelling of worms.

THE ROWAN TREE

The sun takes another golden footstep into the sky, climbing higher each day as they make their way through the vast glacier gorge. The wheel of the year is turning, winter slowly rolling towards spring. But the journey through the gorge is so gruelling that Mara wonders why she brought everyone to such a place.

Why didn't she stay in the caves? Why didn't she stay with Fox? Why didn't she stay on the island and drown? Drowning in her own comfortable bed on Wing often seems preferable to this: a moment-by-moment struggle, fighting brutal winds along the perilous wrinkles of rock that the glacier has scraped into the mountain face. The baby grows heavier by the day, sapping her energy, making a back-aching agony of every blistered step.

Sometimes she wishes she was Tuck, crushed to death in an instant in the caves.

They have climbed right down into the pit of the glacier gorge. It's a place so deep and gloomy the light of the low sun never reaches its ancient ice. Now they have to climb up the other side of the gorge and hope against hope that they find a break in the rock face there, that there are cave tunnels or a mountain pass that will lead them through the mountain to the interior. Mara can't let herself wonder what it will be like there, whether it will be a place they can survive or not.

All she can do is survive here and now, one breath, one step, at a time.

A shrieking wind roams the glacier gorge. It's so harsh that Mara wonders if this is the very source of the North Wind. It fades to bitter whispers as they climb. They take a break in the shelter of a cave where they eat slivers of seal meat, washed down with thin, bitter soup made with lichen scraped from the rocks and boiled up with seal fat in chunks of ice.

Mara's exhausted mind is spooked by the whispering winds in the gorge. She dozes and dreams that the North Wind has hurled the lost secrets of the drowned world into the glacier gorge and imprisoned them in its icy home.

'Another tree!'

Fir is on her feet, pointing at the roof of the small cave, at a tree root entombed there in the stone.

'Long dead,' says Tron.

'But it's a *tree*.' Fir turns to Mol. 'A stone-telling.'

Mara closes her eyes. She's had enough of stone-tellings and signs.

And yet, when she falls back into her doze, her dreams are now crowded with trees. Candleriggs' great nest in the oak tree on the Treenesters' Hill of Doves. The Athapaskans in their boreal forests, around the curve of the Earth, near the top of the world. In the dream she's back on Wing, digging up slabs of peat for the fire. The peat is packed with ancient tree roots that made the soil so rich. The dream turns into nightmare as she's whisked off

297

the island by a screaming wind. Pain grips her as she's ripped from the ground, from her roots.

She wakes up. She can still feel the hot pain in her back and all down her legs.

Rowan is crouched over her, his blue eyes full of worry. 'OK? You cried out in your sleep.'

'Bad dream.'

She doesn't tell him about the pain. It's almost gone now, anyway. She's thinking about her dream and how, like the green wind, trees are the key to the future. She's not sure how but she feels it in her bones.

Rowan stirs up the fire embers and warms her a ladleful of the lichen soup.

'What were you dreaming about?' he asks.

'Trees.' She sips the bitter soup.

'Trees?'

'Yup. We need trees.'

'You've got one right here.'

Mara looks up at the petrified tree root in the stone roof of the cave.

'We need live ones.'

'That's me.'

She looks at him, puzzled, then laughs. Rowan, of course.

'I forgot you were a tree. A rowan tree.'

She sees how he has shed the last of his boyhood. His shaved hair has grown back a much darker blond than it used to be. Always tall and lean, his face and limbs are sharpened by months of hunger and trauma, as her own must be. The ice wind has blazed colour on his cheeks, as the sea wind once did, and his carefree blue eyes are now sharp as flint. Though he's changed, he looks more like

Rowan from the island again than the wasted wreck he was on the *Arkiel*.

Mara sees what the change is. He looks like one of the island men.

'Protector against bad things.' Rowan makes a rueful face. 'Huh. Lots of people on Wing used to have a rowan tree outside their house, did you know that?'

Mara didn't. There were no trees at all on the island in their lifetimes.

'They cut them all down before we were born. My mum called me Rowan after the tree outside her bedroom window when she was small. She cried the day they chopped it down. She said its red berries cheered up the winter and when I was born I was as red as a rowan berry.'

Mara laughs again. Then groans as a sudden deep pain grinds into her back and grips her inside.

Blue eyes meet hers. He is trying hard to look like a protector from bad things but she knows he is just as scared as she is. Mara puts her head down on her back-pack as the pain recedes and tries to ignore the baby's kicks and punches, tries not to think about the pain coming back or the journey through the mountain pass that lies ahead.

KINGDOM COME

The fever strikes as sudden as a winter storm, though Fox has been off-colour and achy all day. He's in the thick of the bookstacks, reading about the creation of nations by flickering mothlight, when the headache strikes and his body is gripped by invisible chains of fire and ice. His skin is shot with hot needles, his stomach spasms with pain and he can't seem to find his way back through the maze of adjoining book rooms to Candleriggs and the part of the tower they've made their home.

Was it something he ate? What did he eat?

Dizzy, Fox grips the edge of a bookshelf. He tries to hold on to the dream kingdom he's been building inside his head. A dream of a cybercity, a place that doesn't exist in realworld, created only of ether and ideals. A gathering of energy in cyberspace, strong enough to cause vibrations of change in the real world. Fox loses his grasp of the dream as the real world seems to tremble, now, as his body tries to burn the sickness out.

He lies between the bookstacks, too ill to move, on a bed of wrecked books. Under the shelves by his head is a pebble-like object covered in dust so thick it looks like fur.

Fox reaches out and grabs it. Wipes off the dust with his thumb. It's sleek and black and flicks open easily. There's a small screen and a keypad inside. What is it? Some old world computer or communicator? Fox presses all the keypad buttons but it's out of power, just like him.

He stares at the glossy screen and all he sees is his own gaze reflected back. Fox can't believe the haunted eyes that peer from a mess of matted hair belong to him.

He feels so ill and disorientated he's frightened. He calls out for help but no one comes. His can't remember where his godgem is. If he had it, he'd send an SOS to his grandfather in the Noos because something awful is happening, he's dying, he's sure.

When he's home in New Mungo and all better he'll demand an airship to go North and find Mara and bring her back. After all, his grandfather is the Grand Father of All the New World, he can do anything. Surely he'll do that for the grandson he loves.

A beautiful child with green eyes, the colour of his godgem, flits into his vision and his head fills with a hiss of white noise. He can't quite remember who she is. The lantern of glowing moonmoths is by his head and as he falls deeper into fever Fox thinks it's his legion of peekaboo moons. They've homed back to him here, among the tower bookstacks.

They're answering his call.

A NARWHAL HORN
IN THE SKY

Day breaks like a spell, the air as sharp and clear as glass. All around them, as they climb, is the crack of icicles breaking off the frozen waterfalls.

'Just as well we got out of that gorge when we did,' mutters Ibrox. 'Wouldn't want to be down there when these waterfalls burst into full pelt.'

They scramble through a chaos of rock. For the first time, the sun almost manages to heave itself over the mountain peaks but gives in at the last gasp. Mara does no better. She can't go any further. Not until the pain that is slicing through her subsides. She leans against a rock, willing the pain to pass.

There's a shout from up ahead, then a volley of excited cries.

'Just a few steps further, Mara,' Mol pleads.

What have they found? Mara forces one foot in front of the other until she makes it into the mountain pass, a gully between two high peaks.

At the far end of the gully she sees what looks like a church steeple. Mara's heart jumps. Bewildered, she rubs the sweat out of her eyes and looks again. No, it's a spiralling narwhal horn, pointing straight up into the blue ocean of sky.

'That rock – it's like a dead giant's finger,' murmurs Fir. 'Are there giants in this land?' She grabs Mara's arm in fear.

It's not a church steeple or a narwhal horn or the finger of a dead giant, but a spire of rock as tall as the steeple of Fox's netherworld tower.

'Water!' Voices ricochet off the gully rocks. 'Water, like a great *sea* . . .'

'Hear that, Mara?' Mol urges, pulling her on. 'We're nearly there.'

Mara hears through a surge of pain. The stomach cramps have been growing stronger and stronger. Now the pain is suddenly red-hot and ripping, as if the baby has grown talons and is clawing her insides.

'Stop it,' she mutters through clenched teeth. Amazingly, the baby obeys and the pain subsides.

The others are at the far end of the gully, running towards the rock spire just beyond. She can see little Wing's bright blue snow suit, bouncing through the gully like a ball.

The baby starts up another agony of talon-clawing her until–

'Ow, w-water!'

'Nearly there, slow-slug.' Mol laughs, then she sees Mara's face and stops dead.

'Something's happening, Mol, something's wrong . . .'

'Oh, Mara.' Mol looks at the hot gush on the ground at Mara's feet and sees what's wrong. '*That* water. It's all right. It's what happens.' But Mara hears the crack of fear in Mol's voice, sees the paling of her face as she yells at the top of her voice to the others. 'Come back! Quick, every-one, help!'

'*What* happens?' Mara gasps, but she is remembering the island women's birth talk.

'*This* happens when the baby's ready to come.'

Mara nods. Of course it does. She just didn't expect it to happen to her, right now.

'We should have talked about it.' Mol's face furrows with anxiety as she takes Mara over to a sheltered shelf in the rock face. 'I thought we had more time.'

'We have – it's too soon – I'm sure it's not time yet – *oh*.'

In a lull between peaks of pain, Mara tries to count months on her fingers then stops as the pain surges back. She has no idea, anyhow, what month this is.

'The baby doesn't think it's too soon,' says Mol briskly. 'All this climbing might have brought on the birth.'

Mara grips on to a rock as shards of pain break inside her.

'Stop gawping, you lot,' Mol shouts. '*Do* something.'

'What?' says Gorbals. They all look blank with panic.

'Oh, just go away,' Mol sighs. 'Useless bunch of dubyas. I'll deal with it.'

Gratefully, the others disappear – all except Ibrox, who makes up a fire in silence, and Fir, who twitters nervously as she breaks icicles from rocks and puts them in a pot to boil. And Rowan, who crouches by Mara's side.

'Go away,' Mara whimpers. 'I want my mum.'

'So do I,' sighs Rowan. He ignores her and stays.

'Hold her hand,' instructs Mol.

And in the undulations of pain and fear that follow, Rowan's hand is the one and only thing that roots Mara to herself.

A HOLE IN THE DARK

Great Skua, he's through!

Bashed and smashed and scraped and bruised, yet he's wormed out of the Earth just like he used to wriggle out of a Salter's grip. He was lucky too. His little nook was near the edge of the landslide and after an age of tunnelling he made his escape.

Now he's stuck in the blind dark. Tuck tries not to panic and feels in the pockets of his windwrap for the little silver firebox he looted from Ibrox. His trembling fingers fumble uselessly on the switch, again and again, until finally the miracle of a tiny flame burns a bright hole in the dark.

Tuck whimpers with relief. He limps around the cave, hurting his crushed foot, but it doesn't matter, he's free! Well, nearly. He scrambles across rubble, kicking up dust, searching for an exit tunnel, and begging The Man, though he's an ocean away by now, to help him find a way out. And he does! Tuck's tiny flame shivers on the upsidedown grin of a skull. Tuck grabs it and lights the small chunk of driftwood inside.

Now he can see the way through the dust and rubble

into the tunnel. All he has to do is follow the trail of bone crosses back to the hot spring. Beyond that, the way is marked with amber fire stones.

Tuck can hardly believe it. Soon he'll be outside under the sky with the ocean wind in his face, not trapped here deep inside the Earth.

He'll be out in the world again, free at last!

THRAWN GLORY

Fox wakens in a slice of sun as it breaks over the city wall. He feels the fuzz on his chin and the fur on his tongue and wonders if he's been asleep for a day or a week. Slowly, he remembers the burning fever, the terrible sickness and the pain gouging his stomach but it all feels distant as if it happened in a bad dream. What was it? A bad egg or some disease from the filthy netherworld sea?

Or the urchin child. She is real. She isn't a fevered dream. She eats rats and birds. Has she given him some disease?

Where is she? Where's Candleriggs? Fox looks around him. Where is *he*?

This is not the usual tower room. He's lying in a sick-crusted bed of paper below a wrecked bookstack labelled *History*.

Gingerly, Fox sits up. He peels off a layer of loose pages that are stuck to his back. He is so fuzzy-headed it takes him some time to find his way through the mess and maze of wrecked bookstacks to the tower room he's made his home with Candleriggs. So weak is his voice that when he tries to shout only a crackle comes out.

'Candleriggs?'

She's not here, only the urchin child, hiding inside a small cave she's built out of books.

Fox kneels down by the child. *Pandora.* The name crawls out of his memory, as if he's been gone a hundred years.

'Where's Candleriggs?'

Blood and a crust of sickness are spattered all down the creases of the knotted tunic Candleriggs made for the child out of the litter of plastic bags. Pandora must have been ill too, but what's the blood? She looks pale and her gem-green eyes are shadowed and scared. Fox sees the dead mouse on the ground that she's been eating. He swallows a surge of nausea.

'Candleriggs!'

He's panicking now. Something's wrong. Candleriggs wouldn't leave Pandora alone eating dead mice.

Pandora points at a mound of books she has made under the tower window at the other side of the room. Fox stares at the gnarled foot that pokes out.

He digs away books, hurling them all over the room until Candleriggs's face is clear.

The only other time Fox has seen death was the shot urchin in the water. That was brutal; this is not. The deep lines on Candleriggs's face have softened as if she is deeply at rest, but death is not something that can be mistaken for sleep. There's no life, no breath, just stillness in a golden lozenge of sun.

She's not there.

Candleriggs is gone.

She left him a note, scribbled in the margins of a book with a bit of charred wood from the dead fire.

Go back to your people. This is all wrong. Maybe it was

enough that Mara found you and I lived long enough to know you, and you could know the truth of the abandoned world. There's nothing you can do from here, I see that now. You've lost too much and there is so much more to lose. Take the child and go back home. Change your world from the inside. Tell Caledon

And there it stops. What she wanted to tell his grandfather has been lost to death or the impossibility of finding the right words.

There's a charred circle around some words in the book.

We shall be as a city on a hill, Fox reads. *The eyes of all people are upon us.*

They are the long-ago words of an Englishman, John Winthrop. He wrote them, the book says, on board a ship called the *Arbella* in the middle of the Atlantic Ocean. He was one of the Founding Fathers of a new world in another age.

Fox stares at the words. Walks over to the window. He looks up at the gleaming towers that dwarf the old world tower he stands in and hears the misery that carries on the wind from the boat camp all around the city walls.

He doesn't really know what the words mean or why Candleriggs wanted him to have them. Maybe, though, they weren't for him. Maybe they're for his grandfather in his city high above. And Candleriggs is right. Though he hardly knows his own parents Fox knows they'll be broken-hearted, as his grandfather will.

Maybe he wants them to be.

Just what *is* he doing here? Getting back at his parents for not being around? Kidding himself that one person in a tower can change a whole world?

We shall be as a city on a hill.

Fox finds the bucket of rainwater. He splashes his face and gulps handfuls of the cold water until his head clears.

He remembers his fever-dream of going back to the sky city, demanding an airship to find Mara at the top of the world. In the throes of deep fever Fox was certain his grandfather, so thankful to have him back safe and sound, would do that for him.

Fox looks over at the dead body of the woman his grandfather once loved yet abandoned in the drowned world. All because she stood against him and challenged the cruelty of his world. Fox knows his fever-dream was fantasy. When the world he created is threatened his grandfather is ruthless, even to those he loves. The evidence is here, right before his eyes.

The only way Caledon would have him back is if Fox denies the truth of the world outside.

How can he? Mara is living the truth he'd have to deny.

We shall be as a city on a hill.

The long-ago words keep haunting his thoughts, recalling his idea of a cybercity, a place with no state in realworld. A place that only exists in the ether because its citizens will it to be.

And what would it be, this secret city, entered through the portal of a peekaboo moon? A place that would open its doors to the truth of the past and the present – to Candleriggs's and Mara's existence, and the life of his baby to come, and to all the lost people of the drowned world.

But though Fox popped a legion of moons into the Noos, no one has answered his call.

It's no use. He can't create a city on his own. And if he did? He reads Candleriggs's message once again. What more there is to lose? Candleriggs kept trying to make him think about the consequences of his plans. *Once you've shocked them with the truth about the outside world,* she'd ask, *what then?* Now, with her dead beside him, Fox feels bound to ask himself the questions he always avoided before.

What would revolution really mean? His heart quickens as scenarios tumble through his mind. For the first time Fox sees that it might not be such a grand and glorious task.

He looks at his torn, grubby fingernails and the netherworld grime ingrained in his skin. It might be vicious, dirty work. Wrecking the old order means destruction.

Fox looks at the towers above him. How much wreckage and destruction justifies the creation of a better world? Could he be sure it would be better? What if the new order were just as corrupt and hooked to power as the old? What if they became so?

There is one question he cannot avoid any more.

What if people died?

Could he live with that?

Mara has to live with guilt of the deaths of people she loved dearly. But they were a mistake. Wouldn't any deaths caused by his revolution be the same? A horrible but necessary consequence of his attempt to rescue the future?

But would Mara ever have left Wing and sailed to New Mungo if she knew it would mean those deaths? *Never.* And yet he is contemplating something with consequences that are just as unknown, involving countless lives.

What if he begins something he cannot control?

What if he does nothing when he could be the catalyst for a new world?

The eyes of all people are upon us.

311

How many deaths, Fox asks himself, would justify the creation of that world? Many or none? Well, Candleriggs, he thinks, I've faced the hard questions but haven't found answers. The final question, Fox knows, is the darkest of all.

What if that's the only way?

In the depths of his fever he thought he heard Mara calling him.

Where are you? he tried to shout.

Above you, came the answer.

Trapped in the fever, he couldn't find her but now he understands what she really said.

Not *above you.*

I love you.

Fox wants to rush and see if, by some miracle, she's on the bridge right now. She is the one person left in the world who might help him with all the questions that are churning him up inside. But there's something he must do first. Nothing in his life has prepared him for this. In the New World, old age and death are dealt with invisibly and tidily behind the Youthnasium's doors.

His hands shake so much it's hard to begin, but Fox makes up a fire exactly as Candleriggs taught, with her flint stones and dry pages from the books. Pandora's green eyes watch through her tangled blonde locks. She hisses with unease, *whississ*, clasping her toy snake tight while he works on the fire until it's fierce and strong and thick smoke fills the small tower room. He tidies every book and scrap of paper from the stone floor and adds them to the fire. Eyes streaming, he takes Pandora by the hand and shuts the heavy oak door on Candleriggs and her blazing funeral pyre.

And it sometimes happens that the stone breaks into flower in your hand.

George Mackay Brown

THIS DAY FOREVER

She is born in a sunbeam, in a flame of agony, just before the sun sinks.

From the moment Mara first sets eyes on her daughter's face, on the soft mouth that opens and closes like a little fish, on the waxy eyelids that flicker like moth wings in the weak candle of spring and on the fox-tawny down of hair, she knows the baby is not the hostile presence she had begun to fear, especially in the tearing hot pain of her birth.

She is the most perfect and beautiful thing Mara has ever seen on this Earth.

A HUNDRED BRIDGES

Stunned by sun, Tuck catapults back into the cave.

He thought the darkness was thinning, but after a sea-son spent in deep night the last thing he expected when he turned the fifty-sixth tunnel bend was a dart of such eye-stinging sun.

Tuck rubs his shocked eyes. A galaxy of sunspots flashes in his head. Shading his face with one hand, the other gripping on to one of the rock spears sticking up from the cave floor, he peers round the very last bend.

Reels of copper light lie like metal rods across the waves in the fjord. The salt wind is in his face and Tuck's spirit soars as he stares at the sunlit sea.

His jaw drops. His heart beats hard. Tuck scrubs the wind-tears from his eyes and looks again, but the light has shifted and the vision, or whatever it was, has already passed.

Yet for a moment there, he saw the most astonishing thing.

The rods of sun, with the waves running through them, seemed to forge into a network. Tuck rubs his eyes again.

He knows it was only a trick of his salt-stung, sun-stunned eyes but for an instant he'd swear, by the eyes of The Man he would, that what he just saw was the glint and weave of bridges.

Bridges, all across the water!

A hundred bridges! Linking the islets of the fjord.

That would beat his Da's seventy-three. Tuck imagines the trademark Culpy crescent branded on every one.

What was that gypsea saying Ma would always nag at him?

Take your father's windwrap and step out into the wind.

Now he sees that Ma was only telling him to loot the best of what his Da had given him and make it his own. If she'd nagged a bit less maybe he'd have listened to what she was trying to say. Well, now he understands.

Breathing heavy and hard, Tuck counts each of the looted and gifted treasures in the various pockets of his windwrap. The vision of the bridges is so strong in him, it's shaken him to his roots. Counting always calms him down.

He'd counted twelve thousand heartbeats trapped in the earthfall. There in the dark, Tuck suddenly knew why he has always counted out the world. It gives him a grip of things his weak eyes don't always reach – and a grip of the world when it feels beyond him.

Maybe now it's within his grasp. Maybe the *Arkiel*'s sinking of *The Grimby Gray* opened up a gateway to the world he would never have had if he was still there with Ma.

Tuck fingers the pages of the book on natural engineering, the cold metal of the camera and the firebox, and the seven tiny moons that are Pendicle's pearls. There's the tiniest tingle in his fingertips when he touches the egg-smooth surface of Mara's globe, with all the secrets of the past nesting inside. And he has his cutlass in its wire-woven scabbard, hanging from his belt.

He misses the smooth glass of Grumpa's three-cornered mirror. It fitted snug and sharp into the crease of his palm. That's gone with Mara, along with a broken piece of his heart. He's got her globe so they're quits, he supposes, though Urth knows he didn't mean to loot it, he was always going to give it back. But he can't now there are mountains between them and a landslide of fallen rocks.

The pirate in him was snuffed out somewhere deep inside Earth. There wasn't too much to snuff out. He's not enough of a pirate to beat the things that make him quake. Things like ice tunnels and unsalty air and the inside of Earth.

He can't be a gypsea now either because he's Landed.

So who am I? What am I now?

The beautiful vision of the bridges glistens in his mind's keep-pocket, beside his memory of the gem that is the Earth. Tuck limps out of the cave mouth and climbs down on to the rocky shore. He lets the salt wind gust through him, overcome with a sharp joy just to be on the outside of Earth once again.

A huge sky billows above the ocean, stacked high with night clouds. The sun has died behind the mountains of Ilira but it'll be back – Tuck is almost certain it will – at the other side of night.

He tugs his windwrap around the warm clothes he took from the caves. The salty gusts blow the dust of the Earth from its folds. He remembered who the windwrap once belonged to when he was tunnelling through the earthfall in the mountain, with an instinct that he never knew he had. It's the windwrap of one of the best bridge-builders Pomperoy has ever known.

In the faded blue windwrap that was his father's, with pockets full of treasure, Tuck limps into the wind and heads for Ilira.

The place of fearful awe.

THE LAND OF DAY

Iceberg ships and castles sail the interior sea under a vivid sundown sky.

So vast is the water that the mountains on the furthest shores can't be seen. If it wasn't for the air, sharp as glass without a tang of salt, Mara would believe that the rolling waves belong to the ocean, not a lake cupped in the middle of a land.

'Trees,' whispers Mol. 'I can smell them on the wind. I'm sure I do. Can't we go to the trees?'

Ibrox has already sparked a meagre fire in a shelter of rocks and Mara hardly has the energy to move. Mol has taken Wing's telescope to scan the shores of the lake.

'There!' She thrusts the telescope at the others. 'Look over there!'

The trees of a young forest hunch together in a valley that leads down to the interior sea. Thick, dark, arrow-shaped trees bend in the wind over a scattering of bare silvery ones. The mountains on either side lean over them like austere parents.

'Where there are trees, there are birds and animals,' says Possil.

'Food,' says Pollock, in case anyone misunderstands.

'It'll be more sheltered there,' says Fir. She pulls Tron's arm around her. 'I want to be *warm* again. I miss the hot spring.'

'The fire,' shouts Ibrox. 'I need something to burn. First things first.'

'This *is* the first thing,' snaps Mol. She's grey with tiredness and her eyes keep blurring with tears, Mara sees, and knows it's because they've made it here but Tuck has not. But still, Mol won't let up on the trees.

'Who are we if we're not Treenesters any more? Who are we now?' she demands.

'This must be the land I dreamed of on the ship, only I never imagined a place so . . . so . . .' Gorbals stares out at the darkening lake. For once, he doesn't have words for what he sees. 'This is the land of Mara.'

'So we're Marans now,' says young Clyde. 'Not Treenesters.'

Mara has to laugh.

'We sound like aliens. I think I'll stay a Longhoper.'

'It *looks* like another planet,' says Rowan. 'Or the moon.'

Ice has sculpted the mountains into infinite strangeness: chaotic cathedrals of stone. A frenzy of spires and turrets, worm-eaten lattices of rock, snow-packed crevasses and vicious, staccato peaks. The great spire of rock that looms high above them points to the Star of the North, just as the narwhal horns did in the ocean. The lake, full of fallen starfire, is like the crumpled silver litter the urchins hoarded in the caves. A silver moon peeks over a crag of mountain and blows the North Wind across the waves.

'Can you walk, Mara? Could you make it down there?'

321

Mara nods. She's more exhausted and sore than she ever thought possible but she's as anxious as everyone else to find shelter from the bitter wind. And though there were none on her island and she was only a Treenester for a short time in the netherworld, the green patch of trees make her feel she is home, at last.

More than anything, she wants a home for her baby.

The baby snuggles against her skin and a beam of happiness surges through her, as pure as a shot of sun; but the flash of joy is spiked by grief so sharp that Mara has to push the pain deep inside, where she has put the grief for those other losses that are too painful to bear.

Fox is not here to see the miracle they've made. She is the lucky one. Mara looks down at her little miracle, tucked tight and safe against her, and the love that sweeps through her is as intense and frightening as the pain of her baby's birth.

'I never saw Broomielaw or Clayslaps in my dream like I said I did.' Gorbals looks as if it's a secret he can no longer bear to keep to himself. 'I lied. They were never meant to be here, were they, or they would have been in my dream.'

Mara glances at his face as he helps her over a spur of rock. She remembers the moment of hesitation when he first told of the dream and squeezes his hand. It doesn't make her own pain any easier but she's not the only one who has lost the person they love.

It's hard to look at Mol and see her pain because then she has to think of Tuck, who wouldn't be dead and neither would his mother, if Mara hadn't crashed into their lives. But even that can't ease her devastation, her disbelieving fury, at his theft of the globe.

*

Life has fastened itself into the most unlikely nooks and crannies all over the Earth. Mara looks at a shrub that seems to be growing out of a cleft in sheer rock. She thinks of the lichen they found in the bleak glacier gorge and remembers the netherworld ruins, alive with insects and creatures and herbs and weeds. She thinks of Fox in his tower there and wills him her love on the wings of the wind.

In this small nook of forest, Mara vows, they will root themselves to the Earth and make a life at the top of the world.

In the shelter of the trees, they fall asleep around a crackling fire, hardly able to believe they are here. When light trickles through the trees a bird flies out of the branches above them, singing a song of impossible joy.

The baby rouses with sharp, hungry cries.

'What will you call her?' Fir asks, stroking the baby's cheek as she feeds from Mara. 'She's as soft as a new leaf.'

'Or a flower.' Mara winces at the force of her baby's hunger but she can't stop breaking into a smile every time she looks down at the perfection of the tiny face. 'I'm calling her Lily. For Candleriggs.'

'Lily Longhope,' smiles Gorbals. 'It's a good name.'

'You're not Longhope, you're Mara Bell,' says Rowan.

'Longhope's my placename,' Mara explains.

'The name of your farm on Wing.' Rowan still looks puzzled.

'It's a Treenester thing,' says Mara, but she takes his point. 'She can be Lily Bell Longhope then.'

'Better,' says Rowan. 'But what about . . . ?'

Mara's face tells him not to mention Fox.

'She has his looks so she can have my name,' Mara says in a voice that's brisk to stop her brimming into tears.

Rowan hesitates, as if he's searching for just the right words. He touches the baby's hand and her fingers open like a star. Then she closes her hand tight around his thumb. 'She can have all of my love and care. Always.' His voice trembles.

And that does it. Mara's tears brim and fall on the baby's fox-tawny head and on to the earthy roots of the trees.

Mara rocks her baby asleep to a rhythm her body seems always to have known. She can't stop gazing at the tiny face. As long as she has Lily she will never be alone in the world. The future seems ever more precarious now that this precious mite depends on her for survival, and yet Mara feels a fluttering joy as she thinks of all the things they will do together in the years ahead. And there is so much she must tell Lily, one day.

In the shelter of a tree Rowan is busy with a pile of fallen branches. Mara walks across the carpet of needles cast by the trees and looks over his shoulder. He is weaving a large basket. After a while, he sets it down and tests it on the ground. He throws a quick smile at Mara and now she sees what it is: a rocking nest for Lily.

'Bit wobbly,' he decides and begins to weave some more.

As she watches his hands working the wood, Mara thinks of old Tain and his driftwood carvings that were famed all over Wing. She pictures her father mending his fishing boat with scraps of driftwood alongside the other island men on the shore. And she remembers her mother rocking her to sleep just as she rocks Lily, with the slow sway of a summer sea.

What she and Rowan are becoming, Mara is not sure.

His familiar presence anchors her where Fox was like an electric storm. He ripped through her life and is scorched into her soul as surely as the snake is branded on her arm. And he is burned into her future through Lily.

Mara remembers how she and Rowan grew up as close as two saplings in this forest of young trees. They sprang from the same patch of Earth; their roots are entwined. And Rowan is still here, alive, in her world. Sunbeams flicker through the branches and land upon the cradle-nest in his hands. The wind ruffles his hair, the same deep, burnished blond as her father's and so many of her island people. He glances up, sensing her gaze, and the look in his blue eyes stirs up a sensation that takes her by surprise, as if a hot spring has burst through the hard grief inside. Mara holds on to his gaze, and the feeling. And she wonders.

Might she and Rowan salvage a future, together, out of the wreckage of their past?

Anything is possible, she reminds herself. It was something she once believed.

MOONSCAPE

Mara is not here. It was only a trick of hope on the back of his fever-dream.

The emptiness of the Bridge to Nowhere leaches all his hopes. His plans are a waste of time. He has lost Mara for nothing. A one-man revolution is just a joke and he's not sure he could stomach what a revolution really means. Candleriggs was right. He should take Pandora and go home. He will risk the wrath of his grandfather and the rooks and try to change his world from the inside.

He'll leave behind a fox-phantom, a dream of himself, to guard the broken bridge. A fox that will bay each night at midnight, its cry echoing all down the boulevards of the Weave. But he can't keep coming back here, night after night, to a bridge that leads nowhere at all. He will exit this ghost existence and find his real life again.

But he's not giving up on Mara. He can never do that. The fox is the guardian of his last flint-spark of hope and he'll leave it here on the bridge. If she does come, the fox will alert his godgem, wherever he is, however far from now.

The ether is full of nervy static, as if he has infected the Weave with his mood.

A light flashes high over the bridge. Fox scans the network for flying cyberdogs or one of the other venomous creatures that mutate out of Weave-rot. But there's nothing he can see. He's about to exit the Weave when there's another flash of light. He looks up.

A moon falls into the boulevards.

A silver glow illuminates the ruins, too strong for a solitary moon.

Another moon shoots over the bridge.

The peekaboo moons!

Fox watches two more moons zip out of the empty ocean of cyberhaze that lies between the defunct Weave and the sizzling cyber-universe of the Noos. He watches them land in exactly the right place. How many have come? How many moons have answered his call?

Time to act or time to go? Now, Fox doesn't know.

But he leaves the phantom fox on the broken bridge and zooms through the junk heaps and the towerstacks, heading for the place he first spotted Mara when they were both just kids who knew nothing of the world and played among the rot and ruin of the Weave.

Fox zips across the ether on to his boulevard of broken dreams.

Just to see.

IMAQA maybe

The Earth turns five thousand times and more.
Sunups and sundowns rise and fall.
In the long polar nights of the Far North many suns
never rise or set at all.
Days pile on days and lives are lived.

THE EARTH SPEAKS

In Candlewood, the tree lamps wink and shiver. Winds burrow through the forest, as fleet as Arctic hares. Above the Lake of Longhope, a cutlass moon sharpens its blade on the eastern mountains, its watery twin broken into pieces on the waves. The stars are so fierce their reflections fizzle on the lake.

Deep in the mountains, winter still grips. But on the shores of the lake at the top of the world, the sun is winning the battle against the longest night, unfastening the fingers of winter, one by one.

There's a rip in the texture of the night. A shift and crack that is nothing to do with the rupturing sky lights of the magnetic Pole. A roar and bellow like a dying iceberg, but this is a voice that is deeper, older still.

The voice of the Earth.

CLAY

In the moon-windy rockways of Ilira, no one hears the Earth speak.

No one hears in the umiaks, the fleet of long walrus-skin boats moving fast as darts up the snaky channel of the fjord. The sea and the banshee wind are too loud.

The tide is with the umiaks and the waves rush them home. The rowers are grateful. Their arms ache after a long shift salvaging bridge metal from the sunken wrecks around the jutting sharks of land where the fjord becomes open sea. As they turn the last bend, the rowers pass under the network of bridges that connect the inner islets of the fjord.

Moonlight makes a glistening weave of the bridges. To Clay, in the umiak at the tail end of the fleet, it looks as if a spider's web has been cast over the wide bay.

A lamplit procession is moving along the unfinished Culpy Bridge. The Pontifix has promised it will be the greatest of all the bridges, an astonishing wonder of metal-weave suspended right across the fjord before it widens out into the bay. The coiling pillars at each end and the graceful weave and sweep of the bridge make Clay think of the sea melodies the wind-pipers play in the market caverns, frozen in mid-air.

Clay pulls on his oar, his eyes following the moving procession of lamps.

'Eyes on your oars!' roars the scut at the head of the umiak. He snaps his whip and his cutlass winks at the moon, while the moon winks on the metal crescents that brand the Culpy Bridge. Clay lowers his head but chances a sly glance upward just before his boat passes under the bridge. The whip tail cracks on his head but Clay doesn't care. What he just saw was worth twenty whips.

The Pontifix was standing on the Culpy Bridge. Clay knew it was him by his wind-straggled hair, the colour of a winter sun, and his bright blue windwrap emblazoned with silver crescents and the crossed wings of a Great Skua on its back. He was examining the bridge's wirework with his silver eyebox. As the umiak fleet passed underneath him, the Pontifix leaned over the bridge to watch. Clay could swear the silver eyebox looked right down at him.

The Pontifix, Bridge-Master of Ilira and Keeper of the Globe, looked through his eyebox into Clay's upturned face.

That's something to tell his mother. It might bring a smile to her weary face.

Up in the mountains the Earth is roaring and shifting but Clay is racing home to harbour, the world's wind is in his ears and he doesn't hear a thing.

PANDORA AND THE GODGEM

Fox is fast asleep at last.

Pandora kneels on the floor beside the bed of shredded books, heaped with ancient clothes from the museum. She pulls on one of the long, grubby dresses, the first that comes to hand, strokes the tawny hair that's strewn with fine threads of grey like cobwebs on autumn leaves and steals a kiss from his dreams.

He's exhausted from a long night's work in cyberspace, outrunning the rooks that are forever on their track. Since Caledon died, New Mungo has lost its dominance of the New World. New forces are rising, says Fox, things are shifting. Insurrection and dissaffection vibrate in the ether. Finally, he says, after all these years, our time has come.

Pandora lifts the lid of the jewelled casket they found years ago among the museum's armour and swords. It's where he keeps the godgem with its headgem that is the same green as her eyes. He's always telling her it's not a toy but she knows that well enough. The game they play is a deadly serious one.

Pandora creeps out of the tower room and runs down the narrow winding stairs. When at last the stairs end, she bursts out through a small door and only stops to rub a stitch in her side. Now she's running through the great halls of the museum, barefoot, long dress rustling, the night air of the netherworld seeping through the smashed window panes and coating her unwieldy tangle of hair with beads of dank mist.

She finds the hall with the huge stuffed elephant and crawls underneath, resting against the thick trunk of its back leg. It's her favourite place and he never finds her here.

Her presence disturbs an owl perched on the elephant's head. It flies off with an indignant *who you!* to join the ghostly hosts of owls hooting and hunting all across the netherworld. Pandora puts on the godgem. The green gem on her forehead looks like a third eye. She gives a happy sigh as she takes a cyberleap to join a night-hunt in another ruined world.

Now she's zipping through the ruined boulevards, no longer Pandora but a green cybersnake, hyperspeeding far faster than she can ever run through the museum's halls. Behind her is the broken bridge where a forlorn fox bays night after night for a mate that never comes. Pandora doesn't bother about him. She is too busy snaking through the flickering towerstacks to play her own furtive part in events that will shake the very foundations of the New World.

And there they all are, waiting for her in a puddle of moonbeams, in the wrecked boulevard where dreams are forged.

CANDLEWOOD SPIRE

In Candlewood, no one hears the Earth roar.

Not those gathering for supper around sundown fires, nor Lily, racing through the trees in the face of the wind. Her hair streams behind her, glinting in the lights of the tree lamps like the tawny tail of a fox.

Beyond the trees, on the edge of the Lake of Longhope, Wing is perched halfway up Candlewood Spire. The huge rugged spire of rock points straight to the Star of the North. Wing is studying the night with his telescope, a grounded star sailor on a stone mast. When the Earth trembles, the thick down of hair on his skin bristles. His hackles rise as he hears the faraway crack and roar.

He has heard that voice before. Once, when he was small, on the journey through the glacier gorge when the mountain swallowed Tuck. It's the voice of the Earth.

Wing sweeps the telescope over the rock faces of the mountains, but there's nothing to see. The tremor came through the rocky pass behind him, carrying ice echoes from the glacier gorge that cuts through the mountains in the world beyond the lake. Often, the land slips and slides and deadly spring tides of snow rumble down from the peaks. But what he just heard is something much darker and deeper than that.

When Lily comes, he'll tell her. Once the stars wheel around the North Star, their anchor, and the great lake throws morning up into the sky, he and Lily might sneak off into the mountains to track the voice of the Earth.

He knows Lily. She'll want to go.

Just to see.

The great waterfall has crashed into sudden meltdown. The huge force of it tears at a weakness in the rock. The land cracks and breaks and a vast slice of the mountain hurtles into the glacier gorge.

The Earth roars as an old ice wound reopens.

A green wind blows over the mountains, fresh from the trees around the lake. It rushes into the opening and snakes through the dark salty air of the tunnels that worm deep into the mountain and lead to Ilira, and the world beyond.